Michael's Black Dress

"Certain, men should be
what they seem"
—Othello

Michael's
Black Dress

JAMES THIBEAULT

SARTORIS
LITERARY
GROUP

A traditional publisher
with a non-traditional approach to publishing

Sartoris Literary Group, Inc.
Jackson, Mississippi
www.sartorisliterary.com

For my Mom, for being my first fan and greatest supporter

Part 1
Red

"My perfect soul shall manifest me rightly"

1

Michael

I stood in front of the mirror in my sister's bedroom, wearing her orange sundress. I'm not sure why I decided on this particular moment to tell her. I guess it was just time, and I needed to come clean. I was finally going to tell my sister the secret I've been keeping my whole life. Well, actually, I was going to show her. When she walked in, I had my hands up—like I was about to be arrested—and I waited for her verdict.

I watched her features slowly transform from astonishment to shock to explosive.

"Shah, don't scream!"

I fidgeted in the tight-fitting dress. The seams near the chest felt like they were going to burst. Each stitch holding on to its very existence, in every breath I took.

"What the—"

I dove at her, pushing her back to the wall. I managed to cover her mouth and slam her bedroom door at the same time. Ma screamed from downstairs.

"Who's slamming doors in my house?"

"Tell her it's the wind, Shah." I begged as she bit down on my finger.

"No, way!" Shah mumbled into my hand and sunk her fangs deeper into my index finger.

"What's going on up there?"

I could hear the couch moan as Ma shifted her weight.

"Please," I whispered. "I'll explain, just get Ma to back off."

Shah pushed me so hard I fell on my back and smacked my head on the bedpost. My chest throbbed, the dress cutting off my circulation. Shah looked at me in disgust.

In that moment I thought coming out to her was a bad idea. I had thought I could trust my sister. We weren't always on the best of terms, but I was the one who was always there for her—the one who listened to every Drum N' Bass album when she broke up with her latest boyfriend. Yes, I mean *every one*. She had all the bass-blaring hits on her computer and we would go through them all while eating late-night ice cream. She was never good at making girlfriends. I was the one elected to wear earplugs while holding the tissues when life sucked.

I had expected some sort of compassion in return, but her reaction was the opposite. Shah stood in front of me and started shedding off her clothes. Sure, I like to wear her clothes, but I'm not a freak that likes to see my sister naked. I held back the gagging sound in my throat and closed my eyes. It wasn't fast enough to hide the image of Shah in her bra and underwear that would forever be burned into my eyes. Jesus, what a huge mistake. I should've never shown her my secret.

Ma kicked opened the door. By the way the door opened, it blocked the sight of me. Shah screamed and covered herself.

"What the hell, Ma! Can't you knock?"

"Oh God." Ma slammed the door shut, breaking her own rule. "I'm so sorry, Charlotte. I thought Michael was in there."

"Why would Michael be in here? At least he has the decency to knock first!"

"Have you seen him?"

"No, Ma. I haven't!"

"All right! Stop with the yelling!"

"You're yelling at me!"

It was getting awkward, considering me and Shah were both half naked in the same room.

"Charlotte," Ma said. She never said Shah's full name. No one did anymore. "I'm sorry. You know I've been trying to respect your privacy."

"I'm sorry, too. I didn't mean to yell."

"Good. Then where is your brother?"

"He went over to Jacob's house. Slammed his door and went out the window."

Wow. She was good. When I was younger, I used to go out the hallway window and onto the roof. I would jump onto the maple and climb down. I could have used the front door, but guys did those sorts of things.

"Great." Ma sighed. "He's doing that again. Well, if he climbs back up and I don't see him, tell him not to slam the doors anymore."

"Will do."

"Love you."

"Love you too, Ma."

As Ma walked down the staircase, creaking on each step, Shah and I both put a finger to our lips, telling each other to shut up. Our similar mannerisms sometimes creeped people out—but I think this particular bedroom moment would have topped it.

When Ma was safely back in the living room—we listened for the squeaks on the old couch—I slowly rose up without making a sound. We stared at each other: her half naked, and me in women's clothes. Then, we laughed. But not too loud.

2

Michael

"What the hell is going on?" said Shah.

I sat on Shah's bed with the skin-tight sundress, feeling dejected. Usually, I went for something that fit me, but Shah just bought the dress and I wanted to try it on. It clearly wasn't going to fit me, but this dress had a retro look that was coming back in style. Sadly, the only new fashion I could wear was what my sister bought. She mostly wore t-shirts and jeans—identical to me in public—and people even confused us at times!

Shah sat beside me on the foot of her bed. "You like to wear my clothes?"

"It's only been recently, I swear! Ma hasn't bought anything new in a while."

"Dude, seriously? Ma's stuff?"

"I don't have a lot of choices."

Ma worked nights at the hospital, so that gave me opportune moments to try her stuff on. Late into the night, when Shah blasted her music, I sneaked into my mother's walk-in closet. The first time, I only pressed the fabrics to my skin, and relaxed into the soothing texture. Afterward, I ran back into my room in shame—as if I had committed a sin. For a year after, I never went into Ma's room. Whenever I had that feeling to try on a dress, I took a cold shower or pushed harder into my workouts. Then, during a sleepless summer night, I had to try again.

This time, I decided to try on one of her dresses. Ma had this beautiful, hydrangea wrap that hung in the back. She never wore it anymore—I'd only see it on her in an old photo. Ironically, it is the only picture I have of my Pa. It's the four of us, and Ma's happily smiling with her two infant kids. But Pa didn't smile—he just looked exhausted and mad. Maybe, Ma kept the picture around to remind us of the tired and irritated man who left his children. After my Pa walked out on his wife and two kids, that dress got pressed deep into the back of the closet.

When I spied the dress, it called to me. It needed to breathe—to flow free in the air. I put it on and twirled around with the hem dragging on the floor. I felt alive. Then, guilt overcame me, and I hastily stored it away.

I teetered on the slippery slope between desire and guilt—waiting weeks, sometimes months until my feelings could not be denied. Eventually, the gaps between my guilt and giving in to my late-night dress raids diminished as my desires grew. Soon, I was wearing dresses almost every night, but even that grew tiresome. I was getting sick of the boxy business dresses with the thin shoulder pads that dominated Ma's wardrobe. Plus, Ma was much larger than me—and all of her clothes lacked the satisfaction of a good fit. I needed something better. That's when I snuck into Shah's room.

Shah turned on the music so we could talk without Ma being suspicious.

"Hey, Michael!" Shah slapped me the shoulder, pulling me back into reality. "Can you answer the question already? Why are you wearing my clothes?"

"Sorry," I said. "It's kind of hard to—"

"—Are we sisters now?"

"What? No. I know it's hard to process, but you remember those late nights when—" I paused to gather my thoughts and Shah interrupted.

"You're a black kid in a white suburb—do you really want to draw *more* attention to yourself?"

"Please, just listen. Back when we were—"

"Wait," Shah stood up and ran over to her dresser. Pulling out the top shelf, she grabbed all of her underwear and threw them in the wastebasket.

"What are you doing?"

"Your boy-toy touched all of them. I can't. No. I can't do that."

She went over to her bookshelf and pulled out her Anatomy 101 textbook. Like a prisoner smuggling a knife in a library, she had hollowed

11

the pages inside to hide her cigarettes and lighter. Shah took a hard drag and kept the smoke tight in her lungs. I had a feeling she smoked, but I could never prove it. I would have never thought to look in her textbook. In my room, I had a copy of *Moby Dick* carved out the same way. Its massive size held my vast collection of magazines clippings of models. While the girls were attractive, my interest was in the styles of the clothes. Eventually, it became a checklist of what I wanted to wear when I finally had the chance. However, that chance was disappearing when Shah put the red ember of her cigarette next to the wastebasket. She was going to burn them!

"Shah, I didn't put them on! Even if I did, I would've washed them first and after."

"You better not be lying. Swear to me."

I raised my hand and knocked on the bedpost three times. We used to do that as kids to know who was really telling the truth, and it still translated.

Shah squinted her eyes at me, then put the cigarette back to her lips. With another hard drag, the flame smoothly burnt to the butt. Shah turned on the fan and threw the cigarette in a mason jar that she kept under the bed. She pulled out a perfume bottle and sprayed the strong scent around. Now it made sense: Shah hated to wear perfume, and I could never understand why her room always smelt so girly.

"Michael," she took a moment to think, "I'm glad you came out to … whatever this is, but I still need a bit to figure this out. Do you want to be a …"

"No."

"Do you now like …"

"No way."

"So you just want   …"

"Yeah, exactly."

"Good," Shah said, "But if you were, that would be … you know …"

"I told you I just like …"

"To wear them, yeah, I get that. But I kind of need a reason."

"Why do I need a reason? I don't really know why, I just like to wear them."

"You can't just decide something like this. Did you bump your head or something?"

"Are you serious? Did we stay out in the sun too long? Is that why we're black?"

"I'm trying to figure this out, okay? Can you cut it with the attitude?"

"Screw you, I'll do whatever I want."

"Oh really?" Shah smirked. "Cause I'll doubt you'll do this again if I let Ma know."

"Please!" I begged. "I don't want her to know."

"Are you going to tell Ma about the cigarettes?"

"Of course not. Why would I?"

Shah craned her head back, surprised.

"Oh, okay."

"Can you keep this a secret?" I said softly. What if she couldn't? What if she told this to everyone at school!

Suddenly, she laughed and then tried to hold it in. Shah kept trying to apologize, but she couldn't contain her laughter. "I'm sorry. I'm just trying to imagine Jacob's face if he saw you like this. It took him months to stop asking black-people questions, so this would blow his freaking mind!"

She was trying to be funny, and I wanted to laugh. Instead, I cried.

Before she had a chance to grab me, I ran out the door with my jeans and shirt bundled to my chest.

3

Shah

When Michael stormed out of my room, I lit up another cigarette—trying to breathe in the bombshell that my brother had just dropped on me. I mean, there were different ways you could tell someone you like to wear dresses.

You know, you can say, "Hey Shah, I like to wear dresses, is that cool?" Maybe I'd say back, "Yeah Michael, that sure is cool with me."

But no, like my ever-dramatic brother, he had to make a grand appearance in my bedroom. I know I'm supposed to be supporting him at this vulnerable moment, but why did he have to tell me in the showiest way possible? That's always Michael's problem: he doesn't think stuff through. He just does what he feels.

Like, last week, Michael was yelling at Ma because she wasn't giving him enough attention. Who says that? What type of grown-ass teenager goes up to his mother and pretends they're on a talk show? Anyway, I was listening from my room—snuffing out my cigarette—when I heard a bottle fly across the room.

"Michael!" Ma yelled. It was late, probably around 3 a.m.

"Do you see that? That's me in pieces. Ever since you took the extra shift at work, I never see you anymore."

"So you throw a bottle?"

"It's like I'm a little kid again, waiting up all night to see you get home."

"Michael, half the time you're not even home!"

"That's because you're not home."

"This conversation is ridiculous."

14

"I'm tired of cooking microwave dinners and ordering pizza. Just get a regular shift like everyone else."

"Oh, so all I'm good for is cooking and cleaning?"

"You know what I mean."

"I don't think you appreciate how much this neighborhood costs. You want to keep living here?"

"I want you here," said Michael.

There was silence for a moment. I tip-toed to the banister. Just like I was a little kid again, I peered over the railing and saw Ma crying.

"Either I work these late nights, or we move. Do you want that?"

"Fine, let's move right now!"

Michael ran up the stairs, past me, and into his room. After five minutes, with Ma still crying at the table, he came back down with a suitcase full of clothes. "Okay Ma, let's go!"

"Do you see what the other towns are like now? This is one of the few neighborhoods that still has a decent public school. You had better damn well appreciate what I'm doing for you."

"And you had better damn well appreciate how I don't give a damn."

Finally, I went downstairs and took the suitcase from Michael. He handed it to me and we both went upstairs into my room. We stayed up for the rest of the night. For hours we didn't say a word, just listened to my music. Eventually, Ma cleaned up the broken pieces and fell asleep on the couch with the TV on. No one spoke a word about it again.

You see the drama? This is what I have to deal with. I get it, Michael's an emotional person. But he doesn't think. Who the hell lets his own mother cry like that? I'll tell you who, it's someone who likes wearing pretty dresses all of a sudden.

I let out a groan and breathed in another puff. This is why I smoke, I thought. How do you explain this to someone? How am I going to walk next to my brother, with his beautiful blowing dress? Am I supposed to give him a high five as we hop and skip together, trading beauty secrets? I don't have the slightest idea. What I do know is that I'm stuck with whatever the hell happens. No, there's no backing out of this one. That's the horrible price of loving a twin brother.

I went into the hallway and knocked on Michael's door.

"Michael?"

"What!" he said like a little kid.

"Just stop, okay? Don't give me a temper tantrum."

"Whatever."

I walked a couple of steps away and took in a deep breath. Even though he wore dresses now, he was still the same Michael.

"Open the damn door, please."

"You can't swear and say 'please' at the same time."

"Please open this door, or I'm going to shove that sundress down your throat! Are you proud of me? No swears!" The door opened. Michael's eyes were sunken and sad. On the bed was his copy of Moby Dick, thousands of magazine clippings scatted around it.

"What? Are you going to keep laughing at me?"

"Please, I do that all the time."

"I can't do anymore jokes, not right now."

"Fine, I just wanted to say—"

"Miiiiiike!" A voice screamed from outside.

"No!" Michael ran to the bed and hurriedly put all the clippings back in the book. "Jacob's going to know something's wrong. I'm so screwed."

I helped him put the magazine clippings away. Michael didn't resist.

"Mikey, Mikey, Mikey! Open your window! You got to tell me how it goes with that girl tonight!"

"Shah? What am I going to do?"

"Relax, I got this. Go take a cold shower and figure yourself out."

"You sure?"

"Yeah, I've dealt with Jacob before."

Michael ran to the bathroom while I opened the window.

"Jesus, Jake. Why don't you tell the whole neighborhood!"

"Oh, hey Shah. What you doing in Mike's bedroom?"

"Michael's in the shower. Why are you shouting like a damn idiot?"

"Can't a brother be happy for another brother? Mike's date tonight is a knockout."

"Woah, you were stripped of your 'brother' privileges, remember?"

"I'm black inside, like an Oreo."

"Oreos have a white filling."

"Whatever, you get the meaning. Hey, do you think I'm going to get sap on my new jeans if I climb this tree?" Jacob shouted from below.

"How about you come through the front door like a normal person. It should be open."

"Will do."

Jacob walked around, and I closed the window. I wanted another cigarette. I got the feeling covering for Michael was going to be an expensive habit.

4

Michael

By the time I got out of the shower, Jacob was already sitting on my bed, bouncing up and down. Even when we were kids, he couldn't stop moving.

"*Moby Dick*? Since when do you read?" Jacob pointed to the book next to my laptop. My breath shortened, but I tried to play it cool.

"Nothing. Bella mentioned she liked the book, so I figured I would brush up on it." I briskly put the book back onto the shelf and flashed a cheap smile.

"Dude, nice move. So what's the battle plan?" Jacob said, eyes wild, waiting for the juicy details.

When he found out that Bella and I were going on a date, he was more excited than I was. Apparently, he went up to a freshman, smacked a textbook out of his hand, and screamed,

"Guess who's getting laid?"

"Um, you?"

"No! You idiot!" said Jacob, completely unfazed, "My main-man Michael. And he's going to have some fun tonight!"

Bella was a junior who just transferred from some other school. For the first week she was there, the boys stalked her in the lunch room, watching her every move. She just ignored them while eating her sandwich.

Jacob had been sitting next to me, jostling with his elbow. "Dude, did you checkout the new girl? Look at how she's eating that sandwich."

"Um, like she's hungry?"

"Yeah, she's hungry for something!"

With bronze skin and wide hazel eyes, Bella surprisingly did make eating a sandwich attractive. She sat alone, and I wasn't sure why she was antisocial. For someone who looked as good as Bella, sitting alone in the cafeteria was a bad idea. With no protection from the girls, guys were more courageous to approach her. Her short hair, ending right at her jaw line, still managed to blow slowly whenever the back door to the cafeteria opened. She also had a nice figure, which Jacob would have thought odd of me had I not pointed it out. But truthfully, that wasn't what attracted me to her. It was the yellow boat-neck tee she wore with faded blue jeans. To bridge the gap between her hair and her clothes, she wore a pair of bumblebee dangling earrings. Bold choice, but it matched perfectly. And her fit. Wow, the stunning yellow tee graciously mounted her breasts and widened her hips just enough. Usually, I'm not a fan of faded blue jeans, but I thought it matched her personality well.

"Hey!" Jacob had said. "Save some of that looking for me."

"I'm going up to her."

"Whoa, relax. She's turned down like eight dudes this week. Even Marshall."

Marshall was the captain of the wrestling team. I wasn't surprised she turned him down. He had more muscles than brain cells. He had probably said something like, "Hey baby, how about I find a way to turn that frown upside down." Did I have a better shot? Maybe not, but it was worth a try. I wanted to get closer to her.

"I'm feeling good about this one," I said, standing up and making a straight line toward her.

The rest of the kids sitting at the table stopped chewing their food. Jacob drummed the table in anticipation. Soon, the rest followed. Bella looked our way, apparently disgusted.

"Shut the hell up," I called back to Jacob.

He silenced his hands. I was impressed how much control I had on him when I demanded it. I walked over to her, and she kept her eyes on her food. For a moment I stood beside her, patiently, like I was standing in line. Eventually, she sighed and lowered her sandwich. I flashed a smile.

"Hey," I said.

"You see I'm eating?"

"What are you eating?" I sounded like an idiot.

"What? You want a taste or something? Get out of here."

I heard Jacob make a wailing noise from the other side of the cafeteria. When I looked over, he had his hand over his mouth. Keeping my eyes on Bella, I signaled with a hand behind my back for him to shut up. He did.

"Look," I said calmly. "I'm not usually the one to come up to girls like—"

"Oh, you aren't?" Bella turned around in her seat, her hazel eyes staring right through me. I liked the way her earrings jingled when she turned. "Cause it looks like you've done this before with the help of your moronic friend." She looked past me and stared at Jacob. Immediately, he inhaled half his sandwich and looked up at the ceiling. *Smooth, I thought, real smooth.*

"Okay, fine," I said, sitting down next to her. A blush of indignation rose on her cheeks as she scooted her chair away.

"Can't you just go?" She sneered.

"I just wanted to say—"

"What? I'm hot? Attractive? Bangable? An amazing ass slash tits slash legs slash thighs? Can you just put the freaking barcode on me and stock me up on the shelf, so I can eat my food in peace? What's with you guys? It's like I'm on the only plate of food left in the restaurant."

"Please, Bella—"

"¡Estupendo! Now you know my name! I suppose it's easier to order something off the menu when you know the name of it."

"I like your top."

"Oh, so you're a breast guy! Congratulations, I'm glad I can give you some entertainment for tonight's mental show."

"No, I like your boat-neck tee."

"Oh." She pulled at her fabric by her clavicle. The way it stretched showed it was clearly cotton. "It's an Ann Taylor."

"I like how it's a three-quarter."

"What?"

"Three-quarter, your top doesn't go all the way down to your wrists. Which is great because—and I'm sorry for pointing it out—but they're way too delicate to be hidden behind some cloth."

"Uh, thanks. I think they're too bony."

"No, they're defined. Big difference." I stood up. "My name's Michael." I extended my hand like I was a car salesman. Apparently, it was goofy enough to get her to smile. Her teeth matched the white in her eyes. Everything about her just fit so well. Bella looked at her hand and realized she had breadcrumbs all over it. She quickly wiped her hands and extended her arm.

"Bella," she said. "Look, I'm sorry I flipped out the way I did."

"No, I get it. You look cute with the bumble earrings, by the way."

She blushed. Her red cheeks blended well with the yellow.

"So … I'm just going to go now. I just wanted to introduce myself." I turned around and walked away. Jacob, with a mouthful of sandwich, awkwardly gave me a thumbs up. He didn't know if it worked or not. I put a finger to my throat for him to cut it out.

"Is your boy wondering if it worked?" Bella yelled to me.

I turned back around. "What?"

"Your friend. I think he wants to know if you got my interest."

"Well, did I?" I asked.

"How about I explain it to you Friday night?" This time, I was the one taken aback. "You heard me. Take me out Friday night."

"Uh, sure."

"And I better be impressed."

I smirked. "So, you aren't right now?"

"Maybe a little, but don't push your luck."

She turned back around—her earrings jingling again. God, the only thing I remember thinking then was wanting a pair.

That was a few days ago and now Friday night had finally arrived. Jacob was way more excited for this date than I was.

"Dude, dude, dude." Jacob slapped me on the back. "What are you cooking in that kitchen of yours? How are we gonna handle her?"

"We?" I laughed. "Do you think that you are coming along?"

"Hey, if you want me hanging back, giving you some pointers. Let me know. Plus, if you mess up, I'll be there to swoop in the rebound."

"No chance."

"You're right, I'll just settle for your hot sister."

At that moment, I had to make sure that my best friend Jacob had his ass kicked, physically and emotionally. I grabbed one of his wrists and turned it inward.

"Ow, ow, ow," said Jacob, laughing and moaning. I managed to stick his head out of the open window. Once Jacob managed to wipe away his tears, he yelled, "Oh God, that hurts! Can you stop it?"

"Just say what I want to hear. Then I'll stop."

Jacob tried to throw a punch at me, but I only twisted his wrist tighter. I wasn't going to hurt him that badly—we've been friends since we were in kindergarten.

"Cut it out, you jerk-bag!" cried Jacob.

"Jerk-bag?"

"If I had my hand back, I could think of a better insult."

"You don't need your hand to think."

"Yeah, but I'm going to need this hand tonight, and you're ruining that special moment."

I flinched back in disgust, and that was just enough for Jacob to break from my grip. With a warrior's yell, he charged and speared me in the stomach. I fell, and both of us wrestled on the carpet. Rug burns covered our elbows and palms. Each of us were decent wrestlers, both starting on the varsity squad for the spring season this year. While Jacob was a better wrestler than me, he wasn't prepared for my wet willie attack. I placed a huge glob of spit on my finger like it was toothpaste. When that viscous dew entered his ear canal, he screamed worse than when he had his wrist twisted. Before he knew what was happening, I flipped him on his stomach and sat on his back. He was in the camel clutch in a matter of seconds, with my hands choking his neck from behind. Defeated, he tapped on my leg, and I loosened my grip a bit. I let Jacob catch his breath, even though I was still on his back.

"What do you say?" I said playfully.

"I'm sorry ... I called your sister hot."

I laughed, and gently slapped him on the head a couple of times.

"Oh, so you're saying my sister is ugly?"

"All I was saying is that I'm running out of options."

I felt bad for Jacob: he was constantly measuring his success with girls to me. I'm not saying I'm a lady's man, but Shah had stopped trying to remember the names of the dates I'd brought home.

"Look, here's the plan," I said to Jake, who was listening eagerly, like a child ready for story time. "I'm going to take her to dinner, then head to the park, and we'll conclude the night back here."

"You sure she's going to make it back here?"

I grinned. He loved when I finished with: "I'll make it work."

"Oh man!" Jacob jumped up from my bed. "Hope you've saved room for dessert!"

Shah came stomping into the room. I smelled the scent of that over-bearing perfume and smiled, knowing she must have had another cigarette.

"Hey! You mind if you don't scream that for everyone to hear?"

Jacob changed his voice to that creepy one he uses to pick up chicks.

"Oh, I'm sorry about that. He just got me all excited. What gets you excited?"

"Jacob," she sauntered up to him. "You have a better chance sleeping with your stuffed animals." Jacob bit his lip. "Besides," Shah poked her finger into Jacobs chest. "Maybe Michael shouldn't be all excited. It's only the first date. Maybe Michael should be more considerate of what other people want in a relationship."

"She knows what she wants!" Jacob shouted. "She wants the—"

"Shut it, Jake," I said. "Shah, I think she'll know me pretty well after a few hours."

"Oh," Shah smirked, "she'll know *everything* about you?"

23

That shut me up, and my stomach burned from the inside. Jacob raised his eyebrow at me.

"What's she talking about?"

"I'm just messin'," Shah said. "Michael tends to forget from time to time that people can be a bit more complex than just flesh and blood." Shah smirked at me. "Isn't that right, Michael?"

"Yeah," I exhaled.

"Seriously, what are you two talking about?" Jacob asked. Shah and I looked at each other and smiled. Immediately, I grabbed Jacob's hand and intertwined it in with mine.

"The truth is Jacob, I love you with all my heart. Be mine."

Jacob violently pulled his hand away. "I hate you two!" he shouted. "You always have some twin thing going." Then he tried to dust off the gayness. "Jesus, I'm out of here." He looked back from the door. "You better cut that crap out with Bella tonight. And don't forget to text me every twenty minutes."

"No promises."

"Fine, every fifty minutes."

"Bye, honey."

"Stop it!"

He ran downstairs and out the door.

Shah burst out laughing. "He has to be the most homophobic man I've ever met. Now, you're sure you're—"

"I told you I'm not gay."

"Whatever. It's all good." Shah looked at me, raised her hand, and tapped three times on my bedpost. "Look, I'm sorry I laughed. That was a jerk move on my part. But you know you can trust me, right?"

"I want to."

"Well then, here we are."

"So, you're not going to mess up my date tonight with Bella? Ma has another third shift."

"Wait," she backhanded my shoulder. "You seriously going to bring her back here after one date?"

"I don't know. I'm good with women."

"Well, I'm glad that you haven't changed that much."

"I haven't changed at all! It's still me."

"Whatever, just remember to wrap it up for this month's special. And don't do anything stupid!"

5

Michael

When in doubt for a date, get frozen yogurt. Ice cream is fattening, and it's going to ruin your figure. Frozen yogurt has less fat, so it's better for you. Of course, that's completely false. It doesn't make much of a difference if you put chocolate sprinkles with Oreos in caramel sauce on top of chocolate-flavored frozen yogurt. Frozen yogurt still has so much sugar, but people believe it is healthier because other people believe it. When a lot of people believe in something, it becomes true. If something is not true, wait until a lot more people agree.

Luckily, Bella and I agreed on frozen yogurt as a good first course for our date. The courses in a date have nothing to do with food, but how they overall affect the person. For example, first course is light and experimental. At the frozen yogurt shop, I asked Bella, "You ever tried dragonfruit flavor before?' Some girls clam up, scared, as if it's a drug. Others say, why not! It's nothing hugely committing, and it's a chance to test the waters. Depending on how the girls react, it's a great way to play out how the rest of the date will go. Don't bother planning the date ahead of time. Have contingency plans in case the girl you're dealing with throws a curveball. Does she like the being bold? Does she act more passively? Try to read the vibe she gives off.

For Bella, she was all over the place, not giving off a particular vibe. I thought FroYo would help give me a better sense of her, because what type of yogurt a girl gets is extremely important. If she's mixing vanilla with strawberries and raspberries, it probably means she doesn't want to eat too many calories. Chocolate with chocolate sprinkles probably means she really likes chocolate or doesn't really care what you think of her. Therefore, there's a good chance she's very bold, daring.

Of course, even though I claim I have this skill, I couldn't for the life of me figure out Bella that night. She put dragonfruit (at my request) with chocolate and a bit of blueberries. What the hell does that mean? It didn't even taste good, because I swiped a spoon full when she went to the bathroom. I needed more time to figure her out.

From FroYo I decided that Course Two would have to be coffee inside a used bookstore. She seemed intelligent, so she might enjoy some books. Just in case she didn't read, we had pricey coffee drinks to fall back on.

When we entered the bookstore, we walked around the dusty, dim-lit books, pushing aside paperbacks that were only a dollar.

"Oh my god," I whispered excitedly. I picked up one of the water-logged books and handed them over to her. "I'm buying you this whole set!"

She stared at the front cover and grinned. *"King's Passion. Part 3: The Sword of Conquest?"* She flashed the cover back at my face. It was a shirtless man with a giant sword up in the air. Beside him were two women in lingerie, grabbing his meaty thighs.

"I figured you were the literate type?"

"Oh, I am, but I'm not partial to someone who unsheathes his sword too early." She playfully smacked the book on my head.

We went our separate ways around the store, having no clue what was filed under what. There was some sort of organization, but I couldn't figure out why Abraham Lincoln bios were next to books on Greenland. That's why I liked about used bookstores—there wasn't a huge amount of pressure to put everything in categories. In my head, there *had* to be a reason why Abraham was vacationing in Greenland, but was there? I pulled out a giant Greenland book that was bigger than my head. With the book wide open, I took a *Vogue* magazine and placed it on the inside. If someone were to walk by, they would notice my interest in the Danish territory and not the latest high-waist dresses the models were wearing. Only honest Abe knew the truth.

In this particular issue of Vogue, Lupita Nyong'o was the featured model—and she was beautiful. Inside the pages, she wore this stunning black and white—almost Zebra-looking—dress that had diagonal stripes. What made it more remarkable was the position of the stripes. Most of the stripes made their way to her stomach from all directions, a subtle X. Casually, her dress created the perfect hourglass figure, elongating her bust and hips. What I loved about her the most was how she had extremely short hair, almost buzzed.

With her arms spread wide, like a fully exposed mannequin, it was like she said in the photo, "I am me, and I make myself beautiful." Something else interesting about Nyong'o is she's not an African American. Even though she looks like it, she was born in Mexico, raised in Kenya, and studied in the U.S. later on in her life. As much as I want to be her, we are not alike. Our skin doesn't magically bind us together. However, if you put me and Lupita on a subway together, it would look like two African Americans were sitting side by side. When I stared at her, there's no labels—just her. "I am me," she says to me in the photo. "I make my own beauty."

"What's a black guy reading about Greenland for?" Bella walked up to me, a pair of books pressed against her chest.

Immediately, I slammed the book closed.

"Oh," Bella stopped walking, "I was just joking. You know, it's funny because..."

"What, black people can't be born in Greenland?"

"Wai t... are you..."

"Yup, I'm Greenland-African-American!" I tucked the book back in the shelf with the magazine inside, feeling strangely apologetic for Lupita for some reason.

"You are *not* from Greenland!" she hit me in the arm.

"How do you know?"

"Because ..."

"Oh, now you have some sort of stereotyping? We Greenland-Africans are *very* sensitive about that."

28

She picked up the sarcasm and smirked. "God, I hate you," she said, rolling her eyes. Bella walked away and headed toward the counter. By the time she was out of sight, I opened up the Greenland book and pulled out the *Vogue* magazine. For a moment, I stared at Lupita, then I put the magazine back on the *Vogue* pile. When I shelved the Greenland book, I hurried over to Bella—who was near the register—and took the books from her hands.

"Now, it's a Greenland-African tradition to pay for a woman's books. You don't want to be culturally insensitive, do you?"

"No, please, I respect your culture."

As I pulled out my wallet, smiling at the clerk, Bella rested her hand on mine. For a moment, we stared at each other, until Bella finally blushed and looked away. The cashier scanned the books and put her books in a paper bag. As we walked out, she laced her fingers into my hands. I couldn't believe how forward she was.

"I would still like you, despite who you are," she said.

I stopped at the exit of the bookstore and released my fingers from her clasp.

"What are you talking about?" I said, my breath shortening.

"If you are Greenland-African, or whatever the hell you said. I'm just saying."

"Oh." Phew, I thought. "That's good."

"It looked like you were about to have a heart attack."

"No, I'm fine. I just thought … you know what, I have one more surprise for you."

"Really? Is it more about the deep inner you?"

"Can we just drop that, please?"

"Oh, sure."

"Sorry, I'm just—"

"Michael, it's fine. I don't want to ruin anything we have right now. So, let's just drop it. Besides," she extended a limp hand to me. "It's time for you to escort me out."

"Oh," I laughed. "You're one of those people."

Michael's Black Dress

"No, I am me, and that's it."

6

Michael

Holding hands, Bella and I walked side-by-side down a paved path in the park—under the bright white streetlights. The fluorescent lights blocked out the night sky, but they lit up the greens and the browns around us. It was the first time I was able to appreciate Bella's red halter dress, which ended just above her knees. Her straps crisscrossed, revealing skin just above her neckline. With the dark earth colors behind her, not only did she pop out, she practically complemented the park. God, I wanted to be in that dress, in that exact moment. My legs free—the hem of my skirt gently touching my thighs. Suddenly, I had to stop walking alongside her. I had to think of a reason to touch her dress.

"Hey, you see that squirrel!" I pointed toward some trees in the dark.

"Where?"

"Over …" I moved in next to her, moving my arm along the sight of her eyes. "… There! In the trees."

I pointed to some spot. It didn't matter where.

"What are you talking about?" she asked. It was too late. My other arm was behind her back, my hand pressed firmly on her back. The dress was so soft, the texture, perhaps velvet? No, it was certainly chiffon.

"Wow, that was pretty lame move, Casanova." She smirked, but she didn't push my hand away. Good sign, really good sign. This was a perfect opportunity for the chess match.

"Sorry," I said. "I think the squirrel was just too fast for you to see."

"Oh really? That's how we're going to play this?"

"I'll tell you what we're going to play…" I moved my chest to hers and stared into her eyes for a while. "Chess!"

Quickly, I pushed her away and ran down the road. It wasn't a sprint, but I wanted her to get the sense she was chasing me.

"Michael! You don't leave a girl in the middle of a park!"

"Then you have to keep up!" I shouted back.

She laughed and followed. By the stone fountain, its water still sprinkling in the night, were eight tables with chessboards. The lamps were placed around the courtyard, and surprisingly the tables were well lit. In the center of all these chessboards was a giant one with gigantic pieces. There were two old men still playing with a boxed chess clock. The two men swiftly moved their pieces and then touched their side of the box. The black man played white and the white man played black. Their figures were almost silhouetted, but the pieces were vividly clear. I ran over to the black side of the giant chess board and adjusted some of the pieces, waiting for Bella to follow. Awkwardly, she stood across from me. She had a smirk on her face and squinted both of her eyes.

"All right, enough of your games. Why are we here?"

"You can't say 'enough of your games' when we're playing chess."

"Ah, but isn't this the part where you say, 'but chess isn't a game, it's a battle?'"

"Damnit, you're taking all of my moves, Bella," I said jokingly. "How am I supposed to woo you now?"

"It just means that you have two games you have to improve on."

The two silhouetted men laughed, but the pieces continued to dance along the table.

"Great," I smiled, "but I think you will find my game, in both cases, is quite skilled."

"You are so pathetic," she groaned playfully.

"Ah, well, I'm sorry if it's too much for you."

"So," she gingerly rolled around the huge knight. "I wonder what move I should start with?"

I walked over to her, ready to pick up on her giant pawns. "You should probably start by—"

She playfully slapped my hand off the piece and adjusted it.

32

"Ok then, I guess you know how to play. Begin."

I gestured my hand with a regal motion.

"You know," Bella said, "you really are a piece of work. Here you are, this whole night, moving me around like these little pawns. Yes, you give me the first move, but it's all an illusion. It doesn't matter what move I make, because you have a move ready for it."

She grunted as she lifted the knight.

"I'm just a Knight to c3, or to d4."

"So, you're a chess player too?"

"I played as a kid, my *Padre* taught me," she said. "But I was sick of the girls making fun of me."

"You don't seem like you would care."

"Well, now I don't. But back then, no one liked to hang out with a chess nerd."

"But I don't see you hanging out with anyone right now."

"Exactly."

"I'm sorry, I didn't mean it like that."

"No, it's fine." Bella walked over to her king's pawn and moved it up three spaces: e4. "Show me what you got."

I countered with d5. The two pawns were in the center of board, diagonally staring at each other.

"You don't have a choice. Defending that pawn is only going to cause you trouble. If you try holding back, I'm going to keep coming at you. There's only really one solid move to make, Bella. You have to take the pawn, whether you like it or not."

The two old men laughed. Bella smirked.

"Seriously? What if I didn't move my king's pawn?"

"Oh, I usually tell the girl that e4 is the best move."

"Why would you tell me that?"

"Because you like me too much."

"I swear to God," she covered her face with her hands. "I should be distancing myself from you right now."

"And why aren't you?"

"Because I want to see where this goes."

Bella took the pawn. Within a few minutes, she won the game. That never happened before.

7

Michael

Bella was outside with me, in front of my house, looking around with her arms crossed. I couldn't figure her out. There was excitement in her eyes, but there was hesitation in her voice as she spoke.

"Hey Michael, I had a great time tonight, but maybe I should go," she said.

"It's okay. My Ma does overnight at the hospital. And my sister's just hanging out in her room."

"Michael, I don't know. I …"

I gently took her arm and kissed the back of her hand.

"I'm not forcing you to do anything, you know that right?"

"Yeah."

"And there's a reason why you haven't left already, right?"

"You're sweet, but … I'm not supposed to do this."

"Do what?"

"Don't play dumb."

"Seriously, you like me, right?"

"Yeah."

"So, what's the problem?"

"The problem is what other people will think."

"I thought you didn't care what other people thought."

She looked away and stared up at the stars for a while. I gently closed the front door. Silently, I walked back to the car and opened the door.

"It's no problem. Come on, I'll drive you home."

"Michael," said Bella. "Do you think I'm a slut?"

I put my hands up in verbal defense. "Whoa, I never said that."

"Would everyone else say that about me? Would your friend think that?"

"Don't worry what Jacob thinks."

"I do worry, because I want you, but I don't want to be a slut."

"Where is this coming from all of a sudden?"

"Look," she covered her face with her hands and began to sob. Quickly, I looked around to make sure no one was around. She knelt to the ground, and I put my arm around her.

"Hey, hey, hey. What … did I do something wrong?"

"No," she said. "You're really sweet, it's just … old drama creeping up on me. Forget everything I just said, it was stupid."

I let out a huge sigh, then walked up to her.

"All right, it's true that I meet a lot of girls. But I don't want you to think that I chose any kind of woman. They need style."

Bella stopped crying for a second. "Style? You're attracted to me because I'm stylish?"

"Yeah, you dress like you own it. I know everyone *owns* their own clothes, but in truth they're borrowing them. It's like they're on loan— temporarily borrowing them from the fashion models. But you, you wear these clothes and say, 'these are mine, and this is my style.' Jesus, it's fifty degrees out and you're wearing chiffon. You're showing a bit too much leg for a first date, and the other girls might call you skanky."

She pulled her hand away from mine. That was a stupid thing to say. She walked down the driveway and waited by my car. I followed her.

"I think you should drive me home now," she said coldly.

"Hey, I didn't mean that," I said, looking in her eyes. "That was stupid. I kind of just say what comes out of my head. Truth is, you wear what you want, and no one has the guts to take it from you. I want that, I want what you have."

I kissed her on the neck. Then I put both of my hands on her hips. I felt her thighs cling tight to her dress. The material had no bumps, not wrinkles, her sides flawlessly smooth. She leaned her head back and gave a soft moan. Then she pushed me away. It wasn't hard, but enough to make me stop.

"We're going way too fast. Shouldn't we go on like several more dates?"

"Is that what you want?"

"Not particularly."

"Then why are you crying?"

"Because girls who hook up with boys on the first date are called sluts."

"Whoa, whoa!" I said, putting my hands up dramatically. "I wasn't proposing that! All I wanted to do was show you my room. Your mind is *so* in the gutter. Really, I'm just an honest boy."

Bella slapped me against the arm. Once again, it wasn't too hard.

"Look," I said, putting my hand through her short hair. She could have had longer hair—black locks flowing down to her chest. However, she exposed her bronze neck, and it was mesmerizing. "I'll take you home if you don't want to do anything. But either way, I want you to know that you are special to me."

With that, I opened the passenger side door. She looked at the inside of the car, and then at me. After a moment, she moved closer to me, grabbed my hand and placed it alongside her neck. Bella kissed my lips and closed the car door with her leg. We tipped-toed across the entrance way—all the time our lips were touching.

We moved together up the stairs, past Shah's bedroom with a pulsing dull bass, and to my own room. When we entered my door, I closed it with her body. All her toughness melted away, and she loudly moaned with relief, finally letting out her pleasure. Playfully, I put a finger to her lips and smiled. She smiled, too. As I pressed her against the wooden door, feeling her back, thighs, and finally chest, she began to push back. Soon, she pushed me back to my bed, and I fell over. Lying on my blankets, I watched her body in the dim moonlight, her red dress looking like the lipstick Chanel Ce Soir. Wearing her smirk just as boldly as her dress, she crossed one of her arms and went to take off one of her straps.

"No," I said, holding out my hand.

Her eyes widened, surprised.

"Leave the dress on. I want to see you in it."

Her smirk resumed, and then she lay down next to me on the bed.

8

Michael

It was three in the morning when I woke up to see Bella was asleep on top of my chest. One of her soft hands was placed on my stomach, while the other was lined across my side. How the hell was that comfortable for her? My arm would have pins and needles in minutes. I put one hand on their back and the other tucked behind my head. The moonlight shined through my window, and I could hear Shah's music lightly bludgeoning its way out of her room.

I thought of Bella's dress—how it clung to her the whole time. It brought shivers down my spine. My sudden movement shook her briefly awake, but then she fell back asleep, unfazed. She thought I was very caring for taking off her dress and hanging it in my closet afterwards. All my t-shirts and sweats where pushed aside for Bella's dress. The streetlamp outside crept its light in and shed its glow onto her red chiffon halter—which shined brightly against my muted clothes.

As her breath deepened and she fell far into sleep, I was finally allowed to stare at her magnificent dress. It was mine. At least I pretended it was. I imagined coming home from a dance, spinning around a couple of times—flaunting bright diamond earrings. Then, I would hang the dress on a lone coat hanger and place it gently onto the closet rack. For a moment, I would sit on the bed, watch the breeze in my room gently sway the chiffon. Chiffon, not like jeans or shirts—anyone can put a hot piece of metal on those materials. Chiffon requires some tenderness. Let the steam do the work—holding the iron just above the material. Like a skilled surgeon, I would alternate between steaming and smoothing the dress out. I used to do this on one of Shah's dresses, so she wouldn't notice I wore it. Frankly, I was doing Shah a favor. She never ironed it once!

39

Michael's Black Dress

I couldn't believe that afternoon I deliberately wore Shah's clothes, so she could walk in on me. Could it have gone better? Probably. However, I wanted her to really know what I felt deep down inside. It was like, a certain rush that people get and spend the rest of their lives chasing after it. For some, that might be money, sex, drugs—whatnot. I can tell you with the most absolute certainty that nothing has made me more special than wearing that perfect fit. I imagined myself in Bella's dress. Right now, while she was sleeping. Suddenly, the thought made me sick. God, I'm a freak, I thought. Was I? Was it so wrong? I wish I could just … have people understand what I mean. There's just a certain thrill about it. A love.

Carefully, I got out of bed and went to my bookshelf. I pulled out *Moby Dick* and stared at some dresses. Many nights, when I couldn't sleep, I would go through all the clippings until I was tired again. However, all I wanted to do was throw them in the trash. I really liked Bella, but what if she knew my secret? It was a sick obsession, and I was going to hell for it. Perhaps, right at that moment, I should stop it entirely.

I stared at her red dress, still glowing in the lamplight. It flaunted its smooth fabric, swaying to the gentle breeze from the open window. What if I were to spin around with this dress? I gently nudged Bella. She gave a soft grunt and nestled deeper into a pillow. Gently, I walked to the closet. In the moonlight, I touched her dress and left it practically melt in my hands. Was this wrong, this feeling?

"Michael?" she whispered, her voice heavy in sleep.

Quickly, I dropped my hand and stared at her. My breath tighten, and I began to shake.

"Yeah?" I whispered.

However, Bella didn't response back, but soon dozed back into sleep. Bella had one brown cheek glimmering from the moonlight, and the other deep in the pillow. She was a beautiful woman, certainly deserving a beautiful dress. I turned to look at the red halter. Any smart person would have gone back to bed, but I ran my fingers again on the dress.

"Come on, Michael," I heard the dress say to me. "You know you want to."

Softly, I grabbed the dress and lifted it off the rail. I swayed it back and forth like I was conducting an orchestra. No, it wasn't enough to stare at magazine clippings. I wanted more from this dress.

"Try me," it whispered. "Get your rush back."

I looked at Bella, who was sound asleep. Perhaps wearing the dress for a few moments wouldn't hurt. Quickly, I shed off my clothes and lifted the dress over my head. My hips were not as wide as hers, but I surprisingly filled out the top. I tried not to make any quick moves, afraid I might tear the dress. Looking into my tiny dresser mirror, I finally saw myself in a beautiful dress. The tears flowed down my cheeks, and I stared into the blurred figure in front of me.

God, it felt so good to wear it. The feeling was pure pleasure—the soft chiffon brushing against my thighs. It was also the sexiness. I wore pure allure on my body. Out of all the clothes I've worn, switching between Shah's and Ma's, this was the first dress that made me feel beautiful. Then, a wave of guilt went down my spine. Why the hell was I doing this? She was only two steps away to me, and I was fully in her clothes. I should take it off, I thought to myself.

"Michael?" Bella groaned.

I ducked behind the bed.

"Yeah?" I whispered.

"Where are you?"

"I'm by the door. I have to head to the bathroom."

"Oh, you're getting up too much."

"Go back to bed, Bella, I'll be there soon."

"… Okay."

The bed squeaked and groaned, and soon Bella had flattened herself back onto the bed. When the creaking noises stopped and the night noises resumed, I stood up and started to remove one of the straps. I looked into the mirror again, catching a glimpse of the dress resting on my chest. This was not a way to see a dress. I needed the full experience. Outside in the hallway was a wall mirror. I looked back at Bella, who had her head deep into the pillow. With soft feet, I tip-toed across the wooden floor and reached my bedroom door. *Creak.* Bella turned her body around on the bed—blankets twirling with her. Before she could see me, I slipped outside of the room and closed the door.

"Goddamnit," I whispered, resting my head on the door. That surely woke her up. I played with the straps nervously. This was a stupid game I was playing, I thought. Luckily, I still had my boxers underneath. It wouldn't be too awkward if she saw me like that—she had seen more of me anyway. What about the dress? If she stepped out of bed, she would look for it. I was so screwed. Then, I felt calm. Since I was already out here, I might as well see how good I looked in the hallway mirror. Down the hall, the wall mirror was grand, with a giant oak frame. In the distance, I could barely make out the red figure that was me. There I was, in a gorgeous dress. I took a few steps closer. God, I looked beautiful. Walking past Shah's room, I was surprised I didn't hear any music, but that was fine. Hopefully, Shah was finally asleep.

I stepped up to the mirror. My hands touched the glass. This was me. For the first time, I didn't see Shah or Ma in the mirror, I saw myself—the real Michael. How could I go back to dressing in secret? This made me so happy. And tomorrow I'd just pretend this never happened? This was my happiness, and I had to keep it in secret? At that moment, I truly knew who I really was—and now I had to cram that person back into a dusty box. I couldn't do it. Me, the boy in the dress, had to keep wearing it. Screw it, let the world see me like this.

"My name is Michael, and I'm wearing a dress," I whispered.

I said it again, louder this time.

"My name is Michael, and I'm wearing a dress."

Fresh blood ran through me, and I felt a hard chill through my body. This was me! I was tired of pretending.

"My name is Michael and I'm wear—"

A door opened. In sweatpants and a black hoodie, someone was staring at me.

"What the hell?" she whispered.

It was Shah.

9

Shah

At the moment, I wanted nothing better than to shut the door and turn up my music. I didn't even want to leave my room. I knew Michael had another girl over, so I didn't want to end up in the hallway with a half-naked girl who was looking for the bathroom. That would be just … absolutely wonderful. I was in the middle of sleeping—like most people do in three in the morning—and Michael kept appearing in my dreams. Both of us were in my room—taking all his clothes and putting them into a pile. Michael started to pour kerosene all over his hoodies, jeans, T-shirts, what-have-you. Then, he took one of my cigarettes and lit it up.

"It's gonna be different now," Michael had said.

"How?" I asked.

"You have to make sure I stay this way, because I'm going to burn all my clothes."

"But—"

"That's your job, Shah. Make sure I don't screw up."

He threw the cigarette on the floor and the clothes went up in flames. Smoke filled the room, but the smoke alarm didn't go off. I couldn't breathe. I coughed and waved away the smoke. Finally, when I fanned all the smoke away, I saw Michael, in a stunning dress. He was smiling, and I couldn't believe how happy he was.

"My name is Michael, and I'm wearing a dress."

"You sure are," I laughed.

"My name is Michael, and I'm wearing a dress."

"Okay, I heard you the first time."

Suddenly, my eyes fluttered opened. I wasn't dreaming, I realized. Michael was just outside my door. And what did you know? Michael was actually wearing a freaking dress when I opened the door. Can people just bear with me for a moment? First, I had to watch my own brother in my clothes. Now, he was wearing his date's clothing. Seriously? I was going to kill him. How in the hell was I going to take a calm and reasonable approach now?

"Get that damn thing off, now!" I hissed.

We exchanged muffled swears, mixed in with hisses. It was like we were street cats in an alleyway. Even though both of us wanted to kill each other at the moment, we were both quiet so not to wake up whoever was in his bed.

"I said, get that damn dress off now!"

"Make me!" Michael baited back.

"Oh, you're asking for it!"

"Try me."

I ran at him, my nails extended and ready to pounce. I went to the face first, smacking him in the head and neck. I left the dress untouched because I didn't want to explain to his date why her dress was torn and ruined. That would have been an exciting conversation: Oh, don't mind that. You see, Michael was just trying on your clothes and we kind of had a little fight.

He had to be such a jerk. When we were kids, he would beat the crap out of me whenever he felt like it. If we were playing cars and he wanted the dump truck, but I was *clearly* using it, he would pummel me on the head until I passed it over. Just because I was a girl, that didn't stop me from punching back. Most of the time, we smacked each other around until both of us were crying. Ma would obviously be pissed when she had to come over to see not one, but two crying children. Her solution was to punish us both. The worst was, she didn't even bother to find out who did what—when it was *always* Michael. We were always fighting about something stupid anyway. Ma would punish us by making us sit in front of the hall and stare at the wall mirror. I guess it was supposed to make us reflect at ourselves, give us this huge guilt trip or something. Instead, Michael and I would just make funny faces into the mirror and laugh.

Soon, we were hugging each other and apologizing for breaking a Barbie doll or reading someone's journal or calling someone a stupid doo-doo head.

When we were in front of the mirror this time, we weren't aiming to forgive. I continued to pummel his stupid, cross-dressing head, while he covered up his face to protect from all the blows I was giving him. I wasn't aiming to really kill Michael, but I wanted him to know how utterly stupid this last impulsive action was. Trust me, he wouldn't be standing if I wanted to do some real damage. I pounded on his head in a violent but loving matter.

"Get ... that ... dress ... off!" I said between punches.

"Quit ... walking in ... on awkward ... moments!" he yelled back. Suddenly, we hushed up. We both said something too loud. We stopped, adjusted upright, and waited for the creaks of the wood. Just like we did years ago, when we snuck out of our rooms at night, we stood breathless and on guard for any odd sound.

Creak.

"It's her," I whispered. Michael's eyes were wide with fear. I panicked, freezing dead in place. Whoever was in there would see both of us, and she would tell everyone. Oh God, Michael would be the laughing stock of the whole school. Who the hell would even want to go near him at the point? I didn't care if he was humiliated at home, but at school? I couldn't even imagine how cruel they would be. People would throw Barbie dolls at him and call him a fag. Oh, damnit Michael. Why couldn't you just be normal, I thought.

"Michael, do something," I said.

"Shah, help me," he whispered, his voice cracking.

Michael's bedroom door opened. Without thinking, I pushed Michael against my door.

"Don't say a goddamn word," I spoke softly. Then I opened my door and pushed Michael into my bedroom. Before he had a chance to say something, I closed it in from of him. Through the wood, I heard Michael's soft whisper. I was right about to open my door again and smack him, when the girl peered her head into the hallway. She was half-awake, squinting to see a dim figure in the hallway. Christ, this girl was probably half naked, peering from the door.

"Michael?"

"Yeah?" I answered, in a deep voice.

"Are you okay, you been up all night."

"Um, yeah, I have a bit of a stomach ache."

"Oh, uh, can I ask a weird question?"

"Yeah … babe, what's up?"

"Did … you take my dress?"

Damnit! I gritted my teeth and gently pounded my door. Why didn't he just take off the dress? Here I was, putting my reputation on the line, while Michael was safely behind my door. No, this was my fault, too. I put myself in this, and I had to get myself out. I was such an idiot, I thought. Why was I talking in such a deep voice? Was I even fooling anyone? I had to fess up. Maybe, if I came out clean right now, this girl wouldn't tell anyone. She looked sweet enough, and maybe she wouldn't find it too awkward. No, I told myself, no one would find this normal. Michael was a freak who liked to steal women's clothes! She would slap me in the face, rip the dress off of Michael's body, and fly out the house in her bra and underwear. Still, what other choice did I have? I took a deep breath and said the first thing that came into my head.

"I didn't want to wake you, you looked so sweet. You got frozen yogurt on your dress. I put it in the wash for you. That isn't weird, is it?"

"Uh, no. Well, a little. But that was nice of you," she said sleepily.

"Okay."

"Yeah … are you coming back to bed because this is reeeeallly awkward talking to you like this."

"Oh yeah, I just have to put it in the dryer now."

"Jesus, Michael, just because we fooled around doesn't mean you have to give me hotel service."

I laughed, and did it with a deep-chested mirth. How in the hell did I know to laugh like Michael did?

"Okay, babe, see you soon."

"Uh, okay."

I heard the door close. Immediately, I opened the door to see Michael's mouth practically hanging down to the floor.

"What did you do?" he said, half angry and have amazed.

"I think I just saved your ass," I said, smirking.

10
Michael

At the pub near our house, Shah smothered our order of steak fries in BBQ sauce. It had been an awkward Saturday morning, and Shah were going to have to talk about it over lunch. Luckily, there was no need to sneak Bella out of the house in the morning. Ma's double nightshift would mean that she would only get home at eight, so there was no rush to leave immediately. Most of the time, the girls woke up early and said they had to be somewhere. Whether or not it was true, I didn't mind because I didn't want them around in the morning anyway.

Bella didn't seem to be in a rush, and I actually enjoyed being wrapped up in her warmth. Honestly, if Ma found out I had Bella over, I don't think Bella would even care. There was a sort-of relaxation with her. In fact, she even asked if I wanted to get breakfast. She acted so sweet that I didn't say no. When I drove her to the local breakfast joint, she never mentioned anything about last night. Instead, we talked about bands, books, and other things that didn't make the time awkward. In fact, she was wonderful. She asked if wanted to keep hanging out some more, but I told her that I had promised Shah we'd get lunch together.

"So, you two are pretty close, huh," Bella had said in the car as we drove to her house.

"Yeah."

"You're lucky. It's just me and *Padre*. Most of the time, he's busy too. Not a lot of time to talk and stuff."

"Well, you can talk with me," I said, surprising myself.

"Does that mean we're still going to see each other? Or, was this a one-time thing?"

"I hope not."

"Good, because I like the real you."

"Excuse me?" I almost drove up on the sidewalk.

"You act all tough with your friends, but you're really a sweet guy."

"Oh. I'm glad you think that."

"Why don't you just be yourself?"

"I am right now."

"But I mean, all the time."

Before I had a chance to answer, I pulled into her driveway and saw a rather large man watering his grass. He was wearing a small tank top, and I could make out some tattoos on his arms. His muscles flexed, even as he was watering.

"Uh," I said. "Is that your dad?"

"Yeah, but he's harmless."

"Wouldn't he be bothered—."

"Don't worry about it." She kissed me on the cheek. "What you need to worry about is me." Bella smirked and opened the passenger door. She walked up to her dad and gave him a big hug. The man looked at me while hugging Bella. His eyes narrowed and starred me down as I awkwardly smiled and reversed the hell out of there.

There was way too much to talk about with Shah. Would Bella's dad kill me? What was even going on with Bella and me? Oh, yeah, and the whole dress thing! I needed to be with Shah so we could go over what the hell happened last night. Shah was thinking the same thing, because when I came back, she was waiting impatiently by the stairs. She called for emergency steak fries. Whenever one of us called for emergency steak fries, we had to drop anything we were doing and head to the nearest fast food place. Shah used it often, mostly due to whatever crap the other girls were saying about her. I only called these types of meetings twice, both for girl troubles. Wait—that was actually a lie. I was going to tell her the truth on both occasions, but I never had the guts.

Before I had a chance to reply, we got into the car and drove to the pub. It was a run-down bar, which didn't allow teenagers at night. But during the day we were allowed to order food there. We sat in a wooden veneer booth with a plastic table in the middle, which wobbled if we breathed too heavily. I wore a plain black t-shirt and jeans while Shah had the nerve to wear nasty blue overalls in public. She accidently smeared sauce on one of her straps and didn't care. What if the guy of her dreams happened to walk in this shady bar in the middle of the afternoon? It was probably unlikely, but still. I don't care how much charm Shah could pull off, no one is getting turned on by her butter-churning, peasant-girl clothes. She had the body to pull off some amazing designs, but she always chose the tackiest things. It was really surprising she hadn't picked up on my secret earlier—considering I usually bought her the only well-fitting and colorful clothes she owned for Christmas.

"What the hell, Shah?" I yelled at her as we ate. "Just keep smudging that stain with a napkin. That's definitely going to get it out!"

"Hey," she pointed at me with a steak fry, "I'm adding some color to the jeans. Isn't that what you always tell me to do? Add some color to my palette?"

I frantically looked around. The place was empty, except for an overweight white guy who seriously liked onion rings. He had a plate just for himself. I stared at him for a moment, and he looked away first. He went back to his onion rings with a look of defeat. Perhaps this was his secret spot, just outside of where he lived. His wife and kids told him to either lose weight or they would leave him. He may have tried, but weeks of kale and wheat germ took the best of him. And here he was now, having an affair. The overweight man lifted his head, making sure I stopped looking at him. Instead, I continued to stare. Before he had a chance to say something, I nodded my head. Don't worry, I said to myself, I won't tell anybody.

"Hey," Shah said, snapping me out of my gaze. "We came here for a battle plan, not so you could make new friends."

"Right," I said, dipping into the steak fries. I tried not to grab one that was drenched in BBQ sauce, but Shah made that incredibly difficult.

"So," she said with a mouth full of potato. "Do you think Bella figured it out?"

"Figured what out?"

"Are you stupid?"

"No, I don't think so. I think she would've mentioned it."

"Maybe she was too embarrassed."

"Trust me, she's not embarrassed at all."

"Ew, I hope that wasn't sexual."

"You be the judge."

Shah threw a fry at my face. Luckily, it didn't have any BBQ sauce. "Besides, that's not important right now. The real question is: How can we get you to wear women's clothes *without* anyone else knowing?"

"Can you not say that out loud?"

"Trust me, Lord of the Rings over there is going to keep his mouth shut."

"I don't care. Why do I even need to keep it a secret?"

Shah smirked. "You're joking, right?"

"What?"

"Like you have the balls to be that open?"

"I do. Maybe."

"Oh really?"

"Yeah, really, Shah. You know what? I should just tell everyone the truth. It would make my life a lot easier."

Shah dug into her grimy overalls and fished out some cash with her sauce-stained fingers. She slapped twenty dollars on the table.

"It's all yours if you can go up to beer-battered man and tell him you like to wear dresses."

"What?"

"Don't stall, you heard me. If you can't confess to that man over there, then what makes you think you can confess this secret you've been hiding for over ten years?"

"Well, more like eleven."

"Well, more like you're out twenty bucks if you don't start making some confessions."

I stood up, grabbed another steak fry, and jabbed it at her face. A bit of BBQ dabbed at her nose.

"Hi, my name is Michael, and I like to wear dresses," I whispered to Shah.

"Am I a plump, hair-line receding, middle-age white man?"

"No."

"Then try again, Michael."

I ate my disgusting fry and turned to the man. After a deep breath, I stood up and walked up to him—chest out. I got this, I thought. I can do this, no problem. He had part of an onion ring dangling from his mouth by the time I reached him. Suddenly, he stopped eating to look at me—puzzled. I cleared my throat and took a deep breath.

"Excuse me, sir," I said overly polite.

He turned his whole body to look at me—his jowls took a second to catch up to his face. His giant pudgy hands gripped tightly over his rings.

"My name is Michael." I sputtered, almost shouting. My face was burning.

"Hi," the man said slowly.

"Would you … like to know …" My pulse throbbed by my neck. I took a deep breath. "My name is Michael."

"Hi … Michael." The man kept looking around the room. Did he think I was going to rob him or something?

"I like … to … say … that …" Before I knew what I was doing, I took the plate of onion rings and pressed them to my chest. Ketchup was staining into my T-shirt, but it didn't matter. I had to run. When my sneakers squeaked past Shah, she stood up and tried to grab me. Quickly, I juked past her and sprinted my way to the exit. Out the glass doors and into the parking lot. When I reached the curb, I sat down and cradled the warm batter to my chest. Shah came out a few minutes later. She sat down beside me and put an arm around my chest.

"I gave the man the twenty and told him he didn't see anything. I think he got the message."

She nudged me with her shoulder, hoping I'd laugh. I didn't. Instead, I rocked back and forth with a damn plate of onion rings. God, I was a freak. My eyes began to water.

"Hey, hey, hey," she whispered, holding me close. "So we find another way, even if it means shaving your head, putting on a wig, and calling you Betty."

I dropped the onion rings onto the asphalt. Soon, the napkins blew in the wind and down the road. I thought of Lupita Nyong'o and her stunning white and black dress. She looked amazing with her buzzed head.

"That's it, Shah," I said.

"Oh, hell no. You are not wearing a wig."

"No," I smiled. "But I am going to cut my hair. You are, too."

11

Michael

On Monday, I was in the cafeteria with Bella as she playfully dropped tater tots into her mouth. Even though the screams and shouts in the cafeteria would make most people deaf, I could hear Bella crystal clear. I needed to hear her voice—that slight drop of an accent drove me crazy. Today, it was particularly fitting because she wore these red and white Day of the Dead earrings. It wasn't even close to November, but she didn't care. She matched those earrings perfectly with her off-the-shoulder dress. I couldn't believe Bella was still into me, especially after I dodged that bullet on Saturday.

"Is it weird that I want you to come to the festival next Saturday?" she asked, popping another tater like it was an M&M.

"Bella," I laughed, "I already awkwardly met your dad, so why not make it official?"

"Yeah," she said slowly. "So, you're not … freaked out that my dad didn't care, right?" Then she stared at her tater tots.

I poked her lightly on her open shoulder.

"Hey," I said. "I'd be freaked out if he came after me with a garden hose."

"It's just, most people would—"

"Look," I said, moving my head low to meet her eyes. "I'd love to come, and I'll eat whatever is on my plate. Don't Mexican people make those corn husk things?"

"Tamales!" Her eyes widened and she smiled. "Yeah, but sometimes we use parchment paper instead. Driving to the Hispanic grocery store is a pain."

"Oh, the one on Belmont?"

"Yeah, the one next to you! How the hell did you know that?"

"I may have looked online to see what Mexican places were around."

"I can't tell if that is cute, or super racist."

"Can we lean to the cute side?"

"Maybe."

"What if I picked up some of that parchment paper-thingy when I come visit you Saturday?"

"I think my grandmother will love you for it."

"Then brownie points it is."

"But you would need to come before the afternoon, because the husks need to soak."

"Guess that means I spend more time with you."

Bella blushed, matching the red in her earrings. It's like she planned to be amused! Good God, I wanted to be her. Here I was with my green football jersey and a pair of faded blue jeans. Both had no fit! They hung loose around me like I was a coat rack. Guys' clothing was like wearing a sleeping bag. One time, I had worn jeans that actually fit well, and the entire wrestling team was laughing their asses off when they saw me in the cafeteria.

"Oh, look at that ass on Michael," Marshall, the team captain, had said. "Have you been working out?" The rest of the team circled around me, like some animal pack, and railed joke after joke. "They're pressed and everything, your momma takes good care of you."

All of them laughed, and they wanted me to laugh too. "Man, quit dressing nice for the white boys." Some of the white players smacked Marshall in the chest—which he joyfully blocked and laughed off. I stormed out of the cafeteria and didn't speak for the rest of the afternoon. When I came home, I cried for a little bit in my room. Then I threw out any fitted clothes I had. Only the 'too big' remained. Jacob had called me that night and apologized for the way Marshall acted, but I wanted something more from him. But what was I going to do? Tell Jacob the real reason why I was upset? That seemed crazy.

"Hey, Michael," Bella said, throwing a tater tot at my face. "Hope you were having some deep thoughts about me."

"What?"

"You all right?"

"Yeah. Hey, can you excuse me for a moment?"

"Oh, sure."

I stood up and looked over at Shah, who was sitting eight tables down from me. It was time for our plan. We couldn't just randomly shave our heads. There had to be a reason, otherwise the school would know something was up. Shah and I tried to think of excuses to shave our heads at the same time, but nothing made sense without drawing suspicion. So I thought, if we were forced to shave our heads, it had to be as a punishment. We had to do something awful.

Our target was Lionel: my old, childhood friend. When we were little, the three of us, Jacob, Lionel, and me, were inseparable. Then, as we grew older, I couldn't stand how annoying he became—he constantly was coming over my house just to hit on Shah. Since we needed a victim, I thought Lionel would do nicely.

I walked toward Shah's group of friends, The Rabbits. I liked to call her so-called friends that because they only had lettuce and carrots on their lunch trays. Collectively, they looked like a college pamphlet: an ethnically diverse group of girls all laughing and smiling together. It was pretty remarkable really. Yet, despite how diverse they were, they were all just the same. If I was blindfolded, I couldn't tell them apart by their voices. They all talked the same and laughed like their voices were hopping. They also all wore the most expensive brands. One girl wore this white blouse that had way too much frills on it. She looked like a pirate and that blouse had to have cost at least a few hundred dollars. I couldn't understand why Shah sat with them. Perhaps the Rabbits were missing one color to their palette and needed Shah to join to complete the set. The whole time, Shah weakly smiled at whatever they were laughing at. She was nibbling at her salad when I walked up to her.

"Oh my God, Shah," I overheard one of The Rabbits say as I got closer. "I have to say, I love that sweater."

"Yeah, it's really cute," added another.

"Where'd you get it?" one asked. "Did you get it from …?" She gave a long pause and slightly nodded her head.

"Did I get it from what?" asked Shah.

"You know, like … Africa?"

"Uh, no. I think I bought it—"

"Shah," I said. "Can I talk to you?"

"Um sure, excuse me ladies."

"Hi, Michael," flirted one of the Rabbits.

"Hi," I said quickly, not interested.

Shah stood up and together we looked at each other seriously.

"Are you sure you want to do this?" she whispered.

"Of course."

"It's just, did we have to pick Lionel? He's not a bad kid."

We looked over at Lionel. He sat in the back of the cafeteria which a bunch of losers. There was a paint set in front of him. He chewed on a baloney sandwich. I didn't feel guilty.

"That creep constantly bugs you all the time. Always knocking on the door and asking for science help. You don't even have the same class."

"I know. Whatever, let's just get this over with."

Suddenly, I shoved Shah. She dramatically fell back against the table. The Rabbits screamed. Dozens of conservations hushed immediately.

"What the hell!" said Shah.

"Don't you give me 'What'. What's this I'm hearing about Lionel?"

Lionel, who was way across over at the other end of the cafeteria, looked up from his paints.

"So, you'll just sleep with anyone, nowadays? Is that right, Shah?"

"Michael, what the hell are you talking about?"

"I have to hear from someone else that you've been hooking up with Lionel, of all people?"

"Will you stop, can't this wait until—"

I slammed the table again and walked over to Lionel, my eyes focused on him the entire way. Lionel, holding his paintbrush in his hand, didn't know whether to drop it or to use it as a weapon.

"Lionel!" I shouted.

"Uh, hi Michael."

"Did you sleep with my sister?"

"What?"

"Don't you dare lie to me! I heard somebody say it."

"Who?"

"It doesn't matter. Let me say this: You don't look at my sister, you don't even think about her. You hear me? Nobody goes out with my sister unless I say so."

"Okay, Michael. But I never—"

"Never meant to for me to find out? Oh, so you admit it. Was it fun, did you enjoy yourself?"

"Uh," Lionel looked around for help, and then looked to Shah. I turned around to see Shah walking up to me.

"Michael, chill. This isn't the place—"

"No, no, no. This is the perfect place to flip out! Nobody is going out with my sister."

"Just because you can't keep a girl for more than a week, doesn't mean you have to ruin it for me."

The cafeteria gasped all at once, and they all waited for me to react. Perfect, it was all going to plan, I thought. I grabbed the red oil paint from his case and squeezed all the tube on Shah's hair. She screamed at the top of her lungs as I rubbed the paint into every follicle. I stepped back, admiring my worked and laughed. Shah, seeing how the assistant principal was speed-walking towards us, quickly grabbed a green paint and smeared it on my head. I was trying so hard not to grin when the assistant principal and the security cop broke us apart and ushered us away from the cafeteria.

When I was pushed past Bella, her eyes were wide. I winked at her.

12

Michael

One new redhead and a green freak sat outside the assistant principal's office. We both sat in silence, as there wasn't a soul near us— not even a secretary. Shah let out a deep sigh, and I didn't respond. After a moment, Shah sighed again, but this time it was even louder.

"Yes?" I said. "Is there something you would like to say?"

"You are the worst brother."

"Oh please, you enjoyed the attention. Admit it. Seeing Lionel's face was priceless."

"That poor kid."

"Oh, he'll be fine. Tomorrow, we'll just say it was a misunderstanding and you were talking ... about how you really liked *vinyl.* How you like to hold it tight against you at night."

Shah smirked. "This was your master plan? I can't believe I agreed to this."

"You look cute as a redhead."

"I can't say the same for you."

Green coated my shirt and pants.

"Thanks, Shah." I stood up and pirouetted in the hallway.

She laughed, "Look at you, all grins."

"You don't get it, I haven't felt this good ... since ... since."

I stopped spinning and stared at a cracked grandfather clock that stood outside of the principal's office. The thing was huge, towering over me by at least a foot. It was a stupid idea to leave something so elegant and regal outside. There was a huge crack down the side of its wooden frame. The clock still worked though, its pendulum swaying predictably back and forth. Someone must have bumped into the side of the clock and ruined it. The crack went from the top to bottom, and another big hit might break the thing altogether. I was surprised no one tried to patch it up.

"What?" Shah stood up and tapped me on the back. I continued to stare at the clock.

"I can't go back."

"What the hell you are talking about?"

"I haven't felt this good since the night I wore the red dress."

"Yeah, you idiot, wasn't this the whole point?" Shah ran her hands through her newly red hair. "I did this for you! My hair is completely ruined! I look like a Cabbage Patch Kid."

"I felt something that night, the shortness of breath, a pulsing of blood through my legs. As I stared into the mirror, it was like I met the most beautiful figure in the world. You hear the expression that when you see *the* one, everything falls into place? That was when I saw me, the one. Shah, I didn't see who I was until that night. Before, it was a secret kept hidden under closed doors—someone who peeked out of closets at midnight. How can anyone live like that, to keep a whole different person locked behind a mirror?"

"So let it out!"

"You can't fix something that's broken. You get what I'm saying?"

I ran my fingers across the crack of the clock. I felt the rough, wooden grooves, and then I punched the clock. I muffled my screams—not wanting to get the assistant principal out of his office—and cradled my hand. Some of the wooden panel came apart.

"What the hell is wrong with you?" She looked at my hand and saw the redness on my knuckles. Immediately, she took the panel of wood and threw it into the trash.

"How can you go back?" I looked at her, tears in my eyes. "When the real me is so torn apart?"

"Michael," she put a hand to my cheek. "Why do you think you're broken? You just said you finally saw that different person."

"Because the old me has to go. Don't you see, Shah? I want to live, but I'm afraid of it."

"Don't you go getting philosophical on me."

"I finally have a taste of it, and now I don't know if I can even handle it."

"Then we'll call this whole thing off, we can still try something different. Maybe I'll buy some more clothes for you, and when you get home …"

"I'm a freak! Can you fix this clock? Well, can you? It's completely ruined now. It can't go back to what it was. Is this better? Is it better to be so broken?"

She grabbed my shirt. "You listen to me. I didn't just get paint smeared in my hair and come across as a nerd-loving tramp for nothing. This is your life, Michael, I don't give a damn what we have to do to make you live it. If you think this plan is the only way it'll work, then we'll do that. If you want to just come out about how you wear—"

"No," I shook my head violently from side to side. "I can't. They won't. There's just no way."

"But how will you know unless—"

"I said no, Shah!"

"Then we'll go with your plan. But I'll beat the living crap out of you if you fall back now."

"What the hell are we doing? This will never work," I said.

"It will, I know it," said Shah. "You're the smarter one of the two."

The assistant principal opened the door, and out walked our mother as well. She didn't look beautiful like she used to, just old and tired. Usually she was sleeping at this hour—resting from the graveyard shift. She didn't even look at us, just stared at the clock—possibly at the crack.

"Well, your mother and I had a little chat," said the assistant principal. "And even if it was aggressive interactions between siblings, it still constitutes as improper conduct. So, you two will be suspended for the rest of the week. You'll start fresh on Monday, and hopefully you'll learn to control yourselves better."

"Yes, sir," we said in unison.

"And also," added the principal. "We have a three-strike rule here. Two more behaviors like this and either one of you could get expelled."

"We know."

"I suggest you control your temper before—what happened to my clock!" He ran over to the grandfather and lightly touched it. "Oh, no, no. I can't fix this! Did you two do this?"

"A bunch of freshman ran into it while you were talking," said Shah. "We were going to chase after them, but you told us to wait here."

"Why is your hand red, Michael?" asked Ma.

"Cause Shah is such a pain." I threw the hardest punch I could at Shah's shoulder. She let out of a groan and punched me back in the stomach.

"Nice one, jerk," whispered Shah.

"Enough!" said Ma. "Thank you for your time, sir." My mother added softly, "Michael and Charlotte will pay for whatever arts and craft thing they ruined for Lionel."

"That would be appreciated, Mrs. Carr."

Without a word, she escorted us out of the school, dragging us each by the shoulder. It was like we were little kids again. She threw us into the back seat and drove off in silence.

"You two are a complete joke," she finally snapped. "There's no way you're going to school like that on Monday. You're heading to the salon right now and both of you are getting complete buzzes."

"What?" Shah protested. "You can't do that!"

"Oh yes, I can."

"But I can dye it black! It will look fine."

"That's not the point. Since I don't have time to punish you anymore, I'll do what I did all those years ago."

"But Ma!" I yelled. "We were just kids!"

"And you still are. When you two covered all of your beautiful curly hair with chewed up bubble gum, well, I thought then I just about saw everything. What kids have a competition to see how much gum can you fit into their heads? Back then I showed you a lesson by buzzing bald your heads. You were the laughing stock for weeks and you don't even look at gum anymore. So, that's how it's going to be. I might not be the best mother out there, but I sure as hell won't let my kids do anything stupid like this and get away with it."

"They won't be able to tell us apart," I whined. "Shah has no chest!"

"Michael!" Ma yelled at the rearview mirror.

"You jerk," Shah slapped me hard across the arm.

"Well, then get used to being mistaken for a while. It will teach you a lesson."

13
Michael

When Sunday night came around, and Ma went to bed early before her shift, Shah and I made preparations for Monday. Our freshly buzzed heads had slight traces of red, in hers, and green, in mine, but our hair was now mostly dark brown like before. Shah was waiting patiently in her room and had her eyes closed. In the new dress I bought, I slowly checked and rechecked myself.

"Oh God, I'm so nervous," Shah said, her eyes still closed.

"Why? Because I might look better than you?"

"Shut up. Can I open my eyes now?"

"I never said you had to close them."

"I know. I think it helps if I see a before and after image. So I can trick my mind or something."

"Just open your damn eyes. I think you'll like it."

Shah opened her eyes and gasped. She put her hand over her mouth and widened her eyes.

"Well?" I asked, but not loud enough to wake Ma.

"Michael—"

"I knew I shouldn't have bought this dress," I said while letting out a deep sigh. "I'm not going to fool anyone. I'm just going to have to stay at home, hiding like a freak."

"Will you shut up and come into the hallway?"

We walked outside and stared into the long mirror. My red dress fit perfectly. It was short-sleeved and had black mesh cutouts along the sides of my body. My toned arms didn't matter—they accepted the sharp color. Having shaved armpits was weird, but I stretched out my arms and let the fabric hug me from all over. Last Saturday I called Bella to say I wouldn't be able to bring the parchment paper for the festival. I said my Ma grounded me for the weekend. In reality, Shah and I went to the mall and shopped around instead. First, we went to some low-end fashion stores, but I begged her to go to look at some real dresses. Finally, we walked by a really chic store with a poster of a tiny model with a beautiful red dress. I knew right there that I had to have it. It had the same popping power that Bella's chiffon dress did.

Together, we snuck into the ladies changing room, so I could try on a few bras. I needed to wear a bra in order for the dress to work. When we finally found some that were comfortable, they didn't give me any curves. How was I going to fool the whole school if I didn't have anything on my chest? We tried using a whole wad of tissues that Shah had in her pocket, but it came out all lumpy and one cup sagged to the side.

"Well, when you cry from embarrassment," Shah had said in the dressing room, "at least you'll have tissues." I could feel some tears building in my eyes. "Okay, okay, I know. I'm not helping with your confidence. Do you think you can hold the fort in here for like fifteen minutes?"

"You want me to lock myself in here?"

"Yeah, just don't come out."

"You better not trick me."

"Michael, you realize if I wanted to mess with you, I would have done it *a lot* sooner."

"Fine, go. But you better have a good idea."

She came back in exactly fifteen minutes and twenty-eight seconds. I counted on my watch. The entire time I sat on the stool with my legs up and hugged to my chest. Thankfully, not a soul came by.

"Where the hell have you been?" I asked.

"Away for exactly fifteen minutes, like I said."

"Plus some seconds."

"Stop acting like a little girl."

"You serious right now?"

"Sorry. Here, try these. It took me a bit to find them."

66

Shah ripped open a pair of triangular push-up pads. They had this strange squishiness to them. I grabbed one and she grabbed another. We alternated squeezing them, back and forth.

"Um, what do you think?"

"Is it weird that I'm slightly aroused?"

"Eh, possibly, but then again I'm squeezing them, too. Maybe we're both weird."

I stuffed them into the bra and moved from side to side—showing off the guns.

"Not bad," said Shah. "The men are certainly going to notice you."

"I'm not picking up men," I snapped.

"Oh, and the sass, it's going to drive them wild."

I ripped one of the triangular pads off my bra and used it to slap her in the face. She grabbed the other one and returned the favor. Brother and sister, slapping each other with fake boobs. That had to be a first.

"Okay," I said, holding back a laugh. "You're going to ruin my figure."

"Speaking of figure, we need to get you a waist trainer too. Another fifteen minutes?"

"Ten."

"Eleven."

"Nine."

"Fifteen it is, Michael."

"You better not leave."

"You know, I did want to get something at the food court."

"I swear …"

She opened the curtain and exited the changing room. On the other side, she continued to mock me.

"You look amazing." she said. "I'm going to get the rest of the ladies over her to look at you."

"Shah, shut up!"

"Honey, don't be nervous. You need to be confident in yourself."

"People are going to hear you," I hissed angrily.

"Oh, but maybe I should get an assistant for advice with the waist trainer? I just don't know how they work."

I punched the curtain a few times, praying that a few might hit her head. Shah let out a huge laugh.

"Relax, killer. There's no one in here. I'll be back with the waist trainer and hopefully it will fit you."

Thankfully, when she returned, the waist trainer did fit. I still had a hard time breathing when she pulled at the strings, but I managed to get used to it after a while.

"Are you going to pass out?" she asked.

"This is what you girls do for beauty, I guess."

"Hey, I don't even come close to dressing like this. Give me a loose sweater and sweat pants any day."

"Yeah, and that's why no one asks you out."

Shah dropped the smile and looked at me.

"Do you think I care?"

"Yeah, I think you do." I matched her sour face.

"Well, I don't. This is me, and I'm going to wear whatever the hell I want."

"Correction. I am you, and I'm going to rock that sexy dress from the window."

"Yeah, about that."

"What?"

"They don't have it in your size, but if we order it today, they'll have it ready for Sunday."

"What if it doesn't fit?"

"We can get something else."

"No. It has to be that dress."

"Seriously? Can't you do something different?"

"No."

"Good, because I already ordered it."

"Then what the hell was the point of talking about it?"

"Because I have to drive you crazy. That's my job."

I went to hit her again, but she ran out of the room. This time I knew there was no one in the dressing room, so I ran after her and bear-hugged her from behind.

"Stop it, stop it!" she yelled.

"Belly-to-Back Suplex," I said, and gently lifted her up and behind me. Whenever I learned a new wrestling move, I used to practice on Shah. She, of course, never consented, but I figured that most opponents wouldn't willingly let you suplex them either. When she landed on the ground, there was a giant thud, and the floor shook.

"Is everything okay in there?" a voice said from outside of the changing room section. We looked at each other. Shah was just suplexed from a man in a waist trainer and bra. The whole thing was so messed up that we had to laugh.

"Yeah," Shah said. "I've been putting on too many pounds. And I just kind of fell over."

I stifled a laugh.

"Oh, well do you need assistance?" the woman said.

"No, but I might need help with some other things."

"Please don't waste my time, Miss."

"Sorry, sorry. We're—I mean—I'll be out in the minute."

That was a close one, but I didn't care. I was just so happy hanging out with Shah. It was also worth it, because when Shah picked up the red dress on Sunday night, I looked amazing. No, I was stunning. And I'd never felt happier.

14

Shah

Judgment day had come: Michael was to wear the dress at school. That morning, we drove together in the Jeep in silence. Don't ask me why he didn't want to try something more conservative. He wanted everything or nothing—that's just the way he is. Why can't he just be normal? Why does he need all the drama? I'll tell you why, it's because I allow for this craziness to happen. Michael, with his crazy mind, thought up this elaborate plan during our wonderful stay-at-home vacation. Sure, I have no problem getting suspended. Absolutely *zero* problems with that. It's not like colleges look at that or anything. I told him this wasn't going to be an everyday thing. He had one chance not to screw up, and if he managed to fool everyone, then maybe we would try again down the road.

To be honest, it was kind of creepy how he was practicing copying my voice. By the end of the week, he somehow managed to do it—for the most part. Apparently, he told me that I have a "salt-and-pepper" tone. What the hell does that mean? All I think of is the salt-and-pepper hair of middle-age men. Is that supposed to be a compliment? That sure is a confidence booster—I was a girl in my prime that had the voice of a middle-aged man. Wonderful. That's what the guys line up for...

I liked to think that Michael and I were alike, so how in the hell did Michael get so many dates, and I ended up with weirdos who said the word 'facetious' in normal conversation? Seriously, it was like a five to one date ratio. God, I was so disgusted with Michael's love life—it's like he bought them in bulk and has to go through them before they expire. I used to think he was a man-whore or something. Now, I wasn't too sure. I remembered all the crazy girls he used to fool around with. There was Blake, who wore the Rockabilly look: dyed black hair, circle skirts, and many tattoos.

Cynthia, the wannabe fashion model who constantly wore the open back dresses. Mary, Beth, Alex … they were all so beautiful. Part of me was jealous that Michael brought home all these amazing-looking women, while I was in my room on a Friday night—chain smoking and listening to Pendulum. Now I realized that they weren't really amazing or beautiful. Most of them were dumb, annoying, stuck-up, or not that great-in-the-face department. Yet, they all dressed in an unforgettable style. It made sense now: It was all for the clothes.

I was still angry with him because he objectified all these women—not sexually, but materially. That was going to hurt my head a bit. No, scratch that. Michael wearing freaking dresses still topped my list of things that gave me a headache. I guess, I needed to get used to it—for like Michael's sake and all. But, this was a completely different Michael. What happened to the old one? Maybe he never changed. But there *is* something completely different. I don't know, this is just way too much.

I tugged at the clothes I was wearing, Michael's clothes. I had on some black jeans and a long sleeve T-shirt advertising a rapper I didn't even know. I don't think Michael did either. I guess he just bought all these shirts just to fit in. Pretending I was Michael was pretty easy. Wearing all of these baggy clothes was pretty comfortable. Hell, I could have played a dude even with my hair long. I wasn't minding the whole buzzed hair thing—relaxing my hair took *way* too much of my time anyway. I actually got to sleep in that morning. Instead of waking up an hour before Michael, I just rolled out of bed, took a shower, and put on jeans and a tee—like every other guy. It was a pretty awesome feeling. If only I could do this every day.

On the other hand, Michael looked amazing. He somehow managed to make himself look better as a woman than a man. I didn't get it. He didn't even put that much makeup on. He didn't want to. That's the other thing that was blowing my mind right then: Michael didn't want to be a woman, but he wanted to wear dresses. I thought those two went together. He wanted to be on both sides of the river. Maybe not—I'm so bad at analogies. It was like Michael wanted the best of both worlds but didn't want to stay on one side. Can you even have that?

I kept trying to block out these questions I had in my mind. Instead, I convinced him that we needed to neutralize his eyebrows as much as possible—much to Michael's annoyance. On top of that, I added some peach blush to his cheeks, and some mascara. Still, deep down, the man was still in his face. However, with Michael's glow and his sexiness— which is a little bit weird to say—it did create an illusion. I really thought he was going to fool people. At least for that day. We were already taking a huge risk.

"Okay, quiz time," I said to him. We were almost at school.

"Shoot."

"Why would I, or you, suddenly be dressed this good?"

"I wanted to make up for the buzzed head, I thought I was too ugly," he said back automatically. Damn, he even nailed my "salt-and-pepper" voice.

"What if you shout some really dumb man-thing, like 'Hey girl, Jello that body for me and wiggle'?"

"Who would say that?"

"I don't know, guys."

"Dumb question. I'm not even answering that. Next."

"What if you trip, rip your dress on a nail while falling down the stairs, crash into a trash-can, and everyone sees your exposed underwear with your thing all about?"

"Will you relax? Nothing is going to happen."

"I think something will happen. And I want to be prepared," I said. I immediately looked away—focusing on the school, which loomed in the distance. I couldn't stop thinking of all the ways this could go wrong.

He slammed on the brakes. I flew forward and almost smacked my head against the dashboard.

"Hey!" he shouted. "I need you right now. It's going to work out fine."

There he went acting all manly again. It was odd to see him so dominant while wearing a pretty dress. Michael didn't care. He spent countless hours making up this elaborate ruse to wear a dress in public, and he wasn't going to stop for anything. Still, that was the thing that really pissed me off the most. Here he was, my sweet brother who just wanted to be happy. On the other hand, he was this commanding jerk that had to get his way. He was a guy and a girl, a tough man and a cry-baby, paranoid-mastermind and some fool. Who was the real him?

We drove into the parking lot and parked several rows from the front entrance. I guess he wanted to walk some ways first.

"You ready?" I asked after he turned off the ignition.

"No," he said. "But what the hell?"

"What the hell," I repeated.

15

Michael

I could have continued to dress in secret, and maybe drive three towns over where no one would know me. But would that be any better than hiding in my room? Truth is, I wanted everyone to know. Sort of. You hear those stories about couples having sex in public because of the thrill of getting caught? Maybe that was me. There I go again, making this sound all sexual, like I have some fetish or something.

I felt good when I stepped on the asphalt with my ballet flats and my red dress. I wasn't turned on or anything. It just felt right. I wanted to show off more skin, but Shah said I really had to cover my back and shoulders as much as possible. No amount of makeup could hide my muscular, broad back. Still—with dozens of people walking by—I desperately wanted to shout at the top of my lungs, *This is me, Michael, and I am in a goddamn dress!* But that wasn't going to happen. The thought of it made me smile, though.

All those thoughts vanished when I arrived in front of the school. The high school was an old brick building that was probably constructed about 100 years ago. The red bricks were also brown, and there were many cracks and chips on the walls. No one noticed or cared. Before entering the aged building, there were twenty-five concrete steps leading up to the front door. These steps were also cracked and chipped, but people talked and laughed while they lounged on the rails and steps—as if it wasn't an eyesore. It seemed liked the entire school hung out in the morning by the front entrance—delaying the inevitable as long as possible. That's why it felt like the whole school had stopped what they were doing to look at me. I could feel the energy, their eyes boring into my soul. They noticed me, and I liked it.

"Hey Charlotte," said a boy. He looked me up and down. Part of me wanted to punch him in the face, but I was blushing at the same time.

"Look at you," Shah whispered, "my femme fatale."

"I'm not trying to do this."

"Then quit stopping traffic."

"Why? You think I can't handle this?"

"No," Shah playfully hit me. "But the more attention you draw to yourself, the better the chance we get caught."

"Oh, so I should just wear a bunch of rags I find in your closet and hope to God nobody talks to me?"

"Hey, I'm the last person you want to piss off right now," Shah punched me in the kidney and continued to walk up the stairs. Shah was wearing some odd sweatshirt with the hoodie over her head. Her long baggy pants hid any sort of feminine charm she had about her—if any. I was right about to punch her back when I saw him standing at the top of the stairs.

"Kill me later," I said. "Because we have a bigger problem."

Jacob was dragging his backpack on the floor like it was a dead dog. When he saw me, his jaw dropped, and he let go of his backpack. He tilted his head to the side and raised his eyebrows. I have to run, I thought, I have to turn around and get right back in the car. Maybe I can move to another school, or just drop out entirely. I could be a migrant worker, working a couple of backbreaking years picking strawberries and whatnot, make a few dollars, and come back to high school when everyone I know was long gone. My heart pounded, I felt the rush of blood trying to escape out of my neck. I tried to turn around, but Shah tightly gripped my backpack.

"Relax," she said. "He always looks this stupid."

When we reached the top of the stairs, I looked at my best friend eye to eye. He stammered and looked down at his backpack—papers and books were leaking out from the open zipper. He hurried to pick them up and kept apologizing. I looked at Shah, who gave me a huge smirk.

"H-hey, Shah," said Jacob. "Um, you're looking, like … not you."

"Um," I said, trying my best to imitate Shah's voice. "Thank you."

"No, I mean … you're looking like … very good." He kept adjusting his backpack strap and looking up at the clouds. He tried acting all cool and stuff every time he looked at me.

"So," Jacob said awkwardly, "You, uh, going to class."

"Yeah," I said, annoyed.

"Cool, cool." He looked up at the clouds again. "Well, maybe I can walk you and then … you can walk me."

"What?" I asked.

"Do I have to kick your ass again," Shah pointed a finger at Jacob. Wow, she had my voice down pat, I thought. Even her finger pointing was spot on. It was like I was watching myself on film.

"Relax, Michael," said Jacob. "And by the way, the buzzed head, it works well on you. I don't think it would on me. Unless I had cancer. Do you have cancer? Do you both have cancer? Do I have to go to some sort of meetings with you, because I will, I want to be supportive—"

"Shut up," I said. Then I realized I needed to be drop back into Shah mode. "Ma made us shave our heads because of the whole paint thing."

Jacob laughed, "Oh yeah. Man, that was awesome. I mean you guys being suspended sucked and all, but man it was so funny. Lionel almost had a heart attack." Then Jacob looked sad for a moment, and then looked down at his shoes. "Um," he stammered after a moment and then said, "Was it true that you and Lionel … had … done … took a swan ride through the tunnel of love?"

"Oh, God no!" Shah shouted.

Jacob looked at Shah, and then at me.

"No," I added. "Michael and I talked it over, and he heard me talk about *jokingly* sleeping with Lionel. Yeah, it was a joke. A pretty bad one."

"Yeah!" he pumped his fist. Then he stared at me and dropped the excitement. "I mean, I'm glad that you restrained from sexual relations with that man. Do you concur, Michael?"

"I'm going to concur a fist in your face," Shah said, still maintaining my voice pretty well.

"Welp, time to run like mad." Jacob ran and Shah followed. She was going to beat him up, a dream she probably always wanted.

"Sha—Michael!" I shouted before she went inside.

She turned, arms extended with her baggy T-shirt.

"And the bird flies from its nest!"

Shah was right. She couldn't be beside me forever. I was alone, with the entire student body judging me, eyeing me. I could do this. I just fooled my best friend. How hard could this be?

16

Shah

As I walked down the mostly crowded hallway and its endless rows of blue lockers, I was lugging Michael's half duct-taped backpack to class. I was feeling pretty good. Not a single person had any idea that it was really me, which I guess was also sad—but not really. Not even his own teachers recognized me. I had four periods where nothing remotely eventful happened. Perhaps this was going to be easier than I thought. But at lunch I was bombarded with a jump from behind. Jacob was on top of me, trying to give me a noogie on my buzzed head.

"God," he said. "It's so much more satisfying when you don't have all that hair on your head."

I didn't say anything back. Still, Jacob kept walking beside me, and kept bugging me about Bella.

"So," he kept nudging me in the ribs. Thank god, he didn't aim higher. "You tried ignoring me earlier. Did you and Bella stick the landing on the pole vault?"

I punched him hard in the shoulder. Did guys do that? Or did they just laugh off a comment like that? Wait, maybe they gave each other high-fives. It didn't matter—I'd already punched him, so I had to commit.

"Easy killer," I said slyly. "I'm not giving out my secrets just yet."

"Geez," said Jacob, holding his arm. "Can you just man-up and tell me if you did it or not?"

"Maybe."

"Maybe means yes! Oh yeah, give some to me!" he extended his hand. I was so tempted to punch him again, but this time in the face. But I sighed and extended my hand to meet his. "Come on, dude. Cheer up." He added, "Bella is a fine piece of—"

78

"Enough!" I shouted. Some kids in the hallway turned to look at me. I let out a laugh and pushed Jacob playfully. "Just drop it okay?"

"Alright," he said sadly. "Hey, your sister is looking pretty cute today. I mean she's always cute and all, but most days she's like a strong B, B+. Today, I'd be so bold as to give her an A."

"B, B+? That's it?"

"It's passing."

"I'll pass you through this locker door if you don't shut up."

"Same old Michael," he smirked. He extended his hand. "I want to run to the lunch-line. Mac-n-cheese day!" He kept his hand out. How in the hell did they shake hands? Did they do some secret boy-scout salute? I wound back my arm and smacked his palm like there was a mosquito on it. "Ow!" he yelled. "What was that?"

"Just … trying something different."

"Well, that really hurt."

"Are you going to cry now?" I smirked.

"You jerk." He smiled back and headed off to the cafeteria.

Alright, so it wasn't perfect, but this was my first day pretending I was a guy. So far, I was nailing it. The appearance was easy. Without the make-up, I already looked like a guy. Apparently, I have the face of a she-devil. Michael and I pretty much have the same face structure and whatnot—but does he have to dunk his face in paint? Hell no, and people like how he looks. Oh, look how pretty his face is! Michael's so hot. Blah, blah, blah. I have to listen to that crap every time at the lunch table. He's my brother and those girls just keep blabbing away at how attractive he is. It's weird, and they know it's weird. Still, they keep on talking because if I made a fuss then I'd be exiled from the table of Rabbits—great, now I was even talking like him.

Michael kept telling me I didn't need to hang out with The Rabbits, but I'm not popular like him. If I don't have a place to sit, I'll have to sit next to Lionel and his baloney sandwiches. No, thank you. Oh man, that was going to be the best part about lunch: I was going to sit with all the guys. It wasn't going to be like a peep show or anything, but Michael's table was always filled with so much energy. They all made fun of each other and were trying to out-do each other with pranks.

Last week, Jacob left the table to go to the bathroom and Marshall put tin foil in his sandwich. That look Jacob made was priceless—he eyes opened mad wide when his teeth bit into the sandwich. Of course, I didn't see it—I had to have it recapped for me by Michael. That day, I had been talking with The Rabbits and they were discussing their plans for Friday—who was going out with whom and who wanted to double date. It was so boring.

"Hey sexy," said as voice in the hallway.

I kept walking down the hall, as I was only a few feet from the cafeteria doors. Shoes kept storming on the tiles, pacing faster and faster. Don't sweat, I thought, just pretend you didn't hear her voice and make it to the door. You can't run, but maybe try speed walking. You're just really hungry, that's all.

"You can't run away from me," said the voice, a bit louder.

Why was there no one in the hall? I wanted to scream for help, but that would call attention, and this whole swap-thing had to be all low-key. A hand grabbed by backpack. It jerked me back and slammed me against the lockers. We were around a corner, where few people would see us. Bella pressed her body to mine.

"You've been ignoring me the past couple of days," she whispered to me, putting a finger to my chest.

"Hey Bella … my mom … said I couldn't …"

"Oh? Your mom?" She laughed coquettishly. "You weren't worried about your mom last weekend." She put her hand on the top of my head and felt the black stubble. "Your hair like this is so hot."

"Thanks, but we should probably get to lunch."

"Lunch? I can fill your appetite." She grabbed my back and pulled me to her. "What's the matter? You're not excited to see me?"

"Um, yeah, I am … but what if someone sees us?"

Bella looked around. The hallway was empty.

"Isn't this what you want? Tell me you want it."

I started to sweat, my chest felt like I had a lead weight inside it. My breathing grew heavy and fast. That was making it worse: Bella thought I was getting turned on.

"Hey, I got an idea. How about we leave through the fire exit and have some fun."

"Or, we could talk about some serious issues, like water purification, or racism in the modern era."

"I'll talk however you want me to talk." She kissed me on the neck.

"Jesus, please no."

"Oh, you're playing hard to get? I like that."

I pushed her away, "Please, not now. I'm really hungry. It's Mac-n-cheese day. Doesn't that sound fun?"

"No, I have a better idea."

She reached down to my belt and I instantly dropped the act.

"Bella, please don't."

"And why's that?" The sultry voice dropped.

"Because."

"Why Shah?"

"Because."

Then I realized what she said: 'Why *Shah*?'

17

Michael

Laughter suddenly brushed upon The Rabbit's faces. The girl who fell onto the ground was a mess. Her hair was disheveled, her food was on the cafeteria floor, and chocolate pudding on her skirt. They should have had pity on her, but they laughed instead. They carried barrels of sweet laughter.

I sat there, fiddling with my dress as The Rabbits continued to laugh at this girl. She must have been a freshman, because I never saw her before. Well, I certainly did, the school wasn't that big. I mean I never met her. Wait, now that I think about it, I think her name was Beth. Anyway, she wore thick brown glasses and some bedazzled purple sweater. She probably sat with Lionel at The Island, but I pretty much bunched all those people together. It was easy to do.

Their table was called The Island because everyone who sat there was stuck there like a piece of land in the middle of the ocean. None of them spoke to one another. Instead, they all just shared the same common truth: that they were all rejects. I felt bad for Lionel and the others who sat there, but if you were to sit at that table, then you would be excommunicating yourself. Also, everyone on The Island somehow all had a bad sense of fashion. That girl was practically crying on the floor, but all I was thinking was why she was wearing a dark brown skirt. Okay, so the bedazzled sweater looked like some vomited disco ball wrapped in string. Fine, I'd let that go. But what's with the purple with dark brown? Some colors just don't go together. Why the hell was she wearing a skirt if it went all the way down to her ankles? You wear a skirt to show off the legs, but if you want to show off the fabric, you wear a dress. The middle-of-the-road skirts don't work, so pick one side and go with it.

The girl continued to cry. The Rabbits and I kept staring at her while the chocolate pudding began to blend in with her skirt. I should have stood up, but that would have brought too much attention to me. I mean, a lot of people were glancing at me even when I wasn't doing anything. Truth was, I looked good. Part of me wanted to twirl around with my dress and dance on top of the tables, but I promised Shah I'd keep it simple, and not change her image. I didn't change Shah, I just accented her—like adding black outlines to a colored square.

"Oh my God, that was just too funny," said one of The Rabbits.

"Yeah," I said back, still keeping an eye on the girl. She looked at me for a moment, and I quickly put my head down. I played with my dress near my thigh until she looked away.

"Shah, can I just say that you look *amazing* today?"

"Yeah, where'd you get that dress?"

Finally, I could talk about clothes and not sound weird. My eyes widened, and I gave a huge smile.

"We—I mean, just me. I was down by the mall and stopped by Mary-Ann's boutique and—"

"It's amazing there, they always have the best sales."

"Yeah … and I didn't find anything that really jumped out. I was looking for more color, but nothing too bold because I didn't want to make that much of a statement. So I was looking for more of a hidden floral, so the dress was more intimate—sort of like cologne … or, I mean perfume—that is, the patterns really come to life only when you're really close. And Mary-Ann's dresses were just so plain and starchy, so we … me … I went to Taylor's instead."

"Woah, hold up. You went to *Taylor's*, like the over-40 shop?"

"Yeah, they had some amazing fabric. It just … melted almost, you know?"

"Shah, you can't let anyone know you went there."

"Why?" I puffed out my chest a moment. Then I realized girls probably didn't do that. I wasn't sure.

"You go there if you're pregnant or something. Or if you have, I don't know, a bunch of kids."

"Oh come on, you guys never shopped there? I was going nuts over the belts they had there. Real leather, not this plastic infusion stuff."

"That's cool, I guess," said one of The Rabbits.

"Aren't you going to ask how much it cost?"

"Shah, that place is a discount bargain. Everything there is *already* on sale."

"I know!" I smiled. "I bought it for seventy-five!" There was no shrieking, no crying out in joy. I thought Shah told me they were always doing that sort of thing. "Aren't you, like, excited or something?"

"Whatever, Shah. Last week, you were acting a little bitchy, no offense. And now you're wearing some grandma dress from Goodwill."

"Hey!" I shouted, a lot darker a tone than I should have used. "I like this dress, so deal with it."

"Wow, cool off a bit, okay? I didn't mean any of that."

"Good."

"You're acting all manly today, but you look more girly. It's weird."

I stood up, raising my voice. "I'll show you weird. You want to see something weird?" I was right about to throw that smug face to the ground, but people around me were staring. Chill, I thought, you have to act like everyone else. I had to keep it cool. But who wants to follow the sequence, who just wants to play the game if the game isn't fun? I sat down. Everyone's eyes went back to their food. Follow the sequence: one, two, three, four. One, two, three, four. If I wanted to stay in this dress, I had to follow the sequence. It was either this or The Island.

Play the game, follow the pattern, stay in line. What was the point of putting on these dresses if I had to look and act like Shah at the time? Even worse, I had to act the way people wanted *her* to act. I want to be me, not her! When the bell rang to end lunch, I stormed down the cafeteria, fists clenched—tightly clutching the two straps of my backpack. I didn't want to hear the chattering of girls, the hollering of boys. I only listened to my own footsteps. Soon, the sound carried me back into the hallway. Am I supposed to keep playing this game? Should I follow this half-ass attempt to be happy? Screw these people, I was going to say something. I stopped in the middle of the hallway. Two of The Rabbits accidently bumped into me from behind.

"Jesus, Shah," they said to me. "Watch where you're—"

I turned around, my eyes pierced through their flawless makeup.

"What?" I snapped back.

"Wow! Relax, will you? No need to act like a—"

"Oh, you better not finish that sentence."

People were beginning to dull their conversations to listen in to ours. My blood streamed through my skin, blushing red my black hue. I felt good. I wanted to knock this girl out.

"Charlotte, we didn't mean anything—"

"So you didn't mean to call me a bitch?"

"I didn't call you a bitch."

"You did now."

"What's your problem?"

"My problem is that I look damn good, and you're going to have to live with that. All of you, are going to have to live with that." I slammed my fist into a locker, causing The Rabbits to hop back.

Lionel came between me and The Rabbits. He put his hands on my shoulders. "Woah, woah, there Shah. Take it easy."

"I'm not going to take it easy. And don't touch me." I slapped away both of his hands with one swipe of my arm. Lionel's eyes widened, surprised by the strength I had. I didn't care. I had to keep yelling. This had to come out.

"You think you had a chance with me?" I shouted at him. "I don't even like you. I never did. I felt bad for you. You want a girlfriend? Go get your paints and draw up a woman who's as much of a loser as you. She'll keep you company."

Lionel's eyes dropped to the floor. His body deflated and seemed to stay afloat by one lone string hanging somewhere above him. He looked so pathetic. It didn't matter. He had to hear it. Shah was too nice, friend-zoning him for years. But now I was Shah, and if I was trapped in her body, then I'd be her new voice. Her true voice.

"And another thing, all those rumors about us sleeping together? I made them up! I thought it'd be funny to get you involved in something. I know, I'm crazy. Isn't it great! You're staring at a freak right now. And I only want to continue being crazy." I leaned in really close to him, seeing bits of straggly blond hair crawling out of his cheeks. "I just want to be me."

The way I said it, dropping my voice low and strong, shattered that last fading possibility I was Shah to Lionel. He tilted his head, and whispered, "Michael?"

The boiling rage had dissipated into the air, leaving no substance in my body. What was I thinking? He knew. Suddenly, my jaw dropped and fear leaked out of my mouth. Lionel smirked.

"Please," I whispered, "Don't give me away."

He thought for a moment. Then the word came out like a flash of lightning. "Michael!"

I ran, dropping Shah's backpack to the floor. I pushed aside boys and girls, who stared at me in horror. Lionel, who was once blind to it all, now could see the real me, the freak.

"It's Michael! Michael's dressed up like Shah!"

By the time I made it outside, slamming open the doors, people turned around and ran out to see me. I was no longer Shah, but the cross-dresser. Lionel continued to shout my name like Paul Revere's midnight run.

"It's Michael in that dress! Michael is Shah!"

I ran down the steps and into the parking lot. Strangely, Shah was waiting by the car, smoking a cigarette. When she saw me, she froze. Then she flicked away the cigarette.

"What's going on?" she said, still in her deep voice.

"They know! We need to go now!"

"But Michael, now's not the best—"

"Just shut up and give me the keys!"

She tosses to keys to me as and hurried across to the driver's side.

I jumped into the car, started it, and screeched the tires out of its narrow parking space. When I made it to the gate, I saw a bunch of students running out of the school—attempting to glance at the freak making its dramatic getaway. In front of the group was Jacob, his eyes wide in shock.

On the road, I repeatedly smashed my hands against the steering wheel.

"Why am I so stupid!"

"Michael …"

"I should've just been you. Should've just played the role and kept my mouth shut."

"Michael …," Shah said calmly.

"I can't be you. I'm not a woman. I'm me. I am me!"

"Michael," Shah said more firmly this time. "We have someone else with us."

I looked in the rearview mirror. Bella sat in the backseat, quietly buckled and looking back at the school we just left behind.

Part 2

Blue

Now forever farewell the tranquil mind

18
Bella

Play it cool, Bella. You're just in the back seat while a cross-dressing maniac is pounding away at the steering wheel—driving way over the speed limit. When Michael saw me for the first time, he slammed on the brakes. Every part of me wanted to choke this fool when my body flew forward and smacked against the front seat like I was a *saco de patatas*.

If I didn't have my seat belt on, my head would have whack-a-moled out of Shah's chest. I was playing it cool, but I was freaking out. I should have never messed with Shah, but I had to know more. I had to keep diving into whatever the hell this was. That's always been my problem: going past the invisible limit. I should have kept my distance when I knew Michael's secret—I should have never punched that girl in the face at my old school. But no, I had to cross that line because everyone else said it was un-crossable. Most people would run away if they knew Michael's secret, but I wanted to know more—to experience it.

"What's she doing here?" shouted Michael.

"I told her to come," said Shah casually, like she was inviting one of her friends over to a party.

"Get out!" yelled Michael. He looked fiercely at the rear-view mirror.

"No," I said. "You want to drag me out of this car with your pretty little dress on?"

He looked to Shah.

"Don't look at me. I had no idea you were going to run to the car right after lunch."

"You both suck, you know that."

"I suck? I could make this a lot worse, Michael," I said back. I didn't want to be vindictive, but he was pushing. I was going to push right back.

That's what that girl did from my old school: she pushed me too far back, so I punched her back. Of course, I act differently now, but I felt the same.

"Make it worse?" Michael shouted into the rear-view mirror. "The whole school knows what I wore today! How could you possibly make it worse?"

"Oh, I don't know. I could mention how you stole my dress and put it on yourself."

That shut him up. He secret wasn't that hard to figure out. The way he looked at me—when he was staring at my chest—I was thought it was sexual at first. But his eyes, they were full of joy, not lust. When he first touched the side of my body, he let the fabric touch his fingers for a little too long. I knew that feeling of pure joy and awe. It was like the first day I saw *Padre* outside—surrounded by trees and cars—and not by guards and Plexiglass. It was the first time I could hold him as long as I wanted, and we could laugh with no one saying "time's up, inmate." *Padre* had said to me years later that my eyes had looked softer than fur. That was Michael's eyes when he stared at me in my red dress. So, when I saw him grab my dress and bring it to the hallway, it all clicked suddenly. I should have been mad, but I wanted him to experience that joy—not strip it away.

"Michael," I added. "I'm not here to hurt you. I know this is crazy, but I'm still into you."

That was true, I had an awesome time that night. I couldn't believe how rushed everything was. Not the sex, that part was great, but our brief time together. One date, then *Bam*! But it was working, you know? He was so passionate, it was hard not to fall for him. Even though I told myself to hold back, I still jumped into bed. If word got out that, I would get the same label as before. Michael could go three-for-three—a new woman every night—and would be called a champion of men. Me? I'd be called a slut, again.

Uh, I should probably mention that. So, at my last school, I traded partners a few more times than the other girls would have liked. Whatever, I loved the deep connection I could have with someone during sex. Late nights, curled up in bed, naked bodies touching—revealing secrets and passions few others knew. Why would you want to block that out? The feeling of two bodies pressed together doesn't happen over 1,000 texts or endless awkward dinners. It's in the moment, the moment where Michael pushed me against the wall and gently felt all the fibers of my dress. Damn, how he sweetly kissed me. We had something together, and I hoped he knew that.

Michael was still silent. Shah knew it was best not to say anything, but I couldn't back down.

"Michael," I said. "I'm not blackmailing you. I want to help."

"You can help by getting the hell out of this car."

"I'm not getting out of his car."

"Fine, then keep quiet until we get home."

Michael continued driving, and Shah turned around to get a better look at me. She gave a wink, and then fooled around with the radio. Shah was pretty cool. I knew she had to be if she was willing to dress up as Michael. She felt a lot like me, so I thought she would get my sense of humor too. She didn't at first. Once she admitted she wasn't Michael, she grabbed me firmly on the shoulders. Softly and with pissed-off eyes, Shah said, "If you even open your stupid mouth about Michael, I will end you." Finally, I cracked and burst out laughing.

Shah's eyes were still mad.

"It's all good." I said. "I have no friends here anyway, so who am I going to tell?

"That's some juicy gossip to the right person."

"Not as juicy as your thighs …" then I turned on the sexual Bella voice again. "Would you like that?"

Shah squinted her eyes at me, then smirked. She pushed me playfully on the shoulder.

"That was not cool."

"Come on," I said. "This conversation was going to be awkward no matter what, so I figured what not have a little fun?"

"Damn …" Shah thought about it for a second. "You're pretty messed up, but I get it."

Michael's Black Dress

We both laughed and started chatting. Soon, we were talking—figuring out the other—and we forgot about the time. Since we were missing class already, and we wanted to talk more about Michael, we decided just to skip class altogether and talk in the car. Before Michael came running in the car, we were laughing like long-lost friends.

There wasn't any laughter the car anymore—only the rumblings of an engine.

19
Michael

I texted Jacob twenty times and called him six. Each voice mail had the same response: "Hey, it's Jake. I can't make it to the phone right now because I'm all aboard the fun train, woo-woo! But if you don't know how to type words into that fancy metallic device of yours, then leave a message."

"Jacob, pick up the damn phone. We need to talk. I can explain everything. Don't shut me out. Come on man, I don't need this." I ended the call and threw my phone across the room. It landed softly on Shah's plaid throw pillow. That thing was disgusting to look at. It clashed with her patterned blue and white bed sheets. Bella and Shah sat silently as I stormed back and forth.

"All right," said Shah, "Just because he's not picking up, doesn't mean—"

"It means everything! Look, I appreciate you being optimistic, and I love you for it, but there's no going back now. It's all over. Jacob won't ever talk to me again."

"Don't you think you're being a bit melodramatic?" asked Bella.

I still didn't understand how the hell Bella managed to end up here. I liked her and all, but this was a problem for just me and Shah. I put my hands over my face and let out a muffled scream.

"Bella," I tried to sound calm, but my voice was shaking. "I'm a straight black man who wears clothes not meant for me. I don't belong to any drag group, a gay community, or whatever. I'm alone with no one to back me up."

"You got us," Bella said.

"Oh great! My sister and some random chick I hooked up with! So supportive."

"That's what you think of me? I'm some random chick?"

"Yeah, you were just a fling. Now get the hell out of my house!"

"Shah said she had a plan to help you, and I want in."

"A plan?" I asked Shah.

"Yeah, about that. I might have lied," said Shah, jumping off the bed. "But, I have just the thing."

Shah ripped open her closet, pushing things around and knocking clothes and bras to the floor. Deep in the abyss, she dragged out a giant notepad.

"Remember this Michael? I got this at the flea market. And you said, 'Shah, that's the dumbest thing to ever buy. When are you ever going to use that?' Well, here we are: A battle-plan board."

"What battle-plan? How can we possible fix this?"

"Why don't we cover it up?" said Bella.

"Cover what up?" I asked.

"You dressing up as a woman," she replied pointedly.

"I didn't dress up as a woman —"

"You pretended to dress up as Shah."

"Fine, fine, fine. I'm not getting into these details with you."

"Good."

"Excellent."

After a moment, Shah wrote on the pad with a black marker: *Covering up.*

"What does that even mean?" I yelled.

"I'm just throwing out any ideas. Here's another one."

She wrote in all caps: *MOVE TO CANADA.*

Bella laughed. I glowered at her. I can't believe I agreed to allow her in this room. Apparently, she knew the minute I was in the hallway, trying on her dress. She admitted she was taken aback by Shah's impression of me, but she knew. I should've been thankful she didn't tell anyone, but it's like she was dangling that favor in front of me. This wasn't her place. She had no reason to wedge her thoughts between mine and Shah's.

"Moving to Canada sounds nice," Bella said and smiled.

"Thanks Shah," I said, steamed.

"Now covering up seems more appealing," she added. "I'm just trying to help."

"Fine, Bella? You want to help? Explain 'Covering up.'"

"I don't know, just say it was a bet. You managed to convince the whole school that you buzzed your head because of a sibling rage. Why can't you pull off something like that again?"

"Oh, she's a keeper," Shah said. "If you don't want her, I think I might make a move on her."

"This isn't a joke, Shah! I just tricked the whole school, why would they listen to anything that I had to say?"

"Because you're crazy, and you made a crazy bet. You and Shah wagered to see who could last the longest without being noticed. Michael, you lost, and you were so embarrassed that you ran out," Bella explained.

"Who'd we make a bet with?"

"Me."

"What?" Shah said. She stopped doodling swirly patterns on the battle-plan board.

"When I saw that you both had buzzed heads, I made a bet that you two could switch places."

"Why would we both agree?" I asked.

"Because I threw down three hundred dollars."

Bella reached into her tan leather purse. She reached into her wallet and started peeling away twenty-dollar bills.

"What the hell?" Shah gasped.

"Who keeps cash around like that?" I added.

"Well, if you must know, I was going to finish up my tattoo."

"With cash?"

"I can't legally get one, so I had to get it under the table—he wanted more to put on the finishing touches."

"What were you going to get?" asked Shah.

Bella blushed. "I can't tell you."

"Oh no, no, no." I snapped. "You know my secret, so we better know yours."

Bella promptly stood up and lifted up her shirt. On the side of her hip was the faint outline of a bare tree. I would have clearly remembered it on the night we hooked up, so it must have been inked while Shah and I were suspended. It was coated in Vaseline, the etches of the tree still fresh and slightly raised.

"A tree?"

"Yeah, I got it the next day, after we …"

Then she quickly hid it away beneath her shirt.

I smiled. "Our night together made you get tattoo."

Bella grinned back, the tension in the air eased a little. "Not really. I wanted this for a while, but you triggered the need to get it." She pointed to the tips of the branches. "See, I'm going back to put individual leaves on the branches."

"Cool," said Shah. "But why are you so embarrassed about a leafy tree?"

"Because, the leaves will be all the people I've ever slept with."

"We talking about a lot of leaves?" I asked, head to my side.

Bella looked down, her fists in a ball. "God, I don't even want to tell you. See, this is why I can't … enough, all right? But it's more than just leaves, it's not just a mark of honor like some tally marks."

"So I'm a leaf to you?" I asked, suddenly offended.

"Yes!" she yelled. Shah jumped back, knocking over the notepad.

Surprised by her quick answer, I sat down on the bed. Bella released her fists and breathed out a long sigh.

"I always wanted a collection of all the people who I've connected with. That night, I felt like I connected with you. It's not just making a collection to display, like trophies on a wall. It's more like a wall of books. Why do you keep all the books you've read? It's not like you're going to read them again. You keep them because they remind you of the stories and the emotions you felt with them."

"Then, why get the tree now?" Shah said, putting back upright the notepad.

"Because … I went to this school to start over. I had a bad experience before, and I thought I could keep my head down here. That past life was over, I was going to be that normal girl at this school—who doesn't sleep around. Then, Michael came along."

Shah suddenly clapped her hands together. "Well that's just great, but how about we move on from the sexy leaves and get back to the plan? Why do you want to fork over the cash?"

"Because I'm willing to hold back on the rest of the tattoo if you want to take that cash. I don't know, throw a party with the money to get everyone back on your side. Parties will do that."

"Really?" I asked.

"Sure, my *Padre* put a lot of money in my bank account—for emergencies. But he didn't think that one through."

"Well, Michael. I say we have a pretty good counter-attack, don't you think?"

I didn't say anything back. I was staring at Bella and her cute smile. She was an amazing woman. It was nice to have another ally.

20

Lionel

I was walking to Michael's house, a giant canvas in my arm, when I thought, "Why am I doing this?" Michael deserved to be humiliated for the way he embarrassed me. My Dad was always telling me that I was too forgiving—that I had to stand up for myself. Meanwhile, my Mom kept reminding me that staying in my room all night was bad for my health. I guess my decision to confront Michael would appease both of them. Outside, in the bitter air, I kept my head down—staring at the white concrete slabs as I walked.

I only lived a few houses down from Michael, but that night the space between our houses on Melanie Avenue felt like a mile. When the wind blew, it caught part of the canvas and pushed me into the road. I'm not even strong enough to hold a painting, I thought. Cars flew down the road, and their high beams blinded me for a moment. I shielded my eyes with the canvas. In the twilight under the canvas, I could still see around me, relying on the glow of street lamps reflecting off the ground. What was the point of street lamps? I wondered. Couldn't we all just manage our way in the dark? I'd like to light my own path, with a single flashlight, instead of following glowing bulbs, like prey to an anglerfish. But there I was, following the street lamps to Michael's house, when I should have stayed home. Finally, after battling winds and cars and lights, I arrived at Michael's. Shah's room was lit brightly.

I've spent so many days at this house. When we were young, the bus dropped us off at Michael's since he was at the end of the street. Half the time, I didn't go home right away. Instead, Jacob, Michael, and I went over to his house and played video games for hours. Okay, Michael and Jacob were the ones who actually played video games, while I sat on the couch and watched. But I didn't mind. I just liked to be in their company. It was around that time, about middle school, when I realized that Michael and Jacob had a tight bond, while I didn't. That didn't stop me from hanging out with them, but I knew I was the odd one out. Eventually, Jacob made it so uncomfortable for us to be together.

"Why do you even bother watching?" Jacob had asked one time while they were playing a fighting game.

"I just like to watch."

"That's gross, what are you a fag or something?"

"Jake," said Michael sharply.

"What, he just sits back there and does nothing. What kind of friend is that?"

I eventually stopped going to Michael's house after that. Still, it was heartbreaking to walk by his giant white house and know that I wasn't invited anymore. I still made excuses to show up at the door, like asking for homework questions and what-not. Part of me told me to just to give up and to let the past go. I was in my room for hours, starring at this stupid canvas—figuring out if I should really give it to him. All of this was too complicated to explain to my parents. Besides, they were too busy with their coordinated workouts. They had two treadmills in the basement. I had a feeling they held hands when the jogged, but I never venture down there. Last year, they gave me a bike so all three of us could ride together—a real family event. I tried to enjoy myself, but they were annoyed with how slow I pedaled. Finally, I gave up, made some excuse about my knees, and threw the bike in the garage. They were pretty disappointed—feeling rejected that I chose painting over fitness. I was a painter, and it was through painting that I was going to apologize to Michael.

I lifted the giant black handle on their front door and knocked. I should have just opened the door and walked in—it wasn't like their mom was home. She was always at the hospital, working late nights, barely connecting with her kids. If Michael's cross-dressing story ever blew up, that would be the first thing people would say: the mom was never in the picture, it messed with the boy's head. They would use some psychoanalytic excuse, like it was some way for Michael to project his longing for his mother. Maybe it was, I don't know.

I remember one time, when I made some excuse to go to the house, I politely knocked on the front door like I was doing now. Their mom—face strained from lack of sleep—said they were both upstairs and left me to venture alone. Walking up the stairs, I heard music blasting from both sides of the hallway. I made an excuse to see Shah, but I went to knock on Michael's door. I knocked on his door with two delicate knuckles. When no one answered, I politely waited and after five minutes knocked again. I'm not exaggerating when I said that I waited a whole five minutes—I looked at my watch constantly. Awkwardly standing in the hallway, I stared at the wood grains of Michael's door. I told myself, Come on, be a man, open the door. Just a crack. You waited long enough. I wasn't trying to be a creep, but I knew he was in there. I heard the soft padding of footsteps. When I tried to call out his name, it came out as a soft creek, "Michael?" Be a man, I thought myself, and I opened the door.

Through the crack, I saw a white dress with black trim along the hem. It was resting on a chair, the open window blowing the fabric like a conductor's hand in largo. I opened the door slightly more and saw a figure sitting at the edge of the bed. Bare black legs dug into the carpet fabrics. They were slim, but alive with muscle and purpose. I moved my eyes up to see Michael in only boxers and a tank top. I thought, I'm dead. Now, I'll be called a pervert. He didn't like you that much as it is, and now you'll forever be a loser. This would have sealed the deal.

Luckily, he never noticed me. He stared at the dress on the chair, swaying like a metronome. The music continued to thump, and Michael kept to the beat, nodding his head to the rhythm. It seemed like the dress had its own melody, and Michael was listening to its performance. His face was so beautiful, entranced in thought, eyes soft and engaged. I heard a flushing from the bathroom. Great, Shah was going to open the bathroom door any minute. She'd see me looking into Michael's room like a freak. I slammed the door. There was a voice from the inside. "Shah?" I ran. I bolted down the stairs, past their mother and out the front door. I never asked Michael why he had a white dress in his room. Apparently, I knew his secret all along.

When the door finally opened to Michael's house, the rest of the twilight had almost drifted away. I still expected his mom to be at the door. Instead, there was that new girl, who I sort of saw around school. She put a hand on her hip, her body contrapposto.

"Is Michael here?" I said as though I was selling cookies door to door. Then I realized she was the girl that Michael was seeing. I saw them walking the halls together. Suddenly, my stomach sunk down to the floor. "Here," I shoved the canvas to her. "Give this to Michael."

"And a 'hello' to you too. Who are you again?"

"Lionel, I live down the street. Can you just give that to Michael?"

"Lionel, like the guy who blew Michael's cover?"

"Yeah … that's me."

"Well, I'm sure he's going to love this … whatever the hell this is."

"It's art," I said, annoyed.

"Oh, how … artistic."

"Whatever. Who are you again?"

"Bella."

"Okay, Bella. How about you quit talking to me and go give that to Michael."

"Oh boy, you're a charmer. How about you give it to him yourself?"

"Uh," I froze.

"That's what I thought. Get lost. Thanks for running Michael's day and I'm sure this … thing … will make amends."

She closed the door on me. I turned around, tears beginning to well in my eyes. I let the streetlamps guide me home.

21
Michael

Bella left soon after Lionel dropped off the weird-ass painting. It made no sense. It was completely coated in black. He must have put layer after layer of black, because I could see how the color was heavily painted on the canvas.

"Some guy dropped this off," Bella had said, holding the painting one-handed like she was serving a pizza.

"Who?"

"Some dweeby-looking guy."

"Oh, Lionel."

Shah and I still sat on the bed, her arm around my shoulder. She lit a cigarette with one hand and carefully blew the smoke out the window. Occasionally, I took a drag myself. I was finally calming down, taking deep breaths until I felt all the air coating my lungs. Bella's plan, while stupid in its own right, was the only way to save face. Sure, I was going to have my friends make fun of me for years, but at least my image with the dress would be just a joke, not the truth. However, when I heard the name Lionel, my body tensed and floodgates of blood roared through my veins. He was the one who ruined everything! I was this close to pulling it off!

"You took a gift from him? What's wrong with you?" I asked.

"Maybe I should just go," Bella said, defeated.

Shah slapped me upside the head. "Hey, you did a great job calming down, so don't blow it."

"I'm sorry," I said softly, completely exhausted.

"I know," Bella said, gently putting the painting on the bed. "Relax, soon 'the truth' will spread like wildfire. Tomorrow, I'll hand Shah the cash at the front of the school stairway. I'll make an obnoxious show of it, and you'll get some ribbing. Then, that's the end of it."

"Thanks, Bella. I don't think I would have ever figured this out without you."

"Don't worry about it, just get some sleep. You've had a long day."

She leaned over and kissed me on the cheek. I felt her lips warm on my skin. My eyes closed and my back muscles relaxed with one heavy drop.

"What about me, love?" joked Shah, pointing to her cheek.

"Honey, I can only give out so much love."

"Now, you're being prudish."

"I never saw you taking me out."

"All right, all right, Michael wins on that category." Shah poked me in the ribs. I flinched and went to push her, but she smiled. I smiled back, weakly. Shah was only trying to cheer me up. Same with Bella. This whole night, I was just yelling at them, taking my anger out on the only people who gave a damn about the real me. I took a deep breath and sighed. I was letting my emotions get the better of me.

"I'm sorry for being so angry today," I said, standing up from the bed.

"Bella gets a free punch then!" Shah quickly stood behind me and wrapped her arms around my neck—locking me in a full nelson. Why the hell did I teach her that move? She was laughing as I tried to squirm away. Bella walked up to me, mocking a fist, and waved it at my head.

"Oh, this is tempting," Bella said. "But I'll settle for something else." She reached for my stomach and practically clawed me with her fingers. It was a violent tickle that had me laughing and screaming for them to stop. I twisted away from Shah and threw her into Bella—both of them falling onto the bed. Both were belly-up laughing, like two giddy sisters. I wish Shah had more friends—it was great to see her happy this way. I laughed with them, holding my stomach since the muscles were taut.

When their laughter grew quiet, Bella stood up and walked herself out. Shah said something about texting her later, and soon I heard the front door close.

"So," I said to Shah, "You and Bella seem to be pretty close now."

"When someone tries to make out with you like that, you get to know each other on a different level."

"That's good."

"I meant it when I said she was a keeper. Bella is just awesome."

"I know."

"Well, I'm going to head to bed. It's almost midnight. Ma should be home in a few hours, and I don't want to be awake for that. She'll chew us out for not sleeping."

"I wish she wouldn't."

"I know, but that's a whole different story."

"Night, Shah."

"Night, Michael."

I hit her on the shoulder with a soft jab. She returned with a hard cross to my arm.

"Damnit, Shah," I wailed.

"I'm not going soft on you," she said, pointing a finger at me playfully. "Oh, and don't forget your painting."

"Thanks," I grabbed it from Shah and closed the door behind me.

In the hallway I looked at the canvas for the first time. I thought maybe there was more to the painting, so I turned the hallway light on. No, it was still all black. I tilted it left and right, like I was trying to find some sort of hidden compartment. I looked behind me and stared at the mirror. Memories of that night came back, and they were going to haunt me forever. Soon, things were going to go back to normal, but I didn't feel as happy as I should have. That time—when I proudly wore that dress out in the open—I had been so happy. Did I want to go back to who I was before? I would be safe, and Shah and I could figure out some secret ways to get my fill. I sounded like a sick freak—get my fill? Was I no different than an addict? Did I need to get help, see a shrink? I put the painting in front of my body, like it was the red dress.

I tried to visualize how I felt that night, with Bella's dress wrapped tightly around me, and closed my eyes. Breathing in, I felt a wave of pleasure—remembering the soft fabric resting on my skin. I needed it. Life was too short to deny myself what make me feel good. I had the right to be happy. It was then, in the mirror's reflection, that I finally saw the blue dot in the painting. It was only a drop of blue on the top right corner, but it was clearly there for a reason. What the hell did that mean?

22

Lionel

I like to paint at night, when all is silent except for the distant sounds of semi-trucks roaring down the highway. They have a distant vibrating drone that I find soothing. I need to be calm before I begin. Starting a painting angry or sad would taint the experience. Instead, I must be relaxed, and devoid of as much emotion as possible. Only then I can begin.

Late at night, when the orange street lamps are guarding the outside, that's when I prepare my paints. Most painters will only have a few colors available, since they have a general idea of what composition they'll be designing. I've never worked that way. Instead, on a large plywood board, I put samples of as many varieties as I can. Even particular colors, like tangerine and olive, can be seen arranged in my neat, compartmentalized rows—as though I was about to cook instead of painting. I don't know what color I'd need when it begins, and I don't have time to think about mixing in the moment. The moment is what matters, and expressing that moment requires all of my emotions, not thought.

When I hear another roaring truck drive by the highway, I close my eyes and breathe in. Michael. He probably threw my painting across the room, kicked it in with one stomp. It was probably broken beyond repair in Shah's room, half of it awkwardly in a trashcan. Plum. That's the color I'll use, I thought. I dressed the canvas with a plum and blue coat. As my wrist danced along the canvas, I imagined that Michael was at his front door, instead of Bella. I hoped that he would be smiling, and I would smile back. I would shyly present him with the painting, and he would hold it to the light and bask it all in.

"It's beautiful," he would say.

"I made it for you."

"That's really sweet of you, Lionel."

"Thanks."

"Listen," Michael would say while putting down the painting. "I understand why you flipped out the way you did today. You were angry. I get it, you think that I don't understand you, but I do. I can see through to the real you, and I saw all those signs."

"Really?"

Then Michael would scour, "No! You're stupid charades fooled me and Shah! For years! Years, Lionel! First of all, I'm never going to figure it out if you keep acting all secret like this. Secondly, why would I ever want a weak joke of a boy like you—I could have whatever man I wanted!"

No, I'm sorry! I didn't mean to keep it a secret. I wanted to tell you. I would scream it from my window for the whole neighborhood to here. I don't care what people say about me? You get that? I'm not like you, so goddamn self-conscious—who cares? Who goddamn cares, Michael! I can't say it because of you. Because, if you said no, then it would be all over. All my hypothetical dreams would come tumbling down. I can't have that. Instead, I cling to limbo. I only imagine there is a maybe between us, because a 'maybe' could have a 'yes' tucked deep inside. With 'maybe' there is hope.

I looked at the canvas, and I saw my masterpiece with my mind's eye. Throughout the canvas, I stabbed at the plum canvas with a bright yellow. The paint splattered like blood leaving a bullet wound. In the center was a ruby-red X, which was encircled by a black ring. I don't remember the process, just the fever of emotion. The whole process is an artistic blackout—never knowing what true form will be created. Some nights, my canvas is destroyed by violent splashes of color. Other nights, specks of blue may scatter on the board, like birds scavenging for food on the ground. The inside of me comes crawling out and is released onto the canvas. If Michael has his dresses to feel real, then I have my paints.

I took a deep breath and stared at my finished work. A purple Michael had his lips sealed by a red X, while bright yellow lights blind his eyes. What does this mean? I thought of Edvard Munch's *The Scream*. I was the lone figure who screams to no one—while the rest of the world walks away. Around me, there was deep anxiety and pain, but only I scream. I was an expressionist mess. I knocked the painting off the easel, embarrassed to look at it.

The phone vibrated on my night stand—its midnight blue screen lit up part of the room. When I reached for the phone, Michael's face was staring at me. I couldn't help but smile. I took this profile picture of him only a month ago. It was when we were in school. He was laughing at a joke Jacob made, and when he cocked back his head to smile at the ceiling, I took a picture. No one noticed, because no one ever does. I used to randomly call him and hang up, just so I could see his picture on my phone. When he asked why I called, I said I accidently dialed him. To make sure he didn't catch on, I stopped calling. This night, however, Michael was calling *me*, actually me!

"Hello?" My voice tried to shake out the tears in my throat.

"What's with the painting?" he said coldly, no welcome or hello.

"Because—"

"You don't just shout on the hilltops about me, and then try to make it up with a stupid painting."

Stupid? Why am I letting him talk to me like this? I spent hours working on that painting. Doesn't he appreciate all the work I do for him? God, give up already, Lionel. But I couldn't.

"It was a painting I made for you."

"It's just a blue dot."

I smiled—he found it. That meant he must have stared at it for a long time.

"Yes, yes!" I shouted. "I made it a few weeks ago, and after what happened today, I thought this was perfect chance to give it to you."

"Oh, you think this was a great day, then?"

"I mean … it was a good … opportunity."

"Just tell me what it means."

What it means? He knows it represents something! He doesn't think it's some mistake, like a slip of the brush. Maybe, this is hope.

"I want you to think that maybe you're the blue dot."

"Why?"

"And the rest of the world is the black."

"Okay, but I'm one of the few black people in this town."

"No, it's beyond color."

"But you just mentioned blue."

"Michael!" I shouted. Then I immediately calmed down. "Let's pretend you're the blue dot, okay. Just humor me."

"Fine."

"That blue dot would be forgettable in an ocean or sky, but on a black canvas it's unforgettable."

"Okay."

"You don't get it, do you?"

"Lionel, I'm going to bed."

"Wait, wait! What I'm trying to say is maybe you're my … maybe you're remarkable—being so different from the rest. This is your chance to be special in a drab world."

"But now I'm just a target," Michael said bitterly. "The rest see me and know how different I am. I'm not remarkable. I'm isolated, alone. Look at how *remarkable* the freak is."

"Michael, I don't think—"

"Just stay away from me for a while. I don't care if you see Shah. Whatever you want to do is fine, but just don't talk to me."

"Oh, okay, Michael. I'm just trying to help."

"You could have helped by keeping your mouth shut!"

"Well you embarrassed me in front of everyone! Twice!"

"Well, I'm sorry about that."

"And I still want to help you!"

"Goodnight, Lionel."

"Be a blue dot!" I said quickly.

"What?"

"Just try, for me?"

"You listen up. I don't owe you anything."

"Then, for the painting's sake."

"Whatever." Then he hung up the phone.

I sat down on my bed and stretched out my arms. The semis continued to drone down the road. Why did I love him? It was obvious that he didn't love me back. He just told me never to talk to him again. Perhaps when he calms down and finally sees the blue dot, things would be better. Maybe, he could be my blue dot one day—a shining, colorful spec of joy. I took that night as still a maybe. One day, he would understand. Maybe.

23
Shah

It was 3 a.m. and I was chain smoking until my whole room was covered in smoke. There was no way I was going to be able to mask this scent when Ma came home, but I didn't care. I had a feeling that she had known all along and didn't mind. That was perhaps the part that pissed me off the most: did she even give a damn about us? I shouldn't say that, I know she's my mom and she unconditionally loves me and yeah, yeah … but it wasn't like we were short on money. We lived in a nice neighborhood and she had a pretty decent job, working the night shift. I would be losing my mind if I had to do that job though. Half awake, patching up psycho drugged-out freaks all night—it would drive me crazy.

"Ma, what's it like to work when everyone's asleep?" I said to her a few years ago when she first started the night shift. She was startled by my voice. I was at the kitchen table, late at night, waiting for her to come home. She was mad that I stayed up for so long, but then she sighed and sat next to me.

"Long." She dropped the rest of her weight into the chair and slouched back.

"Then quit."

"Baby, I got to make a living for you kids."

"But we also want to see you during the day."

"You will, on weekends and stuff."

"Do you need this job?"

"How else are we going to get by?"

"With another job."

She brushed my cheek and then twisted my nose. Ma did that just enough for me to back away and smirk. Then she put her hand through my hair and let it nest in there, like a baby bird.

"We're going to braid your hair."

"Yeah, but not everyone likes that."

"Who cares."

"The ones who make your future."

"Can't I just be myself?"

"No, you need to be who they want you to be." She pulled her hand out of my hair, and then reached into her purse. She pulled out a cigarette and lit it. Mom didn't usually smoke in the house, but she seemed so defeated this particular night.

"I'm so happy that I brought you two up in a nice neighborhood. Do you honestly think we could go back?"

"Whatever," I said. "I don't make a difference."

"It does! I grew up in the poorest slum, eight kids to a dirty two-bedroom apartment. You get nothing. Poor education, poor food, poor future. Sometimes, trying hard can't get you everything in life."

"But that's what you did!"

"I lucked out. When your father gave me the chance to leave, I bit and never let go. I didn't know him that well, but his job paid him well … and I was selfish. You got to understand, sweetie, if I don't work this job, we go back to the dirt and I don't think you'll survive. I don't mean physically, you'll be fine, but the 'you' that I tried so hard to raise."

To raise us? I don't think Ma got it. We saw her only on the weekends, like divorced children. Michael and I practically raised each other—cooking dinner and cleaning the house during the week. It's a miracle that we didn't take advantage of that. Okay, maybe we did a little, but it was a miracle that we were even sane. All right, scratch that, too. Perhaps her absence did mess us up a bit.

I ashed out my cigarette in a glass of water. It was now all brown with floating butt corpses. Usually when I finished smoking, I'd flush the glass of disgusting liquid down the toilet, washing away the evidence. Still, it wouldn't hide the scent. Screw it, I thought, I wanted her to smell it. It was her fault—she gave me this habit. If it wasn't for all those nights watching her smoke in the kitchen, I would have never tried to mimic her. I heard the car drive in, and I checked my alarm clock. 3:30 glowed red in the dark. I breathed in my cigarette, the red embers almost the same colors as the clock.

I walked down stairs with the glow-less cigarette in my mouth and the glass in my hand. By the time she opened the door, I was sitting at the kitchen table. When she saw me, she gave a huge sigh, and sat beside me—like all those other nights.

"Hey baby," she leaned in a kissed me on the head.

"You want a smoke?"

"Sure." She took off her coat and let it hang on the chair.

"You know I'm seventeen, right?"

"It's too late to talk about your teenage angst."

"Then what do you want to talk about?"

"Nothing, baby, I just want to go to bed."

"Oh."

I stood up, and then placed the glass next to her.

"These," I said, "are all the cigarettes I smoked before you showed up. I want to you take a good hard look at it. Are you going to get mad now?"

"Is that what you want?" she said exhaustedly. "Do you want me to yell at you?"

"I want you to do something! I can't … I can't …"

Then out of nowhere, I began to cry. I thought of Michael, pounding the steering wheel and screaming. When he was angry, he scared the crap out of me. I spent all afternoon calming him down, draining the last bit of humor and smiles I had in me. What did it solve? After tomorrow, things would go back to normal and he'd have all that pent-up anger again. It would explode, and I'd get the shell shock. I couldn't do it. I couldn't keep trying to be the comic relief that everyone else needed.

She stood up and wrapped her arms around me.

"Whatever," I whispered, not wanting to wake up Michael. "I'm going to bed, goodnight."

"Charlotte, what is going on? Look, I told you, it's either this shift or nothing."

"Oh, don't act like there's only one choice."

"Then what do you want me to do?"

"Nothing, just keep doing what you're doing. Michael and I are okay."

"Did something happen to Michael? I thought you two were fine."

"No, we're not. And we're going to keep on being messed up."

"You listen here." Ma pulled away from me and grabbed me by the wrists. She dug her hands into my own until our fingers weaved. "I have worked my life away so that you two could have a better life than me. And if that means I have to be out of the picture, then fine. If it means you hate me, then good. If it means that you don't have to live the life I lived, then just go on hating your Ma."

Tears welled up in my eyes. "Do you really mean that?"

She broke away from me and headed for the door.

"I'm going to get some more groceries, we're low."

"At this hour?"

"Yeah, at this hour. Goodnight, baby. Get some sleep."

Ma grabbed her jacket and coat. When she left, she kept her back to me. I lit another cigarette.

24
Michael

Shah and I drove to school the next morning. She wore a yellow cardigan with jeans and I wrapped myself in a large sweatshirt and baggy pants. I felt like a sack of potatoes in this baggy outfit. We listened to the hum of the engine. I gently took each turn, driving well below the speed limit. I tried to slow down time, prolong the moment as long as possible. Except it was time, and it had to be done. Everyone in school was expecting my response, and I was going to deliver it to them.

"Michael," Shah said, "you can always call in sick, you know, take a couple of days. After talking to Ma yesterday, I don't think she'd even care."

"What? You told her?" I glanced at her, ignoring the road in front of me.

"I didn't say anything. It's just, she's so distant."

"Wow, tell me something new."

"She honestly thinks this is good for us, working herself to death."

"We got other things to think about today, and I need you with me."

We went back to listening to the car. Both of us knew we were close to one another, but I was surprised to hear me say that. I needed her? I guess I did. Then a wave of guilt flooded over me.

"Shah?" I slowed down the car and glided it to the side of the road. My blinker, loud and consistent, ticked as we sat in silence.

"What?" Shah asked. "Are you going to make out with me now?"

"Can you be serious for a moment?"

"We both can't be serious. Who's going to keep us in check?"

"Look, you remember that painting Lionel gave me?"

"What, that black thing?"

115

"I called him about it."

"Oh God. Why the hell did you talk to that creep? He's the one who screwed you over yesterday."

"But, I get it. It's not like I was treating him nice either."

"So? What you want to talk about?"

"There was this blue dot on it. And it really bothered me. Did he put it there on purpose? Was it just a spill?"

"Michael, I'm not going to sit here and talk about art. We got stuff to do. Bella's going to be waiting for us at the parking lot. I don't want to be late. So, quit day-dreaming about Lionel. Put this car in drive, and let's meet up with Bella. You can do this."

I sighed, and tightly gripped the wheel. Why did she have to be such a pain in the ass?

"All right," I said, "Let's do this."

I put the car back into drive. We drove past a group of little girls and boys waiting at a bus stop with their parents. A red light caused us to stop right next to the children. It was a beautiful morning, with the girls in little dresses in more colorful varieties than a flavor of lollipops. I loved how they stood still, but moved side to side—the many fabrics waving to one another. The boys, in their superhero T-shirts, jumped off the benches and pretended to fly. Was this the only way a bus stop could be? Everyone seemed so happy. Even the parents, chatting with coffees in hand, seemed content with their kids. The pieces were nicely fit into place. The American Dream could have been painted in this one image. I took a mental picture in my mind, added a frame, and placed it on a wall. Why couldn't I just be one of those kids in the bus stop? My life would be a lot easier for everyone else involved if I was just normal.

Then I saw this one particular little girl. She was sitting on the ground, playing with grass and putting clumps of it on her lap. Her blue dress had green grass stains on it, but the little girl didn't care. Her mom chatted away, while she continued to amass a pile. There was a mound of grass clippings on her lap when her mom finally turned around to look at her daughter. Quickly, the girl brushed away all the grass. The mom knelt down and pointed her finger at the girl.

"Stop that! Don't ruin your brand-new dress."

The little girl looked down and frowned. She stared at the green stain on her dress like she had an accident. Now it was ruined. When the mom turned back around, she smiled at the other parents.

"Kids," she said. "They never understand." The mom grabbed the girl's arm and dragged her away—probably to put on another dress. The girl began to cry. "The more you cry," the mother added, "the more difficult it will be to put on a new dress."

"But I don't want to."

"Of course you do, baby. We need to hurry up, the bus will be here soon."

"Can't I go like I am?"

"No, honey. You look ridiculous."

"Michael," said Shah. "The light turned green."

"She doesn't want to wear it," I said.

"Who?"

"The little—it doesn't matter."

I pressed down on the gas and drove past all the happy children. Perhaps that girl felt the same way I did. Maybe she hated her dress and wanted to wear superhero T-shirts like the boys. The boys never had to change their pants if they had grass stains—that was just 'boys being boys.' She was like me, trapped in expectations. I sped up the car and made the way to the school.

25

Bella

I waited at the school parking lot, my tattoo itching. Only a few cars parked in their neat little rows, but soon the lot would be filled. Eventually, when the spots were filled, cars would park in the grass, the curb, or even in corners barely wide enough to fit anything. These cars had to find every crevasse, every spot, to take their claim. They wouldn't stop until every possible space was filled.

My itch buzzed. I went to scratch it just above my thigh, but then stopped. If I wanted it to stop itching, I had to stop scratching it. Strange concept when I thought about it. The best way to stop the pestering was to completely ignore it. Still, the itch was persistent, a constant nag that practically plead for me to dig my nails into it. I wasn't going to do it. I wasn't going to give in. Instead, I put my hands deep into my pockets and clenched my fists.

Where are they? I thought. I wanted Shah and Michael to show up earlier so we could go over the plan one more time. I would sit at the top of the school stairs—in the middle—and make my presence known. I wore a tight-fitting dress, so I would certainly turn some heads. I hated that part. The whole point of transferring school was to keep a low profile. Before this school, I was officially called the slut. No, seriously, that was my name.

My classmates apparently had some sort of desire to burn a *bruja*, so they picked me. Someone had once completely filled my locker with condoms. When I opened it up, they fell down on the floor like a cascade of water. My so-called friends stopped hanging out with me, and then I became the one who would sit alone at lunch. If someone did sit next to me, it was a guy who usually asked if I was free that weekend. He wasn't interested in me but knew that I put out. He wanted to cash in on the opportunity. It wasn't like I slept with that many people. In fact, there were some girls there who probably slept with way more people. It was just that I slept with the wrong person and was completely open about it.

His name was Tyler. I usually didn't go for the large, muscular guys, but I liked how he smiled. For a guy who was so large, he had such a tiny smile. He barely opened his lips to reveal his sparkling white teeth. His face flushed red when he stared at me. I twirled my hair and giggled, which had him automatically blushing—it was adorable. There was something so sexy about making a guy tongue-twist his words. This Goliath of a man could destroy a whole football team single-handedly, but was helpless to me, a petite David. Finally, he had the courage to ask me out, and I said sure.

For a few weeks, his massive frame hung over me like a coat, his big hands wrapped around my fingers. He kept showing off this macho image to everyone else, but he was sweet around me. I was the one who made the first move, and I was surprised to see him back away. We were walking one night, along a moonlit path in the park. When we came across a pavilion, the rain began to fall. There was no one around for miles. Quickly, we rushed under the cover, our bodies held together for warmth. God, he felt good next to my skin. I grabbed the back of his neck, went up on my toes, and kissed him while the rain fell. Soon, we were peeling away our clothes—we should have been shivering. Then, he pushed himself away—stopping his tunnel-vision of love.

"Are you sure about this?" he asked, his voice quivering. I wasn't sure if it was due to the cold or him being afraid.

"Yeah, I am."

"It's just …" He did his cute smile and looked away from me.

I laughed, touched his face, and grinned.

"It's fine. I'll be gentle. You'll be wonderful." I patted him on the head and that had him laughing. Soon, our bodies were pressed together. The rain eventually was a cool relief to the hot warmth we generated.

When we finished, we cuddled in a pile of clothes, tracing one another's bodies with our fingers.

"Was …" he said. "Was I good?"

I rolled off of him onto my back and laughed. He sat up and stared at me. His eyes were wide, his mouth hung open. When I saw his face, I stopped laughing. I put my hands through his rough hair.

"Oh, I wasn't laughing at you. You were wonderful. You just need to stop being so adorable."

"But was I better than …"

I pulled my hand away, but still kept a smirk.

"Better than who?"

"Your other boyfriend."

"What other boyfriend?"

"The one you lost your virginity too."

"Ha, I guess so. That was awhile back. I would have to think about it." He stood up and reached for his clothes. I put a hand on his back. "Hey, what's the matter?"

"I need to get going."

"No, let's stay awhile. Maybe, we can keep this going, if you're up for it."

"No, I want to get home."

He put on his pants and fumbled with his socks. His wet feet had trouble squeezing into the cloth.

"Tyler, did I say something wrong?" I was now putting on my clothes, fumbling with my bra.

"How many people have you slept with?"

"Does it matter?"

"Yes! I wanted … you know … this to be special."

"*Claro.* And it absolutely was!" I extended my arms and pointed to the roof and sky. "This was better than I thought it was going to be."

"Oh, you thought I was going to be worse?"

"No. It's just, usually it can be awkward when I'm with someone for the first time."

"Jesus, do you need to get a chart out?"

I put my arms to my hips and stared at him coldly, cooler than the night air. "Who do you think I am?"

"I think you're a slut, and I should probably get myself checked out."

My eyes began to water. "Are you serious?"

After a moment, when he finally managed to zip up his pants, he said, "Yeah, I am."

The next day, he told all of his friends that he broke up with me because he was afraid of all of the diseases I had. Friends became enemies and soon I was alone. Then, I snapped. When one girl drew 'Slut' on my notebook while I was in the bathroom, I threw a cross to her face—just like *Padre* taught me. The school decided the slut didn't deserve a second chance, so I was expelled. I moved in with *Padre* soon after.

On my tattoo, a part of Tyler still itched. Even though Tyler was responsible for me leaving that school, the moments I had with him were just too precious to forget. I wanted that tree of mine to be blooming with leaves. Each one would be a cherished memory. I hoped Michael would understand. He wasn't just a leaf, but a part of the tree. Regardless of what happened to Michael, I wanted him to know that we shared a wonderful moment together. Just as I was about to scratch at Michael's branch, Michael and Shah pulled up beside me.

"Finally," I said, and jumped out my car. When Shah saw me, she gave me a hug. It was so good to be around a girl who didn't think of me as just a slut. It felt like we were friends for years, but it was only yesterday when I oddly put the moves on her. I guess after dealing with something crazy like this, we had to stick together. And I was okay with that.

"You ready?" Shah asked me.

I reached into my bag and pulled out the wad of cash. The rest of the leaves would have to wait. At the moment, saving Michael's reputation was far more important.

"How about you, Michael? You ready?" I asked. Michael was in a giant sweatshirt that might as well double for a sleeping bag. He was staring at the front steps of the school with a deep look in his eye.

"What?" he asked dazedly.

"You ready to do this thing?"

"Yeah, but we're doing it my way."

Shah and I looked at each other, then to him.

"Um," Shah said, "You want to fill us in?"

"No," Michael said, jumping up and down like he's about to start a wrestling match. "Got to peel it off like a Band-Aid."

Before Shah and I could get out another word, Michael pulled off his sweatshirt and pants. Head held high, Michael sauntered toward the school—in a dazzling deep-blue, floral lace dress. The crowd began to stare, and we followed a few steps behind. Maybe I would have enough money for the tattoo after all.

26

Michael

They all stared. Their judgmental eyes looking me over as I slowly walked up the stairs. Bella and Shah were a few steps behind, and I know they were confused to all hell. After the conversation with Lionel last night, I couldn't go along with Bella's plan. I would be miserable for the rest of my life—hiding a secret in the shadows. That's what made me a freak: keeping the real me locked away in the basement of my soul. Screw them, I thought, I was going to be out in the open and they had to deal with it. Last night, late of course, I dug into Ma's clothes and found the blue dress hidden deep within her closet. It was old, but it was during a time when she had fashion sense. With some adjustments, I managed to make it fit.

Of course, wearing the dress in public was one thing. The hard part was keeping cool, which was easier said than done. I had imagined walking defiantly down the halls, strutting my clothes while the school was aghast. Still, I would keep my head high, chest out, with my dress bobbing and weaving like a boxer in the ring. I didn't expect disgust, and that's what drained my endurance. For each step I took up the school stairs, their faces were like jabs and hooks. I tried to block them, dodge them with a smile and confidence. However, there were so many people, all criticizing without words. Some did talk, but they whispered to one another behind notebooks and bags. Jacob stood at the top of the staircase. Bella and Shah stood beside me, like lieutenants.

"Michael, what the hell is going on?" Jacob said coldly.

"This is me," I said. I looked over to Shah, who replied with a pumped fist.

"Come on, man. Is this, like, some kind of joke?" he started to laugh uneasily. "You know, I'm all about pranks, but you need to fill me in."

"This is no joke. I like to wear dresses."

"But ... what?"

"It's still me, Jake. Just wearing some different things. No big deal."

"I just ..."

"Look," I said, taking a step towards him. He took a step back. "I don't expect you to accept it right away. I just want you to know it's still me."

"Man ... this is ..." He walked away, moving in a circle. His hands were fluid, moving expressionistically, like he was having a conversation with no one. "What am I to you—was all those women just a—"

"I'm not gay, Jacob."

"You sure look like it."

"Hey!" I shouted, surprised by my sudden anger. "This doesn't mean I'm gay."

Behind Jacob, the door flew open and out came Marshall and our other teammates. He took a few steps back and put his hands up dramatically.

"Jacob," he said. "I'm so glad I finally get to meet your new girlfriend."

Marshall walked up to me and extended his arm.

"It's nice to meet you, and might I say you're looking damn fine."

"Why you son of a—" I said between gritted teeth.

Bella held back my shoulder. "*Venga!* Let it go."

"You better listen to your girl. Now, are you two ladies a thing? What does that make you, Michael, a dyke? Oh, I'm sorry, you probably want to be called something else, like Michelle, or—"

"How about Michaella!" someone shouted from the gathering crowd. That was when everyone finally laughed. Before that moment, there had only been giggles. However, the stairway erupted in laughter. It might have well been toxic gas—I could barely breathe. I had to break away. I pushed aside Marshall, who was still vomiting belly laughs at me. Bella and Shah shouted insults at the crowd, telling them to go to hell and whatnot, but it made no use. Before I made it inside the doorway, I saw Jacob staring at me, speechless.

"Say something," I said softly.

He kept his mouth shut and looked away, turning his back toward me. I didn't move. I wanted to die right there. Why did I think this would be a good idea? Shah and Bella dragged me away from the crowd and into the nearest girls' bathroom.

27
Shah

I should have seen it coming. Man, when my brother acted all odd and philosophical in the car, I should have grabbed the steering wheel and driven right back to the house. I mean, part of me was happy that he just peeled away his old clothes like some caterpillar. But people weren't going to worship him like some butterfly. Once they realized it wasn't a prank, they looked at him like he was a freak. The way they stared at him was so cold, but it could still melt ice.

I could have put a chain of road kill around my neck, and Michael still would have been the center of attention. The worst part was that Bella and I had to stay back and watch the carnage. Thank God she was next to me, because dragging his sorry-ass into the girl's bathroom was a two-woman job. As soon as we pushed him into the room, he had to stare at himself in the mirror. He shook his head from side to side—disagreeing with his mirror self.

"No need to wallow in it," I said, checking each stall to see if they were empty. "You dug your ditch and now you need to lay in it."

"Look, this wasn't my plan, but screw it. Good for you. It's going to be fine now," Bella said. He was still starring into the mirror—ignoring our conversation.

"Nice?" I said. "They're going to tear him apart! We should have done this gradually, let a few people at a time into his world, and slowly expose him."

"You're making it sound like we're developing film."

"We are developing, and too much exposure—"

The bathroom door opened, and a shy freshman girl with a pink backpack and sparkling white sneakers stopped in her tracks and stared.

126

When she saw the three of us, she paused at the doorway—not sure what to say.

"Get the hell out!" I said. She was right about to dash out when Bella grabbed her arm.

"Listen, Shah." Bella guided the girl farther into the bathroom. "I would have agreed with you about the whole slow-exposure thing, but now the truth is out in the open now. We need to show the world that Michael is proud of who he is."

"Michael?" said the shy girl. "Is that the senior, who …"

"What's your name, honey?" said Bella, putting a shoulder around her.

"Um, Beth."

"Beth, I love the backpack, it's really cute."

"Thank you."

"Michael, do you like her backpack?"

Michael stopped shaking his head at his own reflection in order to look at Beth. After a moment, he straightened up, brushing off imaginary dirt from his blue dress. Slowly, he walked up toward Beth. We all waited in silence for Michael to speak. Finally, after a deep sigh, he smiled and extended his hand. "Hey, Beth. I don't know if we met before, but I'm Michael."

Timidly, Beth looked to Bella and then to me. I had my arms crossed, looking at the ceiling and sighing—making it really deliberate. Bella gave some nonverbal encouragement toward Beth, like she would toward a toddler who was approaching a mall Santa Claus.

"Um," she barely whispered.

"Go on," said Bella with a smile on her face.

This freshman barely moved a muscle and kept alternating between looking at me and Bella. Finally, I had enough. "For God's sake, just shake his hand!"

The girl turned around and dashed out of the bathroom. I threw my hands up in the air.

"You see, we just shocked the whole school, and now they're looking at him like some freak!"

"Maybe, if you just gave the girl a moment to—"

"We have to slow it down," I said. "We should start with close friends for a bit, then their friends, then maybe go out on a weekend with his dresses, and then perhaps, *perhaps,* have him come to school wearing makeup, or something that's kind of like a dress. Slow and steady!"

"I don't wear make-up," said Michael angrily.

"I know, I know. But you get the analogy. This is going way too fast."

"Yeah, but Bella's right. I can't just hope that change will happen gradually. I need to do this now, and I need to make *them* change."

"And that would happen, if you just give it time."

"No, slow and steady might win a race, but this is a statement. This statement needs to be heard loud and clear. This is who I want to be and it's happening now."

"Oh, high and mighty Michael!" I cried. "You can talk all noble and brave in a girl's bathroom, but what happens when you go back outside? They're going to rip you limb from limb. They think you're a joke. This is funny to them. You're going to get laughed at, and I don't think you can take it."

"He can," said Bella.

"I like you, Bell, but I know my brother. He's going to crack. It's only a matter of time."

"I won't. I know I can do this," pleaded Michael. "Please, Shah. I need you to back me up."

God, I wanted to support him. I was instantly with him the minute he ripped off that sweatshirt. But after seeing those stares, and the way they laughed at him—how was it possible? They were going to let loose on him, and then I would be the one whom he runs back to. I couldn't keep doing this. I can't hold the walls together, breakdown after breakdown. I didn't volunteer to be his mentor and moral guidepost.

"Fine," I said. "If you need this, then we'll do it."

"Great," said Bella. "They'll come around, we just need to give them time to adjust. If anyone asks us about Michael, we'll tell them the truth and be as peachy as we can be."

"It's not going to be that simple," I said.

"Who said it's going to be?" Bella smirked. I swear that smirk must melt most men. It was hard to stay mad at her.

"All right, Bell," I said. "I'll be as peachy as a cobbler for you. But, are you sure you're going to be okay, Michael?"

"Yeah." His posture was straight, looking as confident and beautiful as when he was wearing the red dress.

"You can't lose your cool. The minute you lose your cool, that's when they won. You hear me?"

"Yeah, yeah. I get that."

"No," I said, grabbing his face with both hands. "You can't flip out, even if they drive you crazy. If you lose it, they'll forever call you a freak, and you'll play into their hands."

"It's not going to happen, Shah. I'll just keep my head high and take a nice slice of the peach cobbler."

Bella kissed him on the cheek. "I'm really proud of you." Michael turned away from the mirror and stared at Bella. Ugh, they both smiled like awkward prom dates.

"Well, ladies. We have a catwalk waiting."

Michael wanted to slug me for that comment, but I flashed him a smile and he gave one back. He coughed, adjusted his dress, which didn't need adjusting, and made his way toward the door. Was he being brave or just stupid? I pointed a finger at Bella.

"You keep an eye on him. Make sure he doesn't do anything crazy."

Bella laughed and then she kissed me on the cheek. "I'm really proud of you, too." With that, she turned and left the stalls. I looked into the mirror and tried see a reflection of the old Shah—the one who never knew Michael dressed up. I wanted to be that other girl who stayed low, who socialized enough to get by. I wanted to be the one who slipped under the radar, not some activist.

"Are you ready?" I asked myself.

Myself looked back at me. The old Shah didn't move a muscle, so I left her behind.

28
Bella

I ran out into the hallway to hold Michael's hand. Truth was, I was really digging the whole dress outfit on Michael—it was his confidence that drove me nuts. It took a man to not dress as one, and I wanted to say that to him, but I don't think he would like it. He kept saying, 'I'm not a woman, or, I'm not gay' very defensively, and I guess he's right.

My whole life I've associated dresses with women, but I guess they aren't two-in-one. Pants used to be a just a guy thing, and that changed—eventually. It didn't happen overnight, but women soon wore pants and showed everyone that it wasn't a big deal—eventually. I guess Shah was right, it all happened eventually. Maybe it was a bad idea for Michael to rush into it, but that wasn't Michael's style. That's what I liked about him—that screw you, I'll do what I want attitude. It was a lot like me before. Of course, my *Padre* made me change what I used to be. He told me to put my head down, but I couldn't anymore.

Mamá divorced *Padre* several years ago—the life he once lived was too much for her. Even though I know he's changed, *Mamá* sees the old him and can't look past it. So the both of us were rejected, and that brought us closer together.

I remembered the first night I moved in with *Padre*. We lived in a small ranch and, for some reason, it always smelled like Indian food. My room was the size of the large closet, but if he didn't mind living here, then I didn't mind either. We were eating a pizza in living room—which could barely fit a couch. Rain dripped through the giant cracks on the ceiling. He looked sad and ate his pizza in silence.

"*Padre, que pasa?*" I asked.

Once he finished his slice, he let out a belch. I laughed.

"Are you happy, *mi princesa*?"

"Of course, now we can hang out all the time."

"But, what if I'm a bad person?"

"You? You cried when I had to flush my goldfish down the drain."

"No, I didn't." I gave him a look, and he cracked a smile. "All right, maybe I did. But I don't want you ending up like me. For real."

"Is that a bad thing?"

"It could be, see this?" *Padre* pointed at one of his tattooed sleeves. He had many tattoos, but they were only visible when he wore a sleeveless shirt—all hidden beneath his clothes. I loved the flaming skulls and beautiful Spanish patterns painted in red and blue. I would spend hours staring at his arms—asking questions about each and every one. However, one was blacked-out. Whenever I asked what it was, he grew silent. "Under this is my past. I did some terrible things, some things that are unforgivable. We have the same blood, the same skin. You could easily get the same tattoo as me."

"How am I going to know if you don't tell me what it is!"

"Because you are better than that!" He suddenly screamed. I moved away from him, and for a moment I saw how dangerous he could be. It scared me. Then, he relaxed and was his regular-self again. "Don't be me."

There was a silence in the room—except for the barking of dogs in the distance. He looked away and began to stand up, but I put a hand on his shoulder. When he turned to look at me, I hugged him. "We're the same: blood, skin, crying when goldfish die. I'm going to be you no matter what. Hopefully, the part you want me to be me."

He kissed me on the top of my head. "*Que Será, Será.*"

"What will be, will be." I said in English. "Isn't that tattoo on your back?"

"That one is very special to me. It was my first tattoo."

"Really?"

"*Sí.* That's what your *Mamá* would say to me over and over again." He rubbed the top of my hair—like what he used to do when I was little. "She explained to me that things are and are not. Some things will be and others won't be. You have to accept what's thrown at you, embrace it and work with it. You have to be cool, like your *Mamá*. That night, I asked one of my guys to ink the words onto my back. I thought she'd be impressed the next day, but she only laughed at me. I don't regret it."

"So you just let people walk all over you?"

"No, work with it, not against it. This is what I'm telling you, I pushed back, and it landed me in jail."

"Oh."

"So be you, but less you at the same time."

"What does that mean?"

"You're going to be trouble-free at this new school. No guys, no punching, and especially no tattoos."

"But you said I could get it!"

"Let's wait another year for that tree of yours. Prove to me you can reserve yourself. Just be cool. Now, let's finish this pizza."

So I did. I never caused a problem in school and was the perfect student. I didn't want friends because I couldn't be myself around them. What if they too called me a slut? I was alone for weeks, afraid to be myself. After the night with Michael, I finally decided I had enough. I was going to be me. The next day, I searched for tattoo parlors. I found one downtown: a dirty store where the owner lived upstairs. When he saw me, he smiled, and looked me over.

"What do you want?" he asked.

"A tree, with giant leaves, like banana leaves."

"I don't know if I can do a banana tree."

"Just anything, a tree with branches." I was beaming, visualizing a memorial of lovers on my skin.

"How old are you?"

"I'm seventeen."

"Sorry, I need a consenting parent."

"Please, I'll give you cash. All of it."

Desperately, I pulled out the money.

"Fine. But I make it on-the-fly, nothing fancy."

"Great!"

The needle ranked into my skin, bleeding black ink into the fresh scars. I winced with pain. Finally, he took a break and wiped away the blood. He gave me a mirror to look at my side. I saw a hollow tree, with black and lonely branches.

"What is this? This is the saddest tree I've ever seen!"

"You wanted a goddamn tree!"

"Not some Halloween stump!"

"That's it, get out."

"No, fix it."

"That's what you get. Give me at least a few hundred more and I'll make it nice."

"*Pendejo*. I'm going somewhere else."

"Everyone else in this town will never ink someone underage, especially if I call them."

For the next couple of days, I gradually withdrew money from my account, bit by bit, saying it was for clothes, make-up, or feminine products. Now I had the chance to make it right—to immortalize Michael and the others in beautiful green leaves. Holding Michael's hand, as we walked down the hall, me in my skirt, and Michael in his blue dress, I was alive. The girls gave me a different stare. They were not the same disgusting looks they gave to Michael, but the slut stare. I was the freak who was into this type of thing, and in only a few weeks I was back to where I was: different school, still a slut. A *zorra*. This was different though, I wasn't going to hide who I was anymore. I was going to flaunt it like Michael. Soon, I would get a larger tree, with brighter colors. I would wear shirts with mid-drifts to show my stomach and side—let them see the tree growing from my body. I would make roots with it.

"Hey fag!" someone randomly shouted. Michael continued to walk, ignoring the comment. Still, he gripped my hand tighter.

"*Que Será, Será*," I whispered to him.

"What does that mean?"

"It means we're going to work through this, not against it. Together."

29

Michael

It was a nightmare. Suddenly, everyone changed. Once the initial shock wore off, it was as if I was a spider. First, people had jumped back, afraid I might bite. Then, they all said to their friends, 'Look at it, look at it!' Finally, they wanted to squash me. People won't let a spider do its thing, even if it never bothered anyone. It just wants to live its life. Still, it will always get killed—not because it's threatening, but because it's in their living space. I've made them uncomfortable, and now they're mad.

Those first few seconds walking down the hallway changed my tone as fast as a light switch turning off. Bella ran up beside me and held my hand. It felt good to have someone beside me, defiantly facing the world together. Then, I felt the change in the air.

"Hey fag!" someone shouted.

All of these people once loved me, thought of me as the cool kid in school. I thought they were my friends.

"Jesus, Bella. You must be into some weird stuff," said another.

"Hey Michaella! You want to give me some fashion tips later?"

"Freak," someone yelled in the crowd. I couldn't hear who any of these people were. They all created a toxic cloud—smothering me.

Still, Bella and I kept walking down the hall, trying to keep our heads up and smiling. But our smiles grew heavy the more stares weighed down on us. The happy mask was beginning to peel off, and soon I felt that I would be raw and naked among the crowd. I couldn't have that. Something smacked me hard on my back. I turned. A small planner was on the floor. I could have picked it up and looked at the name, but I didn't want to know. Maybe it would be someone I once knew, someone who once liked me. I kept walking, but my smile had finally fallen. Whenever we passed people, crumbled up balls of paper hit us from behind. No one threw them in front of me, which was the worst part. No one openly showed their disgust. They had to wait until I was behind them. Still, we kept our heads up.

The worst was when The Rabbits walked by—five of them—and one held out a giant dry erase marker. She waved it around like a sword. When The Rabbits brushed by Bella, one slashed the marker across her chest. Christ, it was like a prison stab—so subtle but violent. A giant black mark was right across her heart.

"Oh my God, I'm so sorry," said one of The Rabbits, clearly not.

I looked at the mark. Across her beautiful embroidered blue and white top was a black stain. It would never come out.

"You fu—" I said, head down and fists clenched. Bella jabbed me in the stomach. She stopped me from screaming my head off at them.

"Oh, it's okay," said Bella cheerfully. "This old thing was going to Goodwill anyway soon. So don't feel bad." The Rabbits looked at each other, confused. "Hey," she added. "Could you do me a favor, could you just put another mark on the other side. Just to even it out for me? It doesn't have to be perfectly symmetrical, but it will balance it out. You know, black, white, and blue will do pretty well together."

The Rabbits—particularly the one in the center with her marker extended—didn't know what to say. They stood there awkwardly, while the crowd waited for a response.

"Don't be afraid. I'll do it." Bella quickly grabbed the marker from her hand and made a huge gash into her top—even bigger than the one before it. "There, now that's some style. Thank you!" She handed the marker back to The Rabbits and kept walking, dragging me forward.

As soon as we were past them, all The Rabbits started to laugh. It was loud and obnoxious, and it had my heart racing with rage. Perhaps they were embarrassed and decided to laugh it off. Maybe they were laughing because they couldn't face their real guilt. Honestly, I thought they were laughing at how dumb Bella looked. It didn't matter. The fact was they were laughing while we were not.

"Relax," said Bella, squeezing my hand again. "Don't lose your cool, just like Shah said. Embrace it, you're done hiding."

"I can't believe you let them do that to you," I said, my voice completely empty.

"Yeah, it happens. But don't let them take you down. Come on, this is your day." She nudged me, and then tickled me on the stomach. I started laughing, and then tickled her back. Together both of us were dancing around each other, trying to get the other to squeal. Soon, I lost patience, and wrapped her by the chest and lifted her up. I spun her around in the air. Then I realized everyone was still staring at me—it never stopped. Still, I was alive and truly felt it. I kissed Bella, letting my happiness drain onto her lips. When she pulled back, I smiled, the truest one all day.

"Thank you," I said.

"Don't mention it."

"Ladies," said a deep voice. "Can you quit rough-housing in the hallway?" It was the assistant principal. When we broke away, he instantly saw it was me, not Shah.

"I'm sorry, Michael ... it was just ..."

"Oh don't worry about it. Don't I look beautiful today?" I said with a smirk. Bella was trying to hold back her laughter.

"Um ... well ..."

"Don't be shy."

"Yes ... yes, you do."

Bella and I laughed and walked past him. Could I really do this? Could I keep up this happiness up the whole day?

Well, I was going to try.

30

Lionel

I couldn't believe Michael was still smiling while sitting in the cafeteria. I thought by now he would break. Throughout the day, I overheard all the stories, from class to class, all the nonsense that Michael was put through. Each horrible class, when the teachers had their backs turned, the people teased him—calling him names and throwing pencils, papers. Whatever people had, they threw it at him. Someone even tossed their backpack at him. That was practically assault.

Of course, Michael didn't rat out to the teachers—he had his pride. Whenever a teacher did confront the students, Michael said they were just playing. Did they seriously buy that? I have no clue. I think most of them were just confused. Michael was supposed to have a detention for ditching the second half of school yesterday, but apparently he was excused. This pissed off the student body, who thought it wasn't fair that a *transvestite* got special privilege. I heard one girl yell at him, "Go home and skip more school you tranny-bitch." Who were these people? I thought. All of them loved Michael only yesterday, and now it completely changed. They were fickle and fragile, all of them—just a bunch of jerks who couldn't handle the real Michael. I could handle the real him, but I overreacted yesterday. I felt guilty for how I acted. The moment he needed me, I betrayed him. That wouldn't happen again.

How could I even help him though? The worst part of it was when he was on his way to lunch. The people in the hallway, building up their confidence, had been tapping on the lockers—building a crescendo chant, shouting, "Tran-ny, tran-ny!" Still, Michael and Bella courageously walked down the hall, smiling at everyone like they were in a procession. Didn't they get it? Smiling was only going to make it worse.

"Can't you see?" I said silently to imaginary Michael—holding his strong and soft hand. "The more you ignore them, the more they want to break you. You're holding back a river, and it will only push and push until it breaks through."

"No," said my Michael. "Give it time and they'll get used to it."

"They won't. This is who they are. They are shallow and used to certain things. If you change that, they will break you."

I imagined him putting his hand over mine. "We're going to be patient, and soon everything will be alright."

"But I don't want you to get hurt."

"Do I look like I'm hurt now?"

I looked over at the real Michael. He sat at a table, empty except for his two women: Shah and that girl, Bella. She was crazy, parading him around while soaking in all the attention. Why do you let them pull you around like this? Do what I do, Michael. Keep your head down low and stay out of the spotlight. Sometimes, the light will glance off of you— you'll have to deal occasionally with bullies and torment—but you'll have a relatively pester-free life. Sit with me, and let's be alone together—the Island at the lunch table.

Even though he was the most ridiculed person, he still didn't have the nerve to sit with me and the Islanders. We never asked to be called that, but we didn't deny that word either. It was true, I was stuck with the rejects. Only yesterday, one of the Islanders, Beth, tripped and spilled all of her food on the floor. The Rabbits, as Michael called them, were laughing at her. They laughed at a little innocent freshman. Was it those people that he wanted acceptance from? I certainly wouldn't want that. They were the real monsters, they didn't have a conscience.

They will never accept you, Michael. Fight all you want. Instead, be with me, isolated from the world on our own little island. We'll be islanders where no one will hurt us. We'll be alone and forgotten, but can escape this entire struggle. Give in to being who you are, a loser like me. You are different, and either you change the crowd, or you change yourself. My sweet Michael, don't fight the current. Be you, and be with me.

As if he could mentally hear me, Michael stood up from where he was sitting and looked at me. I blinked a couple of times, trying to de-trance myself from daydreaming. No, this wasn't a dream. Michael was walking toward me, his blue dress dancing through table and chairs. My heart raced, I stood up straight, and I could feel my palms sweat. How could a guy look so beautiful in a dress?

"Hey," said Michael, his voice silky yet dark.

"Hi."

"I just wanted to thank you for the painting. It really gave me the courage, you know?"

"Yeah," I stammered. Oh no, I thought. I was blushing.

"It was really nice of you."

"Thanks."

"So, I guess I should also apologize—"

"Stop, it's fine. I'm just glad to see you happy."

Michael's smile grew wide, so bright it could light up a room. I will be painting this image tonight, I thought. I want to keep this moment forever. Perhaps I didn't need to paint it, as it would be nestled inside my head like a warm blanket in the winter.

"Hey," said a voice. "Is that your new boyfriend?"

Michael turned and I looked past him. I couldn't believe it. I thought it was Marshall or some other of those dumb jocks who were giving him trouble all morning. But it was Jacob.

Despite the soft dress he was wearing, when Michael wanted to act tough, no dress could cover it. I swear, he grew two sizes, and batted away any chairs that stood in his way as he challenged Jacob.

"What did you say?" Michael said, their faces neck-and-neck. The rest of the student body rose from their chairs and cheered. Their eyes lit up like children on Christmas. Finally, they got want they wanted: Michael was going to lose it.

"I said," Jacob said, cold and void of humor, "is that your new boyfriend?"

That wonderful smile left Michael's face, and in its place was an ugly sneer. Why in the world did Jacob have to transform such a lovely face? Bella and Shah rushed over to try and hold Michael back. They weren't going to make it. Even if they did, Michael would have brushed them away. I could save him, or curse him forever.

I stood up and shouted for the whole cafeteria to hear. "Would that be such a bad thing?" The tension dropped and now the spotlight was on me. I walked up to Michael and put my hand on his shoulder. "Would it really be so bad," I said for only him to hear. Michael looked at me, his eyes confused. I was never this close to him, and I felt the warmth of his breath. Please, I'm sorry, I said to my imaginary Michael, don't pull away. Let me stay this close, even if it won't last. The spell was broken when Jacob shouted, "You're gay now too? What else did you hide from me? Do you two like to switch roles for fun?"

"I'm not gay!" Michael roared and pushed me away. I fell hard against my seat.

Suddenly, Michael charged at Jacob, shoving him so hard he bent backwards against the table's edge. After the initial shock, Jacob quickly grabbed him by the waist and tried to throw him to the ground. Michael dropped his weight and his stance. Everyone was cheering, yelling, "Fight, fight!" This was the explosion they were waiting for. Did I cause it, or was this going to happen eventually?

31

Michael

I exploded. All the smiling and cheeriness I put on vanished the minute Jacob opened his mouth. We were rolling on the cafeteria floor, knocking over trays and soda cans. This wasn't like the matches we had in my backyard, where we both were playfully holding back. We were really trying to rip each other's heads off. A crowd towered over us, leaning in, blocking the fluorescent lights above. We kicked and squirmed, trying to get the slightest edge. The people who were too close were in the crossfire—receiving blows to the shins by our restless legs.

I was going to explain it all to him. It was still me, Jake, I was still the same person who lit a garbage bag full of gasoline on fire—just to see what would happen. That one time, I had lit the bottom of the bag with a lighter and was surprised there wasn't an explosion. The flame just melting the plastic, not igniting the gas. Jake had been growing impatient, so I leaned in some more to see what was wrong. Then the whoosh of flames exploded from the bag, fire billowed up in the air and almost singed my eyebrows. Part of my long sleeve shirt was on fire, so I spun around in circles—hoping that the wind would blow it out. Instead, the flames crept up my arm and I screamed. Jacob had been rolling on the dirt, unstoppable laughter frothing from his mouth.

"Help me! It's not funny!" I had screamed, but I was strangely laughing too. My maniacal laugh, deep in the middle of the woods with flames around us, would have made a great urban legend if anyone happened to hike by.

"Roll! Roll on the ground," Jacob had said, holding his stomach like it would fall out any minute.

Finally, I knelt down and pummeled the ground with my arm. Jacob stood up and threw chunk after chunk of sand. After all the flames were smothered and the black smoke blew away, Jake ran around me with his arm extended.

"Ahhh, help me! It's going to eat me."

"You jerk!" I tried to tackle him, but my arm was sore from the burns. Luckily, the fire only ate away at my sleeve. When we came back to his apartment, his mom soaked my arm in ice water while scolding both of us.

"Don't. Ever. Play. With. Fire!"

Getting yelled by her was actually a compliment. She only yelled around family and growing up with Jacob made me a part of hers. Now that was over. My ex-best friend was positing himself to come from behind with a rear choke. I was reacting physically, but the only thing on my mind was how different the holidays were going to be. There would be no Jacob on Thanksgiving, inviting Shah and me to his house while Ma had to work a double. No Jacob on Christmas, giving me a terribly wrapped gift. I lost my best friend, and I was angry for it. I wanted to kill him.

Jacob quickly spun around me and threw me to the ground. My cheek pressed against the sticky cafeteria floor. He leaned in really close, and I thought it was just for leverage, but he whispered, "I don't want to be friends with a goddamn fairy faggot." I reached for a tray that was on the floor and smashed it on at his head. He let go of his grip and I continued to beat him with the tray. He put his hands up, but I continued to wail at him. It was all over, no more holidays, no more friends or family—I just lost the closest friend I ever had.

The assistant principal was yelling at us to stop, but he didn't dare to break up the fight. The last thing he wanted to do was to ruin his suit and his jaw. I crawled on top of Jacob—continuing to smash him with the orange tray. After I saw bruises and blood form on his face, I tossed the tray aside and looked at everyone. My dress was torn, and a part of my hairy chest was shown. If they didn't think I was a freak before, now they were certain. I looked over at Shah and Bella, and they looked away—too embarrassed to support me now. The only person that came up to me was Lionel.

"It's over now," he said. Then, he gingerly put a hand on my arm. What did he say? 'Would that be a bad thing.' I pushed away his hand.

"Get away from me, Lionel." He looked hurt, but I didn't care. I was alone now. When the assistant principal noticed that the animal wasn't going to attack anymore, he walked up to me. Just before he reached me, I shoved my chest out and startled the assistant principal. I laughed, but not in the way that I did in the morning. It was a bitter laugh.

"Michael," the assistant principal said, "you need to come with me."

"Well, certainly. Sorry if I'm a mess." He pulled me up from my armpits. No one said a word. "Hold on, let me fix my dress. I wouldn't want to mess up my appearance." I let out another bitter laugh. Nothing was funny, but I kept laughing.

Part 3

Black

Put out the light and then put out the light

32
Jacob

He had to ruin everything. Or was it she? *She* had to ruin everything? No, there's no way I'm calling him *she*. That's just not going to happen. I'm not even going to call him *him*, ever. Because I'm done talking to him. It's done, I'm never talking to that loser, cross-dressing, something, something—I was never good at coming up with insults. I mean, how the hell could they suspend both of us? He was the one who hit me with a tray, like some crazy animal.

Ok, fine. I messed up. Calling him out in front of everyone was probably a bad idea. But man, he knew I had the somewhat awkward hots for his sister, and then he dresses up as his sister? Hell, I was flirting with him! That's just … I just … how can you maintain a friendship after that? Oh, hey Michael? You remember the time I hit on you, because you were pretending to be Shah? Wasn't that cool? Yeah, you didn't embarrass me at all in front of the whole school. No way. All right, don't take this the wrong way, but I think since Michael looked pretty—I can't believe I'm saying this—attractive as "Shah," people flipped out when they realized it was Michael. It's like you're eating this awesome candy bar and then all of a sudden someone tells you it's just dirt with some sugar mixed in. Everyone would just lose their minds.

So when I was sitting at the cafeteria and Michael was wearing the blue dress, I was keeping my mouth shut. I thought I was doing pretty well. What I wanted to do was scream at his face, but I had no idea what I was going to say. For most of the time during lunch, I kept rehearsing: Hey, Michael. If you're gay, whatever, but I'm not gay. Second, I'm not dressing up with you, like some tea party. Did he like tea parties now? Did he dress up so he could talk in some fancy British accent? "Oh, hello …

British person … would you pass a biscuit?" I was in my own universe, hoping I'd finally come up with something smart to say to him. That was when Marshall jabbed me in the arm.

"Hey, Jacob, your boy's looking pretty good today." I didn't say anything. I just kept my looking at my food and hoping Marshall would get bored and move on to something else. "Wait a minute," he said slowly, like he just came up with the best thought in the world. "Weren't you talking a mile a minute about how good Shah looked yesterday?"

"Shut up, Marshall."

"It's all right, man," he patted me on the back. "No one's going to shame you for being gay. I mean, I don't know if it counts if he's wearing a dress." All the other wrestlers laughed.

"Let it go," I said, not looking up from my soggy sandwich of mayo, ham, and cheese. It was great when Michael and I used to sit together in middle school. Both of our moms were always too busy to make anything great, so my mom just slopped together this mess while his mother gave him ten freaking dollars. Ten dollars for the school lunch was a feast. I used to throw away my lunches and we would buy all sorts of candy, cookies, and drinks. As we got older, the money got tighter, and we had to go back to soggy messes of white bread. Even in high school, we traded food like we were young again. I always had cases of soda in my house, while he had some candy bars. We swapped those often because his mom didn't like soda in the house and mine didn't allow candy bars.

"Hey Jake," Marshall poked at me again. "Looks like he's talking to his new boyfriend."

I turned around, and saw Michael chatting up a storm with Lionel. Really? Lionel? The creep who always followed Shah around? Man, I once grew penises all over his arm during a sleepover at Michael's. He's a weird kid.

"Oh, oh," added Marshall. "Maybe, they've been undercover lovers all this time! Hell, maybe he was trying to get you to join all these years. I mean, maybe that's why he's on the wrestling team. Makes sense for him to be the top seed—he's used to rolling around with men."

Before I knew what was happening, I turned around and punched Marshall in the arm. It landed well, with a nice thud. Instantly, Marshall threw up his arms.

"Hey, dude. Don't be mad at me. He's the one who's messing with your head. He and his new boyfriend."

Then I saw Michael smile at Lionel. It was a wide smile, a bit too happy. Wait, I thought, was Michael and Lionel—no way, wasn't he with Bella? And damn, Bella was hot. What the hell was going on?

"You got to say something to Michael," said Marshall. "Say something like, 'How's your new boyfriend?'"

The rest of the team egged me on. I tried focusing on my soggy sandwich, but eventually Marshall took the sandwich out of my hand.

Marshall said, really seriously, "If you don't ask him, I will."

I don't know why, but I wanted to be the one to ask him. I knew Michael better than anyone—well, I thought I did—and this question would set him over the edge. If anyone was going to get beat up for asking, I wanted it to be me. Part of me wanted to duke it out with him. Also, they were right—I needed to know some answers.

"Hey, Michael," I said. "Is that your new boyfriend?"

Suddenly, we were going at it. I should have won it, since I had the better position on the floor, but then I thought, 'Was this what he wanted?' Was he grabbing me because he liked it? It was hard to really keep going because grabbing his dress and body felt all wrong. With the adrenaline, I had to keep going. Then, he grabbed the tray, and wailed on me. That left me with a cut on my eyebrow and some bruises on my arm. That fight got us both suspended for the remainder of the week. This was Michael's second suspension in two weeks! If he even sneezed wrong, he'd get expelled!

"He's not a boy!" I had said back at the house. I was sitting in the kitchen with a bag of cold peas on my face. My mom was making dinner. "He's a girl now."

"So?" my mom said. "He's still your friend since first grade." My mom, with her wheelchair, rolled back over to the oven to check on dinner.

Ever since the accident, about three years ago, my mom never thought to do things differently. While some people would wine about being disabled, she never let me know how she really felt. I mean, I can't imagine anyone being happy in a wheelchair, but she acted as happy as she could be.

"Well, he's not my friend anymore," I complained. "It's like I don't know him anymore."

"Maybe you should try to know him now?"

"No way."

My mom rolled back to me. On the kitchen table was my mom's bright pink notebook. I wasn't allowed the touch it, or even breathe on it. Occasionally, I managed to sneak a look inside the cover, but it was only filled with random words, and my name often. She picked up the notebook, held it in her hands for a minute. My mom stared at the cover like she was reading it, but there wasn't any words on it. Slowly, I leaned in to see if she was okay. Without warning, she smacked me on the head four times with the notebook.

"He. Is. Your. Friend."

The cut opened up again, and my mom put her hand to her mouth, guiltily. Then she kissed my head and put the peas back on my skull.

"Remember when your dad passed away? Michael slept over every night for a week. He never left your side. That's the Michael I know. And I also know that even if he maybe puts on different clothes, inside he's still the same person."

I sighed and didn't say anything.

"Here's what you're going to do," added my mom. "You're not going to speak to him for the rest of your suspension. Cool off a bit. Think about all the great times you had with him. If you still think it's not worth saving the friendship, then fine. If you do think it is, then go over to his house on Sunday. Deal?"

"Okay, Mom."

She kissed me on the cheek. Then she dropped the notebook on my lap.

"I'm giving you my notebook for a while. Do you understand how much a big deal it is?"

"Yeah, whatever. I get it."

"No, you don't."

She wheeled away from me and went to look out the window. I heard tiny gasps. Was she crying?

"Mom, are you alright?"

When she turned around, her cheeks were red, and tears were beginning to drop from her eyes.

"I'm sorry, it's just that I gave you that notebook and you don't even know how special it is to me."

"I know if I look at it, you beat the crap out of me."

She laughed, but dryly. "That notebook saved my life."

I stared at its pink cover. It was worn and very plain. It was just a notebook.

"What are you talking about?" I asked.

"I'm going to let you in on a secret. I'm sorry if this adds on top of Michael, but you finally need to know. After the crash, I didn't want to live."

"What?"

"After losing your father, did you expect me to be happy?"

"Of course not, but you wanted to…?"

I felt sick to my stomach. Suddenly, Michael's dress stuff didn't seem that important.

"Relax, baby." She put a hand to my cheek—the one that wasn't cut up. "I don't want to do that anymore, and it was all because of this notebook." She pointed at the pink cover—it hurt my eyes to even look at it. "One night, when I had all the pills ready, I wanted to leave a goodbye note. So, I grabbed whatever I found on the table, and it was my notebook. Back then, I just used it for shopping lists. For some reason, I thought I might make a check list of all the great things that happened in my life— you know, to end my life on a happy note."

She smiled, but it was hard to return the gesture. I was about to throw-up.

"After I made that list, I didn't feel as depressed. Whenever I feel sad, I write down a bunch of things that are great. Like toasted marshmallows, late nights with friends, and of course, you."

My eyes began to well up. She began to tear up but took a deep breath and smiled. Before I had a chance to really cry, she kissed me on each eye. She used to do that when I was a baby, and I finally smiled. Michael's choice didn't seem that important anymore.

"So, number one, you're grounded. Two, no talking to Michael, or Shah. Three, write down all the great stuff you did with him. If that notepad isn't full by the end of the week, I know you're lying."

She went back to the oven to check on dinner. My face was practically numb from the peas, so I placed the bag down on the table. Instantly, the table was damp with water. I reached for the pink notebook and found a pencil on the table. I stared at an empty page—trying to think of something that was great about Michael. After a moment, I wrote, *Stayed with me after Dad died.* Then, I thought of a stupid thing we did: *Ate ghost peppers and screamed in pain for hours.* I started laughing, but my mom didn't turn around. I think she wanted me to be in my own world with Michael. Soon, I was thinking of every fun moment we had. By the time Sunday came around, I had filled up the rest of the pages.

33
Shah

Michael had it easy. He had to flip out on Jacob, get the rest of the week off, while Bella and I had to deal with *his* aftermath. We sat on top of my car, Sunday evening, sharing a cigarette and staring at the setting sun.

"I don't think I can do another week of this," I said, inhaling a giant wave of smoke. I held it in deep in my lungs and never wanted to let go. Just choke me in tobacco, I thought, just give me a moment. Having my body struggle for oxygen was a nice distraction. It kept my mind off of Michael and the hell which was that week. Finally, I had to give in and let out the smoke. It blew softly up in the air and faded into the twilight. I passed the cigarette to Bella, who happily accepted and breathed it in just as deep.

"You can do it," she said casually. "It gets better."

"Will it?" I wasn't so confident. All week, we had become the new targets. With Michael out of the picture, and Lionel hiding in whatever goddamn shadows he was in, the school targeted us. It was like they needed to feed their hatred on somebody. Suddenly, Jacob was a martyr who stood up to the monster and was defeated. Now, the school had to remember its fallen comrade. Someone filled my entire gym bag with rotten eggs when I left my locker open. Everyone suddenly remembered that I, too, dressed differently—I was the one who fooled everyone into thinking I was a boy. They created a new game for me: how many pictures of cock and balls could Shah find around her things? Or, my other favorite, how many times could I bear the word *tranny* before completely losing it?

Every night, I tried to hold back my tears. I didn't ask for this—this was Michael's war and he started it! Whenever Michael knocked on my door, I instantly lit up a cigarette and wiped away my tears. If he asked if

152

I was crying, I said the smoke was getting into my eyes. I'm not sure if he bought it or not, but he left me alone most nights. He spent hours just staring at dresses on-line, ordering boxes of clothes to our house. He seemed calm, like he didn't try to kill his best friend on a dirty cafeteria floor. I overheard him talking on the phone with Bella one night.

"No," I heard him say, "that was one breakdown and it won't happen again. I know what I have to do. I have to be calm."

I couldn't do the same. This war was tearing me apart. I held Bella's hand as the sun began to set.

"How did you stay so calm during all of this?"

Bella had it far worse than me. She was the Ms. Freak who was dating Mr. Freak. The Rabbits continued targeting her at random times—slashing her clothes with markers whenever she passed by them. Since she never complained, they kept harassing her. At lunch, someone managed to coat her seat with superglue, so when she went to sit, she was stuck to the chair. Bella knew the minute she sat down and had whispered to me to not yell. She had told me to hold tightly on the chair. With a quick jerk, she torn the fabric off her skirt and stood up.

I stood staring at her purple underwear, and luckily the chair was blocking most of the color. Still, some people saw it, and tried to pull out their phones in time to take a picture. Before I knew what was happening, Bella grabbed my sweater and wrapped it around her waist. Quickly, she sat back down on a new chair and went back to eating like it was no big deal. I saw The Rabbits giggling a few tables away. I gripped my tray, and I was ready to smash their heads in, just like Michael did. Then Bella held my hand. There were tears in her eyes, but she was smiling.

"Don't," she had said. "Stay with me."

She was breakable. I saw it with those tears. Of course, neither of us told any of these stories to the teachers. We were afraid it would make it worse. Imagine the payback afterwards! Besides, what could the teachers actually do? Everything was done so secretly, so discreetly, that we couldn't actually pin any of this to anyone. Instead, we took it all with stupid smiles on our faces. More importantly, we didn't tell Michael. He seemed so happy during his second suspension—blissfully ignoring anything posted online about him during his hiatus. He didn't seem bothered that the school probably wasn't going to tolerate a third suspension. He only had one more chance, but he didn't seem worried.

Bella finished the last of the cigarette and flicked it away onto the asphalt. I saw the red embers spark, then die. She stood up on the hood of the car.

"We're going to keep on taking it until they come around. They will. I know it."

"I can't, Bella. Just thinking about tomorrow is making me nauseous. Plus, Michael's finally going to see what we've had to put up with."

Bella breathed in the last rays of light. She stood tall, staring defiantly at the remaining bit of the sun.

"We have a chance to make a difference. This isn't just about Michael, but about everyone like him. We can change the tide."

"I never wanted to change anything," I said, looking up at her.

"You just want to keep living a carefree life, cracking jokes, and letting those jerks dictate how we live our lives? Maybe there're others like Michael who are too afraid to speak out. We can spark a movement!"

"What? No. I only did this because Michael's my brother. I don't care about the others. I can't keep taking these ass-whippings week after week! We're not going to start anything. And even if we did, it's not going to last."

"Yes, we can. We're going to do this together. Look at the sun." Bella pointed at the barely visible red glow in the distance. "If you stared at the sun during the day, you'll never see it move. In fact, it will burn your eyes out. But look at it now, and I swear you can see it move like a mile a second. It's only at the end can when you see the progress. Wait and it will surely move. It may not be as fast as you like, but it's moving. And soon, you, me, and Michael will be watching a setting sun."

I pretend to throw up over the side of the car. "Oh God, Bella. Way too much cheese on that."

"I'm trying to motivate your sorry-ass."

"I'll give it a B+."

She sat back down and then put an arm over my shoulder. Together we watched the remaining sunset. It was beautiful. But then I imagined watching it rise early in the morning. Could I sit on the roof of my car, in the middle of an abandoned parking lot, baking in the sun, watching it move the entire day? I wouldn't have the strength or the patience. Sure, the sun moves, but it's painfully slow. How slow was this fight going to be? I knew I couldn't last much longer, and I don't think Bella could either. But she still made a great speech.

34

Lionel

Walking down the sidewalk toward Michael's house, I was carrying another painting. Once again, the bright, orange lights guided me to the moment that I've dreaded for a long time. Tonight, I would explain everything: how I pretended to like Shah, how I dreamed of him for years, and how I couldn't imagine a day without Michael's smile on my mind. For too long I had let my fantasies live in purgatory.

This night, my paints exploded onto canvas, a massacre of love and hate. Michael scared me—the way he could implode, the way he beat up his best friend. His old self was fading away, like construction paper that's been exposed to the sun for years. As a kid, I used to cut images of dinosaurs and giraffes—anything that had a fascinating shape—and tape them onto my wall. Dozens of vivid blues, greens, pinks, and reds decorated my white walls.

A colorful zoo guarded me while I slept. Then, as I grew older, I ripped them all down—Michael and Jacob thought they looked stupid. The tape peeled away the white paint, leaving brown splotches in its wake. What bothered me the most was the backside of the construction paper. I thought these animals had such rich colors, but when I turned them over, I realized what they used to look like. Over time, I forgot their true self— their true bright colors. Maybe I haven't seen Michael's true self in years. Perhaps, there was a richer and brighter self that had been kept hidden from me.

I knocked on the door, expecting Shah to answer. Instead, Michael opened the door.

"Hi," I said a bit too chipper. "I mean, how are you feeling?"

"Um, good. I've had a lot of time off recently."

156

"Yeah, how is your mom taking it?"

"She, uh, still doesn't know," he said. "When she came to pick me up the second time, Shah managed to get my old clothes from the car. Ma didn't even want to talk to the assistant principal. Instead, she just took me home."

"That's it? No punishment?"

"No."

"Don't you think you should tell her why it happened?"

"No. She wouldn't understand."

He stepped aside to let me go through his doorway. When I brushed past him, I felt the warmth from his skin. Even that could chill me all over. I couldn't play this game again. I had to tell him the truth once and for all.

"Michael, I wanted to talk about Friday. When I said—"

"Oh, is that another painting?" He grabbed the canvas and walked away from me—up toward his room.

"Uh, yeah, I wanted to explain it to you this—"

"No, I think I get it this time."

Awkwardly, I followed him up his front staircase and toward the hallway into his room.

"Um, is Shah here?" My heart raced, hoping there was a way out. Maybe Shah would interrupt us, make a joke, and find a way to end whatever this was. But wait—why did I care? I was alone with Michael, and that was the reason why I came over. Wasn't it?

"No, she's out with Bella. She said she'd be back later, so it's just us for a while," he said, still intently focused on the painting.

When we entered his room, I was amazed to see how much it had changed since the last time I was there. Covering the walls were dozens of pictures of models wearing beautiful clothes. Also hanging on the wall was my painting—the black canvas with the blue dot. I almost started to cry.

"You put it up?" I asked.

"Of course, I really like it." Michael smiled.

I was trying my hardest not to blush, but I felt my cheeks grow warm.

"Remember when I used to cover my room with pictures of animals with construction paper?"

"Oh yeah! Jake wouldn't stop ragging on you about that," he said with a laugh. It was so golden, and his eyes seemed to glow.

"But…"

"But what?"

"You laughed at me when you saw it, when we were kids, so I ripped them all down."

"Oh." Michael walked around his room and paused to look at every photo on his wall. "I'm sorry I said that. You've always deserved better." He peeled off some of the magazine cuttings and moved them over, so there was a rectangular space free on the white wall. "I think I'll put this painting right here." He grabbed some tacks from his desk and mounted it on the wall.

The canvas had two hands, one white and one black, in a dove hand-gesture. Each fingertip had tears dripping down—falling into a violent sea of red. I was crying and screaming when I painted it, but I wouldn't let Michael know that.

"I didn't think you'd put it up—it's a little terrifying," I said softly.

"Oh God, no. I get it, I really do," he said back. Then he turned to me, his eyes were so warm. What was going on?

"Well, I should be going."

"Why?" he asked, holding my hand. His callused hand felt so strong in my palm. Suddenly, he was walking toward me, and I slowly retreated. Then I was up against the wall. His chest pushed against mine, and he pinned my hands with his muscular arm.

"Michael…" I said weakly, my lips dry and my throat pulsing.

"I treated you so badly, for all these years, and now I want to make up for it."

He kissed me on the neck. His lips burned into my skin—igniting a fire that roared inside of me. Again and again, he placed his lips along my body. Each time I shuddered, my breath erratic in rhythm. Then he pulled back and looked me in the eye. I felt a tiny spark as our noses touched.

"Is this what you wanted?" he said, not passionately, but as a start of a contract agreement. It gave me a second to snap out of the trance he gave me.

"What about you?" I asked back, trying to smile. But some of the magic flew away—and I didn't know why.

Michael thought about it for a moment, and before I had a chance to respond, he put both of his callous hands to my cheeks and pulled himself to me, pressing his lips against mine. The mood was absolutely perfect, but something was odd. I mean, I couldn't say no. Isn't this what I wanted for all these years?

35

Jacob

Okay, apology time. I was right outside his front door—psyching myself up to go inside. This wasn't going to be pretty. I could start off with something like, "Hey, man, what it's like being a chick?'" Could I high-five him now, or do I have to hug him with my butt awkwardly hanging out? Do I have to squeal like, "Oh my god, I'm so happy to see you!'" Please God, no. That would be really uncomfortable. I mean, him wearing the dresses is already uncomfortable enough, but if he started acting the part ... I don't know. It's like he ripped off the mask, and shouted, "It was me all along! Fooled you!" And everyone comes out from trashcans and from the walls and from the ceiling and then they all laugh at me.

"Come on, Jake," I said to myself, "you can do this."

He hasn't *changed* changed, just ... changed—if that made sense. Of course it made sense, he's your best friend and he's still going to be. That's why you're here, ready to make a long-ass speech about acceptance and goodwill towards men or something like that. Maybe, I could just punch him in the face, and then he could punch me in the face, and then we would be all cool. That sounds a lot easier.

I kept knocking on the door, but nobody was answering. I couldn't call him or text him because this had to be personal. I wanted to see his face when I said I wanted to make this work. Truth was, I missed my best friend. We did everything together. Hell, one time he even convinced his mom to let him go trick-or-treating in a clown costume because that was what I was forced to wear. My mom's disability check didn't come in that month, so she couldn't afford the really cool superhero costumes. All she found was a discount rubber clown mask. That didn't bother Michael. No sir. With a smile, Michael put on a rubber clown mask like mine. It really pissed me off how he was always there for me. Filling up that notebook really put everything in … perspective, you know? And what did I do in return? I called him out in front of the school and threw mashed potatoes in his face. But he could have trusted me. I would've kept it a secret, damnit! Yeah, I would have flipped out for a bit, but eventually I would've been cool with it. But no, he had to let little Lionel in on it before me. Seriously? That dweeb that was obsessed with Shah, like stalked her and everything! Well, then there was that weird interaction with Michael before we fought. But no, he wasn't gay. Was he? No, I knew Michael, like *knew* him and maybe he forgot to tell me the whole dress thing, but he hadn't lied to me about everything. Right?

I pounded a couple of more times on the door, and then decided to walk around to the side of the house and climb up the tree like I usually did. The reason I even knocked on the door was because I figured he was changing into his lady clothes and I didn't want to be staring at him like a pervert. Would it make me a pervert? Seriously, I was going to grab a pen and paper later, so I could make a list of what was and what wasn't cool to say to the new Michael, because I had absolutely no idea anymore.

As I was walking around, I noticed Michael's bedroom light was on. Oh, so the big man was too cool to open the front door? I listened for a moment and heard the faint sound of some music. Alright, so maybe he couldn't hear my knocking or whatever. Maybe he was busy with dress … things? When you put on a dress, do you need to concentrate? Maybe you need to concentrate like a surgeon and he's like trying to save this guy with blood gushing everywhere and he can't hit an artery. Oh, and then there was a bomb going off too, and he can hear the seconds tick away. Tick, tick, tick. That sounded pretty stupid, but if Michael and I were talking— that would have sounded awesome.

Michael and I used to talk for hours about the movies we'd direct one day. I was always the big fan of that idea we created: *Sexy Monster Island*, where all these really hot girls were really gigantic monsters but they were able to put on these flesh suits that would make them attractive. Michael loved the idea too and we even wrote a couple of scenes. We stopped when I said we would have to make the monsters be really evil and then kill all the guys who end up there. Michael didn't argue, but he lost interest after that.

At the base of the tree, I tried to lean my head up toward the window. I heard some noises, but I couldn't figure out what it was—like the floor moving or something. Maybe he had a girl up there? A part of me wanted to shout out his name, but I was afraid he'd look out and slam the window on me. In wrestling, you've got to be an animal in the ring—the first quick move can really decide the match. You can wait and counter his attack, but it's that nice swift strike that creates the tempo. Michael was always good at that. Taking his advice, I wanted to be close enough so that he couldn't block me out—he'd have to confront me.

I started climbing the tree, being as quiet as possible. As a kid, I thought this tree was higher than a mountain, but it's only about the size of their house. To get up to his window, I had to hop on the first branch, and then swing my right leg to the second. After that, it's like climbing a ladder. As I climbed higher, I heard some faint breathing. Maybe he was with a girl—but it didn't sound right. Trust me, after wrestling with someone for so long, even someone's breathing has its own DNA. When I was high enough to peer over the window frame, I saw Michael's back was pressing someone to the wall. I was right, I stupidly thought, he's too busy to answer the door because he's with another girl. Classic Michael. I started to smile, and I was right about to climb down the tree when Michael pulled back from whomever he was kissing.

It was Lionel. Suddenly, I had the urge to climb into the window and punch that stupid face in. So, they really *were* together after all? There was *another* huge secret he kept hidden from me? Were all those nights of talking up women just a show? Who was this person? Michael wasn't really Michael, maybe he was Michaella—that stupid name Marshall came up with.

Shaking, I climbed down the tree without making a noise. At the base, I looked back up and stared at the glowing light above in his room. I told myself that I had no right to be calm—I needed to be angry. Without thinking, I punched the base of the tree with all my might. I wanted to scream but didn't—not even when I noticed my whole hand was scraped up and bleeding.

36
Michael

I heard a dull vibration. Abruptly, I pulled away from Lionel and looked toward the window. Attentive, like a dog, I swiftly craned my neck and kept deathly still—hoping there would be another sound, a tick. Nothing came, but that didn't stop me from going to the window. Pushing Lionel away, I peered out into the night. It was hard for my eyes to adjust to the darkness, but I thought I heard some rustling in the bushes. Great, it was some fools trying to catch me in the act. Well, I'll show them, I thought.

"Yeah, that's right!" I yelled at the bush. "How do you like it? Come back up, take some pictures while you're at it."

I closed the window, even though my room was already humid. I took a deep breath and tried to calm down. After a moment, I turned to Lionel and put on my best sexy face—I didn't actually know how I looked.

"Where were we?" I said to Lionel, walking back up to him.

"Um, I think I'm just going to head out."

"Why?" I stood back, surprised. Isn't this what he always wanted?

"Because ... this doesn't feel right."

"What are you talking about?"

"Michael, why are you doing this?"

"Because I like—"

"You've never hit on me before."

"What if I just realized—"

"The truth, please." He pushed me away and crossed his arms.

I held my head back and sighed. Who was I kidding? I wasn't turned on by any of this. I kept imagining it was Bella. Lionel smelt of paint and sweat. Still, I kept going—hoping that maybe the moment would spark something. I remember when I was little and gagged at the smell of coffee.

Then, the more I was around it, I grew to like it. Maybe I could have become gay if I kept trying. After all, wouldn't it finally make sense why I dressed up in woman's clothes if I was gay? It would answer a lot of questions.

"People can't wrap their head around me," I said. "Maybe if they knew I was really gay, it might explain some things."

"Are you kidding me? That's insane! What the hell would it explain?" Lionel snapped. I never saw him this angry before. He looked extremely uncomfortable.

"I don't know," I said defensively. "Right now, I'm a contradiction— I wear dresses but I'm straight. Being gay gives me some protection— there're a bunch of gay guys who do drag."

"Oh! My mistake!" Lionel put his hands up in fake shock. "Please, let's continue to make out because you need some protection. I haven't even come out to my parents! Being gay doesn't protect you, Michael!"

"What do you expect me to do?"

"Do? How about be yourself! Is that a crazy idea? It's far saner than what you just did. You're messed up, you know that? I've loved you *for years*, and you're just going toy with my emotions just so you can have something to fall back on? Christ, were you going to throw me under the bus when your 'gay phase' was over?"

"But maybe I really am gay. Think of this obsession I have with dresses. I could've been repressing some stuff, I don't know. Why can't we try?"

"Because I've seen how you look at Bella, and other girls in the past." Lionel's eyes began to well up. "I know how you want them, when they smile and touch your skin. I knew all along, but I wanted to be them. You're straight Michael, but I wanted to pretend otherwise. It was a fantasy of mine, but now that I've lived it, it's not the same."

He walked out the room. I followed a few steps behind him, but I didn't have the courage to say anything. When we reached the bottom of the stairs, by the front door, he turned to me.

"You know, I have to thank you. I liked living in a dream, imagining a sweet Michael who would whisk me away. Now I'm waking up, and I see the real you— a manipulating, selfish bastard who doesn't care about anyone but himself."

"Lionel," I said weakly.

"You broke the spell, congratulations."

"Are you going to tell—"

"Unlike you, I care about other people, so no, I'm not going to tell anyone. You want my advice? Lay low, don't make a scene. Be boring. Boring makes you safe. Soon, high school is over, and you'll never see any of them again."

"You know I can't do that."

"Then you'll fall apart. Goodnight, Michael."

He closed the door and left me in the dark foyer. I went back upstairs, slammed my bedroom door, and pulled down the latest picture that Lionel gave to me. It was a stupid picture anyway, I thought. I broke it across my knee. It didn't make me feel any better.

37

Jacob

I waited outside for him. I watched Lionel close the front door and head toward his house. The street lamps were lit, but there was no way he could see me. Lionel walked with his arms crossed, his hands tucked into his elbows. He looked as though he was cold, but it was a warm night. I had to admit, he fooled me. For years, Lionel was just that awkward kid. Who knew he was playing this secret game with Michael? Is that why Lionel always tagged along when we were kids? Who were these people? Michael and Lionel, people I knew my entire life, were putting on a show for me. How come I couldn't see through it, see the strings on the freaking puppets?

When I was a kid, I could never figure out how all the wooden puppets danced during the first-grade assembly. Michael and Lionel laughed at my stupid face because I could never figure it out.

"They're moving with magic," Michael said, laughing.

"No way."

"Yeah, there's a magician behind the curtain who's waving a wand around and saying 'hocus pocus,'" said Lionel.

"That not true!"

"I'm telling the truth. Cross my heart."

When the assembly was over, I had walked over to the performer and shouted, "When I grow up, can I be a magician like you?" He laughed, in a mocking way, the way when older people don't want to hurt your feelings because you're being so stupid. "I'm not a magician, kid, I work the strings on the puppets."

"So how do you make them float?"

"I pull on the strings, see?"

I turned around to see Michael and Lionel uncontrollably laughing on the ground. My face blushed and I ran away from both of them. Of course, I made up with Michael during lunch, when he gave me his pudding. Lionel never apologized.

"Lionel," I whispered behind a bush. He turned around, looking into nothing. I waited for him to walk a couple more steps before I whispered again, "Lionel."

This time, he knew it was a voice and shouted, "Whoever is doing that please stop."

I kept quiet and let him sulk in the silence. Once Lionel began walking, quickening his pace, I moved out of the bush and flew past him in the shadows. Since Lionel was directly under a lamppost, he never saw me. I was just a figure moving quickly away, too blurry for the eye to see. By the time I dove into another bush, he was running down the street.

Soon he heard my footsteps behind him, and he didn't dare look back. Something deep inside of me told me to keep chasing him, like a lion. The lampposts stopped for a couple blocks, leaving darkness for him to run through. That was when I sped up. Lionel tried to run faster, but he was no athlete. Soon, he was sucking in breath and slowed down. That was when I tackled him from behind. His face smacked against the asphalt, breaking his glasses. Before he had a chance to turn around, I pushed his head against the ground with my knee.

"You could have just told the truth," I said, gritting my teeth.

"Jacob?"

"Shut up!"

"Let me go!"

"No, now shut up."

"Please, you're hurting me."

"You could have just let me know he was gay. That would've been fine. And he could have worn whatever stupid dress he felt like. But no, it had to come to this. It all had to be a secret. How long has this been going on?"

"It's not what it looks like," said Lionel, gasping for breath.

"I saw you two. What kind of mind games have you been playing with everyone? I'm sick of everyone treating me like an idiot. Tell me the truth. Did you even like Shah?"

He didn't speak. I shook him until he spoke.

"No."

"It was all about Michael?"

"Yes."

I stood up and walked away. That was when Lionel started laughing. I could see his skin was scraped, and his glasses were cracked and bent, but he was laughing while lying on his back.

"What's so funny?" I asked, stopping to turn around at him.

"Is this how you solve all of your problems, Jake? You're just going to beat up anyone who messes with your tiny little brain?"

"Shut up!"

"Aw, little Jacob's all sad. He doesn't understand what's happening."

"I'm going home."

"Oh, did I hurt your feelings, Jacob? Were you hoping to spend some quality time with Michael?"

"Go home. Before I—"

"How does it feel? Your best friend is nothing but a fraud who wants me—the quiet dweeb."

"Shut up!"

"Oh yes, I've known Michael far better than you ever can. I've felt him like you've never known. We've been seeing each other for years, right behind your back. That whole thing with Shah? That was just an excuse for me to come over. All those nights he said he was with another woman, no, it was just me! How does that feel? You want to laugh at me now! Go ahead laugh! But you've been the idiot the whole time. Or, maybe *you* wanted to be the one pressed against the wall? Is that it?"

I dove back onto his frail body and pummeled Lionel's face. My fist still hurt from punching the tree, but all the pain went away when I connected with Lionel's cheekbone. He laid limp on the ground, not even bothering to put up his hands. It didn't matter. I continued to punch him. I saw blood coming out of his mouth, but that only motivated me to hit him more. When his wire glasses jabbed into my fists, I ripped them off of his face. I broke them in half and threw them into the asphalt. The entire time, I wasn't hitting Lionel—I was smashing in Michael's stupid smirk. Why wouldn't he trust me? All this time it was a trick? A goddamn trick?

"I'm not an idiot," I shouted. "You hear me? I'm not an idiot!"

38
Shah

It was three in the morning when Bella and I came back home. I wanted to say I felt better after hanging out with Bella, but I still felt empty. I didn't feel any better about going to school the next day—just thinking about another day of hazing made me want to throw up. That week, the only subject that distracted me was learning about the Civil Rights Movement in history class. I wanted to connect to all those people who stood up for what they thought was right. Yet, I kept thinking how could all of those people get so many ass-whoopings and barely see results?

Oh, but Shah, said the argumentative me, aren't we better off now? Do I have it that well? Is it really great to be black in this day and age? I remember only last year when I was flirting with this white boy. He was a cute, slender guy with red hair and way too many freckles. He played the bass and was in a rock band. When he finally made a move, he said to me, "You're very hot, for a black chick." For a black chick? Did I not fall in the same category as other girls? I don't know what came over me, but I slapped him right in the face. I felt bad afterward, because I really liked him. Michael and I stayed up late that night and listened to Goldie's *Timeless* while I sadly ate a pint of ice cream.

Was that the absolute worse I had to deal with? Not by a long shot. When Michael and I were kids, we got to represent any African country we wanted during World Day. Seriously, the teachers thought we would be delighted to "represent our native land" by selecting one of the many African countries. Truth was, I knew next to nothing about Kenya, Benin, or even South Africa. In school, we only studied European countries, so I really wanted to do the Netherlands. I loved all the engineering and inventions that went into forming their country. However, the teacher really pushed me to do an African country, because they already had too many people picking European countries. I ended up doing Sudan while Michael reluctantly did The Gambia.

All right, so that's some subtle racism, but the absolute worst moment was when Michael and I were called niggers. We were out for dinner with Ma two years ago, enjoying our cheap burgers and fries, when she left for the bathroom.

"You gonna be fine alone?" she asked. We looked around. The restaurant was practically empty.

"Yeah Ma," I said. Michael nodded his head. She grabbed her purse and headed over to the bathroom. She crossed paths with two men who were sitting at the bar. Ma didn't notice, but the two men were giving her the eye. This wasn't anything sexual—they both had this evil look, like she had knocked over their drinks and didn't apologize.

When she had passed, the two drunks looked at us. I don't remember what they looked like. All I remember is their eyes. They both had piercing blue eyes. The whites in their eyes blinded me. All four of us stared at each other for a moment, and then the two men went back to their beers. Michael smiled and stiffened out his neck—pretending to act so tough, like he just won a fight.

"Yeah," said Michael softly, "that's right."

"Michael," I hissed.

"What?"

"Keep it down."

"You saw how they looked at us."

"It doesn't matter. I don't want to cause a scene."

"I'll cause a scene. I don't care."

I suddenly grabbed Michael's burger and took a giant bite.

He looked at me in disgust. "What the hell did you do that for?"

"What are you going to do about it?"

He jumped towards me, grabbing my plate. He took all of my French fries and shoved them into his mouth. Fries were thrown and hamburger mess was all over the cheap plastic table. We both started howling in laughter. Thankfully, Michael forgot all about the two guys at the bar. But they were still watching us. Michael was too busy shoving his burger into his mouth to hear the two guys, but I did.

"Goddamn nigger kids."

It was the way he said it—this dark and nasty crack to his voice. I instantly lost my appetite. Michael was still throwing French fries at my face, but I didn't retaliate.

"Hey, what's wrong?" he said.

"Nothing."

I never told Ma or Michael what they said. I was afraid of how Michael would react. It was better just to keep the peace I thought. The point is, all these years after the Civil Rights Movement and we still had issues like that. It amazes me how fast the world can change, but so slow at the same time. How fast was Michael's plight going to be? Were there still going to be two men who stared at him with disgust for wearing woman's clothes—even years and years later?

What if standing up for my brother leads to nothing, other than some sort of case study for others to look back on? They'll all be like, "Remember back when that boy dressed up in women's clothes, you see how poorly they reacted to it? Yeah, people were so stupid back then." That whole week of ridicule might be for absolutely nothing.

"Arg," I said to the fridge with a combination of pure exhaustion and frustration. I pulled out some ice cream from the freezer and sat at the kitchen table. I had to get up for school in a few hours, but I didn't care about sleep. No matter how hard I tried to calm myself down, I thought of all those staring faces. How long would it take to break down all those people, one by one? Maybe they'd never change. Maybe everything I was doing would mean nothing in the end. Hell, if anything, we just made it worse. It was amazing how so many of those people turned so cruel. When the freak and the defenders of the freak arrived, that's when I saw the true colors of people. How do you fight back against hatred? We were at the mercy of them being kind. Didn't it show how horrible they really were?

My phone buzzed. The text was from Bella.

—You still up?

—Yeah

—Go sleep!

—I know

—Seriously, everything will be fine.

—You sure?

—No.

—Awesome.

—Just trust me, no one's losing any limbs, okay?

—Okay, night.

—Night Shah.

I reached into my pocket for a smoke, but I realized I smoked my last outside. With a deep sigh, I stood up and shook out my arms and tried to shake all the stress out. It didn't work. As I was walking up the stairs, my phone buzzed again. I smirked—I guess Bella didn't want to go to bed. I kind of liked having a friend like this—it was mostly Michael who I talked to for hours on end. It was nice to have someone else to talk to. When I looked down at the phone, I saw Lionel's name. The text read:

—Hlepps.

"What the—" I whispered. Then, I heard a faint knocking on the front door. Was it Ma? No, she wasn't due home for another three hours. I tip-toed over to a drawer and reached for the largest knife I could find. If some loser was going to play a prank on Michael, then he'll get the scare of his life. When another soft knock was at the front door, I looked through the peephole. No one was there. Great, they were playing ding-dong ditch. I threw the door open, knife in hand, and whispered as loud as I could, "You can bother us all you want at school, but don't bring it here. You hear me?"

That's when I looked down and saw Lionel curled up into a ball on the front porch—bleeding from his face, his shirt all red.

39
Bella

My phone vibrated the dresser. The sound was so loud, it managed to make the dresser sound like an airplane was landing in my room. The phone's bright glow might as well have been the sun popping into my room. I shielded my face with a pillow and grabbed for the phone, just to shut it up. My heart was pounding me awake. I looked at the screen with one eye. It was Shah.

—Come to the house, NOW!

—Why?

—Lionel's beat up bad. He doesn't want to go to the hospital.

"Jesus," I whispered.

I tore the bedspread off my body like it was infected with bedbugs. Whatever clothes were on the floor, I threw them on. Since I didn't have a car, I would have to grab *Padre's* car keys. I opened my door a little and sure enough *Padre* was asleep on the couch. His keys were usually on the kitchen table, but he startled over any sound. You'd figure he couldn't hear anything because he snores like a lawnmower. However, any creaking of wood, any tap of a glass, would wake him instantly. He claimed this was due to his time in prison—he had this fear someone would attack him in the middle of the night. I don't know whether this is true because I don't remember him before prison. I was just a *niña pequeña* back then. It was only after years of visitations did I understand who my father really was.

Mamá told me stories of him for years—awful tales of how he stole from the poor and murdered for fun. She thought she knew him when she was a little girl, but that boy had disappeared. Once he landed in jail, she filed for divorced, and I was forbidden to see him.

"But *Mamá*," I had cried years ago, "What if he gets lonely there?"

"He will rot in there like the *perro* he is. My daughter will not be a bone he can gnaw on."

So, for years, I obeyed and had this evil image of him. Once time I drew a picture of him in elementary school: a devil-horned skull with tattoos all over his face. My teacher was worried and called *Mamá*. She never chastised me—she was proud. Then, a few years ago, *Mamá* finally gave me permission to visit him: he tried to hang himself in his cell. *Mamá* refused to go.

I was only a few feet from him, but with the glass, it felt like I was miles away. Suddenly, the skull had a smile. It had sad eyes and my exact same noise.

"Bella?" he said as question, but he knew the answer.

"Hi," I said quickly, I was shaking all over. Was he going to break through the glass and kill me?

"How are you?"

"Good."

"Are you afraid?"

"Yes."

"I've been here for a while, and if you never see me again, remember this: fear is good. It shows you the danger. Do not fear it, use it. Understand what it is you're fighting."

"So, should I fear you?"

Tears, suddenly, streamed from his face.

"Yes, I think."

"But what if I try to understand you?"

More tears streamed down his face. He smiled.

"Then you can finally be my daughter."

I visited him every week after that. He taught me to face my fears and to be myself. I never told him what myself truly was: a slut. That's what *Mamá* called me when she found out about Tyler and then all the other boys. It didn't matter if I used protection, or if I knew them all so well before we fooled around— *Mamá* said I was 'The Slut' and was just as despicable as *Padre*. He never heard the true story why I was expelled—

he only heard about the punch and thought I was his badass little girl. Truth was, I still feared how he might react, even after all this time.

When I gently lifted his keys off the kitchen table, I heard his snoring stopped. Slowly, I placed the jingling keys into my pocket and tip-toed out the door. He probably heard me, but it didn't matter. I had to rush over to Shah's as quickly as possible. There was no one outside, just the lampposts lighting a silent parking lot. The silence was broken when I revved the car down the road and toward their development. Surely, *Padre* had woken up now, but Shah needed my help.

Was the attack on Lionel some sort of retaliation? Did someone attack him because of what I did? If anyone was to get hurt, it should've been me—I was the one walking into the crossfire. Maybe they went after Lionel because they wanted to break someone, and they couldn't do it with me. Is this what it came to? I didn't care about ripped pants and names, but actual violence? Maybe Shah was right—what if they came for us next?

When I came to their street, I pulled to the side of the road and walked two blocks. Shah said not to pull into the driveway, because she didn't want to wake Michael. Great, I thought, we had to deal with more of Michael's crap while he just sleeps away. No, Bella, you can't be angry. This is a moment, I told myself, and you have to let the moment pass. When I went to the door, I noticed dark spots on the concrete stoop. Oh God, was that from Lionel? I braced myself by the door and took a few deep breaths. You have to be strong, Bella—I said to myself. Embrace the fear. When I opened the door, I saw Shah sitting in the dimly-lit living room, looking over Lionel. Even though the lamp barely lit his face, I saw the damage someone had done. His face was all busted up, with a giant bruise on his cheek.

"*Madre mía,*" I whispered. My hand went to my mouth.

"Sit down," Shah said, "and help me with these bandages."

I sat down and put my hand on Lionel's leg. He was barely conscious, mumbling something to himself over and over. Looking above, he saw the ceiling fan spin, watching it in a daze. I watched his lips move but couldn't figure out what he was saying. Leaning in, I put my ear to his lips.

"It's my fault. It's my fault," he said so softly. I had to listen to his voice a few times until I could understand.

"Why is he saying that, Shah?" I asked.

"He won't say who hurt him."

"What the hell?" I said a bit too loud. His head jerked up like it was pulled by a string. "Who hurt you, Lionel?"

"Don't tell Michael," he whispered, "I made it worse."

"We'll go after whoever did this to you. I promise." I gripped his leg tightly, until I noticed he was wincing. I looked at my hand clawing at his thigh and pulled away. Who attacks a harmless kid like Lionel? What sick freak beats up someone so innocent? They should've gone after me.

"Bella," said Shah, "what about what we said tonight? About staying strong and…"

Suddenly, the room seemed hot—filled with the stench of blood.

"I need to go outside."

I left the table and opened the door. Out in the cool night air, I still couldn't make myself feel cold. Could I keep doing going along with this whole mess? I looked at my skin to see if heat was floating off of it. There was nothing. Still, I felt I was on fire and something was burning inside of me. What if these people were going to attack me next? Shah? Michael?

Suddenly, I was a little girl again—drawing pictures of my evil father. His demonic face was staring at me. The unknown is terrifying—fear permeates within it. But, I thought, embrace the fear, understand the danger, and fight back. I had to keep doing the right thing and fight back— whatever the cost.

40

Jacob

I was hiding under my porch, telling myself it was an accident. I guess it would be hard to call it an accident, since I punched Lionel twenty-three times. Each time I put a fist to his face, I counted softly, one, two, three … and on and on. The blood on his face and his pathetic attempt to block some of the hits didn't bother me—I just wanted to count to twenty-three. It didn't make sense to me while I was hitting him, but as I was curled up into a ball—brushing off cobwebs and dirt from me—I figured out why I picked that number.

Twenty-three was the number I counted up to when we were in the park all those years ago when we were little, playing hide and seek. We were supposed to count to thirty, but back then I always liked to cheat. I gave up counting after twenty-three and ran around the park, looking under every park bench and in every bush. What really made me mad was how they clearly were moving from spot to spot, because I swear I looked at every possible hiding place. Little me was almost crying because I was so frustrated.

"Guys!" I yelled. "Quit moving!"

That's when I heard a giggle. I moved softly to the sound. Under the brook, there was a crawl space beneath the bridge. When I peered into the crawlspace, I saw Lionel on his stomach looking up at a tree. He had his hands under his chin, and he was playfully kicking his legs. When I looked up at the tree, I saw Michael looking around—trying to find me. He looked like a pirate at the top of the ship, surveying the whole sea. Lionel didn't seem to care if he was caught—we were doing the tag rule, and if you were tagged, you were it. Nobody could run away if they were on their stomach like that. He was just smiling, like he was watching a really funny movie.

I walked over to him, not softly, but at a regular pace. He didn't move and kept his eyes on Michael. When I tapped him, he craned his neck in horror. Suddenly, he put his legs up and looked away from Michael.

"I wasn't doing anything."

"Um yeah, that's why you're it now."

"Oh, okay."

"Why were you looking at Michael?"

"Uh, what are you talking about?"

"Michael, he's up in the tree. Why were you staring at him? What are you going to do, marry him?"

His face turned red. He looked away from me and pulled out of the crawl space. Before I had a chance to say something, he said, "Hey, do you like Charlotte?"

"What?"

"Do you, you know, like-like Charlotte?"

We were still kids back then. I had no idea how the birds and the bees worked. Shah would hang out with us from time to time, but we all thought girls were gross—and Michael didn't want to hang out with his sister back then. When we did hang out, when Michael's mom forced us to, it was actually pretty fun. Shah didn't act like the other girls. She liked to push and tackle and that was always something I liked to do. The first time Shah punched me in the arm, I laughed, but I was a bit scared—it was a good punch.

"Uh … why? Do you?" I asked.

"Do you?"

"I asked you? Do you like-like her? Were you just thinking of her? Oh my God, you like Charlotte! I'm going to tell Michael. You're so dead!"

I don't know why I ran over to Michael and screamed Lionel's secret love. I thought that maybe if Michael knew, he would put a stop to it. Truth was, I was jealous. Did I like Shah then? No, but if Lionel did, then I wanted to as well.

Lionel was right—I was jealous. I was jealous because they had some secret that was completely hidden from me. That bastard. The way he was laughing at me. I was glad I punched him, even if it was twenty-three times. Suddenly, my phone rang. Who the hell was calling at four in the morning? I looked at my phone. Its blue screen lit up the whole ground under the porch. I saw Shah's face on the screen.

"Hello?" I said. I sounded way too awake. I said "hello" again, but far more sleepily.

"Hey," she said practically whispering. "Look, I'm sorry to wake you up like this."

"Oh. Yeah, it's not a problem."

"I have no one else to call, and you might know something. It's about Lionel."

The hairs on the back of my neck rose. Why did he go to her?

"He's been hurt really badly. Someone attacked him in the middle of the night. He doesn't want the police involved and he won't say who did it. I don't care if you're still mad at Michael, this is about Lionel and I need your help. Do you know anyone who had it out for him? Was any of your douchebag wrestling friends saying anything?"

Tell the truth, I thought. You made a mistake. Don't let this get any worse. Then I thought of Lionel's stupid face, and I didn't care.

"No. There were a lot of people joking about Michael."

"What about Marshall? He's always looking for trouble."

"Marshall?"

"Yeah, that big guy who's always ragging on Michael."

"Oh, yeah probably."

"Probably what? What the hell do you … look, I'm sorry, but Lionel's hurt pretty badly, and we're going to try and pass it off as some sort of drunken stumble. That's what he wants, but I don't think anyone's going to buy it. Unless we can figure out something else, the police probably will get involved."

"Jesus, he's hurt that bad?"

"We need to know who did this. Do you know anything? You said Marshall, right?"

Tell the truth, idiot! Say what really happened. It didn't matter what my head thought, I wasn't going to admit what I did. Lionel was covering for me, but why?

"Yeah, maybe Marshall did it."

"Oh God. Why are people so messed up? Thanks Jacob, sorry to bother you." Then she hung up.

I turned off the screen and rested on the dirt. Man, as I child this was my favorite spot. It was so important to me because when my dad died, I stayed under the porch for a couple days. Michael was the first person to really drag me out of there. Since my mom couldn't get the wheel chair near the porch, she sent Michael down.

We had a sleepover under the porch—as gross as that sounds. Soon we were laughing, and I forgot about the pain, at least for a while. We told secrets to one another. Right there was the time that I first told him I liked Shah. He punched me in the arm and laughed. At that moment, he could have told me how he felt. He could have said everything he wanted to, and I would have punched him back and laughed. Instead, he kept his secrets with Lionel. Then fine, I thought, I'd never tell Michael what I did. After all, we weren't really friends anymore, were we?

41
Michael

I was in the middle of the dark room—with no windows or light. In the center of the room, there was an apple on a desk. There was nothing on the desk except for the fruit. I walked around it several times, and it seemed good enough to eat. I picked it up, checked for bruises, and saw none. When I went to bite it, Lionel whispered from somewhere, "Liar."

"Eat it," said Bella from out of nowhere. "It's fine, there's nothing to worry about."

"Keep looking around it," said Shah. "Poke it a few times, I don't know."

"Why would he poke an apple?"

"It might be rotten inside."

"You can tell by the outside!"

"No you can't."

"Liar," continued Lionel.

"Eat the apple," whispered Bella and Shah.

"Liar."

"Be patient."

I bit into the apple. It tasted sweet—its tanginess buzzed the inside of my cheeks. When I looked at my bite marks, I saw a black spot. The entire apple from the inside was black. How could something that tasted so sweet be so black?

"Keep eating it, you liked it!"

"For Christ's sake, it's all black. Why would you eat it?"

"Liar."

"Shhh, shhh. Lionel, it's all right."

Suddenly, we were all in a field. There was grass for miles and miles. The sun was shinin, and the birds were chirping very loudly. Under a tree, Shah was beside Lionel, petting him on the head. He was fast asleep, mumbling to himself. How did I get here? Is this because I ate the apple?

"Just close your eyes and relax, everything is all patched up," Shah said to Lionel.

Bella was pacing around in the field, admiring the beautiful countryside. Shah just rested with Lionel beside the lone tree in the field. I didn't feel a part of them, but an outsider who was uninvited.

"We need to get him," Shah said to Bella. "We need to find out who hurt Lionel."

A crazy jester appeared from behind the tree, he kept laughing at Shah and Lionel.

"Are you crazy?" Shah said, looking up at the jester and then at Bella. "We stick to the plan. I'm not going to flip-flop now because you're afraid."

"And you're not?" Bella poked the jester in the stomach, who was giggling. "I thought we were dealing with petty pranks, but this? You want to deal with attacks?"

"We have to be strong. Why do you think Lionel didn't want us to know who the attacker was? Do you think he wants us to attack him?"

Bella lifted the jester up from the ground and threw him far away from the grassy fields. Her strength was immense, and she tossed him with ease. The jester flew into the sun and vanished.

"You're right," said Bella. "How is he?"

I looked at Lionel. He was sleeping peacefully next to Shah. Suddenly, he lit into flames—like a marshmallow over a fire. His skin was black and charred. Shah didn't seem to care and continued stroking his hair. Despite the flames, Shah lifted Lionel's head gingerly off her lap and rested him against tree. Soon the tree lit on fire, but Bella and Shah didn't care. It was still a beautiful day in the grassy pastures.

"I've patched him up the best I can," she said. "We have to call his family."

"Fine," said Bella. "Here's the plan: He was drinking, and we found him passed out when we came back. We didn't think it was that bad, so we patched him up at your house. Wait, does he even drink?"

"Maybe? Hell, I didn't even know he was gay."

A lone rain cloud came from the sky. It rained upon the lone tree and doused the flames. The tree was black and stripped of all its leaves. Lionel's body was charred black, but the girls didn't care about that. Instead, they continued to argue. It was then that Lionel's charred body rose from the base of the tree. Bella and Shah walked away, arguing over something, and eventually they both faded into the endless grass. That left me alone with the body, which was rising to meet me.

"Liar," Lionel whispered. His bony black fingers were reaching for me. I tried to back away, but he kept after me. No matter how far away I ran, there was endless grass and nowhere to hide. The black body kept after me, gaining distance. When I ran out of breath, I collapsed into the grass. When I turned around to look at the blue sky, I saw the black body above me.

"You. Are. Him." He pointed.

"What do you mean?"

"You. Are. Him."

"I don't understand."

"Do not be him. The boy in black."

He touched me on the leg. I felt the blackness of his touch run through my body. My black skin became blacker—coal-color skin rose up through my body. Soon, I'd be completely burnt in blackness.

"Please, Lionel. I don't understand!"

"Do not be him."

My body up to neck was completely black. I couldn't breathe. The blackness was filling my lungs. How could I die, right here, in the grassy fields? Everything is so beautiful, and yet the blackness…

I woke up. Quickly, I looked around to see if there was green grass around me. There was nothing. After my eyes adjusted and the confusion lifted, I realized I was in my bedroom. That was some messed up dream, I thought. Once my heart stopped pounding, I listened for some faint noises. There was someone talking downstairs. Was it Shah?

"… I'm sorry to wake you up like this…," Shah was saying.

I ripped the sheets off the bed and opened my door. Strangely, there was a door closing at the same time. I kept still, listening for any sound. A car turned on and went down the driveway. Wait, it didn't sound like the Jeep, I thought. Who was here in the middle of the night?

"Look I'm sorry, but Lionel's hurt pretty badly…"

The dream. Bella was just here. Did she…? I was still in a daze, not yet awake. I turned back to my room to read my alarm clock: 4:15 AM. What happened to Lionel? The black body in the green grass flashed in front of my eyes. Why did the blackness come on to him like that? Why did it come onto me? Perhaps it meant nothing. Or, I wanted it to mean everything. At this point, I just wanted something to make sense. But I was confused as ever, and Shah talking on the phone at four in the morning only made it worse. If I couldn't get any answers from my dreams, I would sure as hell figure out what was happening downstairs.

"… do you know anything? You said Marshall?" continued Shah.

Marshall? What the hell did he have to do with this? I walked down the staircase and into the kitchen.

"Thanks Jacob, sorry to bother you."

She hung up and took in a deep breath. Shah stared at the wall for a while, taking in the emptiness. When she turned her head and saw me by the refrigerator, she gasped. I must have looked terrifying because Shah's eyes were wide and afraid.

"What did Marshall do to Lionel?" I said coldly.

"What?" said Shah defensively.

"Don't play me, Shah. What did Marshall do?"

"You don't want to know."

I thought of my dream. Lionel's burnt body. The blackness got to him. Would it get to me to?

"Tell me everything, right now," I said.

42
Bella

It was 7 AM, and I waited by the school parking lot—wondering if Shah or Michael were going to show. Chugging down a large black coffee, I could barely stay awake. I didn't get a chance to sleep and driving Lionel home so late was the absolute worst. He was asleep, but he looked like a rag doll—limp and lifeless. Once Shah managed to patch up the cuts and reduce some of the swelling, Lionel still looked awful, but she said he didn't need stitches. Thank God for that.

"You could make our lives a lot easier by telling us who did this," I had said to Lionel as I drove down the road. He didn't respond, so I kept talking. "*¡Mira!* I know you have a thing for Michael, but you're not helping him by keeping quiet. He's going to find out, and when he does, he's going to lose it." That was the part that scared me. I could control myself, even Shah—although I was close to the edge. It was just, if Michael lost control, what was the point of me keeping it together? Was Michael going to break no matter what happened? There was no point holding rank if he would be the one to break first. I felt like an idiot. I punched the top of the steering wheel.

"Damnit, Lionel," I said. "This complicates things. Who knows if Michael can keep it together!"

When we came to his house, the lights were on. Great, I thought, I hope they didn't call the cops. I pulled into the driveway, and immediately a man and woman opened the front door. They didn't seem to look like Lionel's parents—they were tall and pretty muscular. While the husband seemed to be a decent athlete, I was terrified by his mom. She had this intimidating stance and practically snarled at me when she saw Lionel in the passenger seat. She was about to punch through the window to get to me.

"What did you do to my son?" she barked.

"Lionel was … a bit hurt, but I patched him up. He should be fine."

"What the hell?" said the husband, who pulled Lionel out of the passenger side. He carried him inside like he was just a baby who had fallen asleep in the car.

"Who in God's name are you?" asked the woman. "We were right about to call the cops. Lionel always says 'good morning' when we go for our morning run! He's always up at five! You better explain yourself!"

"I convinced Lionel to hang out with me tonight. We snuck off into the woods."

The man quickly returned. Did he just dump Lionel on the couch and run back to yell at me? "You listen here. I don't know who you are, but I don't want you ruining my son's future. He's a bright boy and you're—"

"Look," I cut him off. "I'm sorry, but—"

"Oh, don't you try apologizing," said the woman. "You're a little delinquent who tried to sneak out with my little baby boy. What are you getting with all of this?"

"Ma'am," I said, trying not to lose my cool. "Lionel snuck out of the house to see me. He told me to go to the woods, and he was the one who brought the beer, and finally, he was the one who accidently fell down the hill."

"Well, he's safe now," said the husband. "No thanks to you."

"You don't go near my son, ever again. You hear me?" The woman pointed a finger at me.

"Yes, ma'am."

"Come on," said the husband. "Let's go inside."

They walked inside, and I heard his mom shout, "That bitch!"

I pulled away and headed back home. I felt my throat quaver. Don't cry, I said to myself, don't you dare cry. But the tears came anyway. I had to stop the car a few times because I couldn't see the road in front of me. Finally, when I got home, I parked the car in the massive lot and walked back to the apartment. My father was reading the paper when I opened the door.

"Where were you?" he said calmly.

"It's complicated."

Gently, he lowered the paper and placed it to the side.

"Were you seeing this Michael again?"

"What? No. This was different. There was a boy—"

"Another boy?"

"*¡Espere!* Hold on a minute. That's not what—"

"My daughter is a whore!"

"What?"

"You think I'm stupid? I heard how you were sleeping around when you lived with your *Madre*. I didn't say anything because I gave you a second change—like what you did for me. When you told me about this Michael boy, I didn't judge because you don't judge me. We are fair to one another. But now you have the nerve to tell me you're fooling around with any man you please."

"So what? I'm careful."

"So you admit it? You're a whore?"

"Look!" I lifted up my shift and showed him the tree. "You see this? I want to fill this tree with all the people I've slept with. Yes, I guess your daughter is a *puta.*"

"You got a tattoo behind my back?"

"There's a lot of secrets you keep from me!"

"Because you wouldn't understand!"

"Maybe you don't understand me!"

"Get out of my house." He opened the door.

"*Padre,* please try to understand."

"You have been living another life behind my back, now go."

"We have the same blood."

"This, who is see here, is another person. You are not my daughter."

I walked out the door, and continued walking. By the time I arrived at the school, it was close to seven. I sat on a stone wall, at the entrance of the school, and waited for Michael and Shah to arrive. Soon, cars drove by. All these faces were staring at me. I didn't care, let them stare. My eyes were tried, exhausted from lack of sleep. They also were fighting back tears, but I promised myself I wouldn't cry. I had to be strong. Whatever Michael and Shah wanted me to do, I would do it. If everyone thought of me as a whore, a slut—then fine, I would be that.

That was when I saw the Jeep quickly drive past me. I thought they would have slowed down when they saw me, but they must not have noticed. In the parking lot, the car flew and also crashed into a parking space. I didn't like what I was feeling, but I kept on walking toward the car. Shah stepped out first on the passenger side—wringing her hands. She looked completely anxious.

"No," I whispered, "I need you too." Then, I saw why she was so anxious.

Michael jumped out of the car, wearing a black A-line cocktail dress. He didn't look regal, like he did with the other dresses. He was threatening. How in the Hell did someone look dangerous in a black dress? Somehow, Michael pulled it off and flaunted what he had. Keep it together, I thought, keep it together for Michael—do what needs to be done.

43
Michael

My dress whipped back and forth—my walk was wide and with long strides. Both of my fists were clenched, and I made sure to have my chest out. Third time's a charm, I thought. As I walked up those long staircases, people stared again, but no one was laughing. I smirked, keeping my eyes wide and white. Bring it, somebody laugh, somebody say something this time around. This was now survival, and if I were to maintain who I was, I had to fight it all the way.

Finally, I heard a girl cackle. I craned my head, looking for where the sound came from. As I walked toward the sound, people moved aside for me. When I reached the girl, she was still laughing with her friends. By the time she noticed I was starting at her, she was quiet. Ends up, she was one of The Rabbits.

"Hey," I said, casually.

"Nice dress," the rabbit said quietly. The rest of the girls were trying to hold back their laughter. I turned around and saw Bella at the bottom of the stairs.

"Bella," I said, "she was the one of the girls who tagged you, right?"

Bella immediately shook her head, begging me not to do it. It didn't matter, I needed to make a show. It was perfect that The Rabbits were the first to be in the crossfire. From under my dress, I pulled out a giant black marker. I pointed it at the girl for a moment to really dig home the point.

"So," I said, "you think you can do pretty much whatever you want, huh? Am I supposed to pretend that you haven't been messing with my sister and Bella all last week? Well, I'm back now, and I'm not going anywhere."

"Michael!" shouted Shah, but I didn't care.

191

"Not now, Shah! I got this." I opened the cap, and let the girl smell the strong aroma. With a quick flick of the wrist, I slashed her on her cheek.

"You asshole!" she screamed.

"Oh, I thought I was a bitch? Now which one is it?"

The rest of The Rabbits pulled her away and went inside the school. They'd probably head to the bathroom, and aggressively address the cosmetic wound like doctors in a war zone. As they walked away, I let out a nice deep laugh. It was great to see everyone so disgusted around me. It wasn't like the last time, where I tried to take in disapproving faces. This time, I was going to win this. I didn't care about their approval, because they didn't care about me. I was going to shove their ignorance and petty discomfort right in their stupid faces.

I walked up the school stairs one glorious step at a time. Most people stepped aside to let me through. No one was laughing anymore. When I reached the top of the stairs, I extended both of my arms and shouted, "This is me, people! Does anyone have a problem?"

No one responded. I laughed so hard, I felt my stomach vibrate. I waved for Bella and Shah—who were at the bottom of the stairs—to come up and meet me. They were hesitant at first, but I kept waving them upwards.

"Ladies, let's go," I commanded.

They awkwardly went up the stairs, like they were regal subjects. Even though no one was laughing, the students continued to stare at Bella and Shah like they were some contaminated creatures. Screw them, I thought, screw everybody. I didn't care what anyone thought of me.

"Michael," Shah said went she reached the top of the stairs, "I really think we should take it a bit— "

"No, this is my life. Either you're with me, or you're going to stare like the rest of these losers."

"That's not fair. I just think—"

"Bella? Are you coming?"

"Yeah, I'm with you."

Bella walked past Shah. Together, Bella and I held hands and walked into the school. Whatever happened inside, we would fight it together.

44

Shah

Once we entered the school, we immediately walked into the girl's bathroom.

"Ladies," Michael shouted. "Get the hell out!"

Thank God there was no one in the room. My fingers covered my face—I was way too embarrassed. After a second, Michael walked up to the mirror and checked his dress. From his backpack he pulled out a lint brush and scrubbed any lint he saw on the black cloth. Bella put a hand on his back and looked like a proud mother. I didn't feel the same way.

"All right," said Michael. "If anyone messes with you, let me know between periods."

"What are you going to do?" said Bella.

"You just leave that to me."

"Don't you think you'll get in trouble? You're already on thin ice."

"It doesn't matter. Now's the time to strike."

"What the hell is wrong with you two?" I shouted and pounded the counter with both hands.

"Quit yelling and help us with the plan." Michael said.

Before Michael had a chance to react, I pushed him up against a stall. "*We* had everything taken care of. We were going to win everyone over eventually. And now, in a matter of five minutes, you ruined everything Bella and I were working on this week! You don't care! All you care about is getting your revenge."

"This isn't about me! This is about Lionel. Marshall and his stupid friends beat him up and now I have to take care of it."

"We don't even know that! Jacob just guessed!"

"Jacob was on to something. Marshall's been riding on this the whole time."

"You didn't even check on Lionel this morning! All you've been doing is plotting."

"And it's about time," snapped Michael, and pushed me away. Bella looked at me, and then gazed awkwardly at the floor. What the hell was happening? How could we have fallen apart so easily?

"Is this what you want too?" I said to Bella.

"You saw how Michael took care of The Rabbits. They won't bother me again."

"What about all that stuff you said yesterday, about not letting them get to us?"

"Shah, I don't know anymore. Last night, it dawned on me just how many lies we've been telling others and ourselves. I don't know anymore, and since Michael broke rank, there's no point anymore, right?"

"Well, I'm not going to partake in this," I said, "I've been pulled in so many directions. Find someone else to go along with this mistake." I turned to Michael. "I know you're angry, and you're hurt. What happened to Lionel is messed up, but you're using it to justify something that is completely against you. We had something here—Michael, you're not a freak." I turned him around to face the mirror. The three of us looked into the glass. I was in my ratty denim jacket and jeans. Bella wore yoga pants with a blue top. But it was Michael who was the most stunning.

"You're beautiful, Michael. And if you continue to retaliate, you're going to let everyone know that you're a complete psychopath. If you want to be that, fine, but it won't be from me."

I stormed out of the girl's bathroom. Some girls were waiting outside in the hallway, staring at me.

"Is he in there?" asked one of the girls.

"Yeah, but he'll be out in a minute."

"Well, we're not going in there until he comes out."

"Fine. Then wait."

"We're tired of waiting," said one of the girls. She brushed past me and opened the door slightly.

"Hey," she said to Michael, "grow a pussy somewhere else."

I pushed the girl away from the door and held her shoulders. It was Beth, the freshman girl who came into the bathroom a few days earlier.

"Beth, he's not going to hurt you. Why do you want to hurt him?" I asked. I did everything I could to hold back tears, and I could feel my heart pounding.

"Get off of me!" She tried to pull away, but I held on.

"He's a human being!"

"Let go!"

"Just let him be!"

The rest of the girls tried to pull me away from Beth, but I held on. Michael and Bella came out of the bathroom. Instantly, I let go. I didn't want to see them lose control the way I did. Before I had a chance to say something, Beth slapped me in the face.

"Don't touch me," she snapped.

Instead of retaliating, I dove toward Michael, who was about to tear her to pieces. I pinned him against the wall. It didn't matter, because Bella pushed Beth so hard, she fell to the ground—her purple backpack sliding across the floor. When everyone looked at Bella, she had her hands extended, ready for a fight. No one moved.

Then Bella bent down to Beth and whispered, "You don't look at us, you don't touch us, and you don't think you're better than us."

"Bella!" I said angrily.

"What?"

"You're going to let Michael boss you around?"

"We need to protect ourselves, Shah. When will you get that?"

"You're better than this!"

"I'm not."

With that, Bella took Michael's arm and they walked down the hallway.

I tried to help Beth up, but her friends grabbed her before I had a chance. When she stood up, she said, "All of you are just a bunch of freaks. The sooner you leave the better."

She was right. With those two completely loose, someone could get seriously hurt. It was only a matter of when.

45

Jacob

Breathe dude. Just take a deep breath and walk right up to Shah. You've known her for years, and she'll get it. Right? You just lost your cool, and accidently punched someone into oblivion. She'll understand … maybe. I was twenty-five lockers away from Shah—I had counted, many times— and had my head tucked inside my own locker whenever she looked my way. You have to do this, I whispered to myself.

I didn't sleep that night. Instead, I stayed under the deck until I saw light creaking into the cracks of the wood slats above. I sneaked in through the rear sliding-glass door. When I was walking through the kitchen, I saw my mom, sleepy-eyed, wheeling herself toward the refrigerator. I froze, hoping for some miracle, that if I didn't move, she wouldn't see me. Turning around with a gallon of milk, she blinked a few times to get rid of the sleepiness, and then looked at me.

"Wow, you're up early," she said.

I looked at the kitchen clock. 5:30 AM.

"Um," I stalled, "I couldn't sleep."

"Oh," she frowned. "Was it because of Michael?"

"Yeah … it was about Michael."

"Did you go over there and apologize?"

I thought of Michael pressing Lionel against the wall. Their bodies rubbing together, swapping spit.

"I … it's not going to work out."

She reached for the coffee pot. "What are you talking about?"

"It's over, Mom." I tried to walk past her, but she held onto my arm. She lifted up a finger.

"You see this? This is one finger. This is the amount of friends I have. Now I have a lot of people who will talk to me, maybe hang out with me, but none of them is my friend. I only have one person in the world whom I can trust."

"Who's that?" I asked, having no clue.

"You never met her. We stopped hanging out when we were too busy with kids. Eventually, we never spoke. When I got into the car accident, I could have really used a friend, but I hadn't spoken with her for ten years."

"Then why do you have a finger up, if she's not your friend?"

"Deep down, I still know where friends. I just don't have the courage to speak to her after all these years."

"What was her name?"

"Jessica."

"How come Jessica never tried to talk to you?"

"Probably because she said to herself 'it's not going to work out.'"

"Oh."

"So, you suck it up and make it work. Otherwise, you'll be stuck with no fingers." She pretended to bite at my fingers, and I pulled away. I smirked and kissed her on the forehead.

"Please make it work," she added.

"I will."

With my head in the locker, I kept whispering 'make it work, make it work.' I came out of it when Shah walked up to me and playfully smacked me on the back of the head.

"What are you doing?" she asked.

I pulled my head back and stared at her. We were only a few inches from one another. She had her hand propped against the wall and was leaning towards me.

"I was trying to see if the smell in my locker went away. I put an egg sandwich there last week and it kind of smelled up the place." She smiled, but it seemed so fake. Her eyes looked so hurt. "Are you okay?" I asked.

"Can I just, hang out here for a moment?"

"Sure, what's wrong?"

"Oh, it's Michael being Michael, you know."

Even though I didn't see Michael yet, I heard about what he did that morning. He and Bella were causing a storm—barking at anyone who called at them, or even looked at them. It was the exact opposite of last week. People kept saying he was giving this look. I knew exactly what it was. Michael had a way of charming people, but when he was on the mat, he turned on his animal mode. When that look flashed on his face, whoever was wrestling him had a bad day coming.

"How's he doing?"

"Bad, very bad. I think he's going to do something awful soon."

"To Marshall?"

"Yeah."

"Then why aren't you stopping it?"

"Because I'm tired." She slumped against the lockers. "And I could really go for a smoke."

"Wow."

"You're not bothered by it?"

"Like I would be bothered by you." I immediately looked back into my locker, hoping to God that there was still a smell from that sandwich. Shah laughed, it was so soft.

"Thanks, Jacob. I needed a laugh. I don't know. Maybe this is just all bark and no bite. Except for when you two duked it out last week."

"It was a good match."

"Then you two need to make up."

I thought of my mom, her fingers. Then, I thought of Lionel's battered face.

"I can't. I need to go." I slammed my locker and walked away from Shah. She ran up in front of me.

"Okay now it's *your* turn to tell me what's wrong."

"Nothing. I got to get to class."

I moved past her and hurried to my next class. Hopefully, Michael would just act all tough but forget all about Marshall. I knew that wasn't true, but if I pretended it was true then maybe it might come true. God, I was an idiot. The way that Shah laughed, it was so beautiful. I already broke Lionel—I couldn't break Shah, too.

46

Lionel

I was fascinated with the ceiling for a long time. There was an ice packet on my face and a bottle of aspirin beside me. Years ago, when I was a kid, I flooded the bathroom and the water was seeping through the floor. Soon, water was dripping from the ceiling and into the living room. There was a huge brown spot on the ceiling for weeks, until a crew came by and dried it out. Then, someone repainted the spot, but I could still see the outlines of the brown spot from where I was laying on the couch.

Before I had made that brown spot, I was in the bathtub with all my GI Joes on the edge of the tub. My father thought it was good for me to play with more manly toys, so he always checked to see if I was using them. When I took them to the bathroom, they weren't really soldiers, but explorers. The three action figures I used were Jacob, Michael, and myself. The three of us would explore the seas and ridges in an uncharted land. As Michael and Jacob grew up, they were less interested in my games, and they stopped hanging out with me. They became best friends, and I became the old friend at the end of the street.

I was pretty angry for a bit and did some pretty strange things. One time, when I was probably a bit too old for action figures and baths, I splashed around the water as GI Jacob was caught up in an undertow.

"Oh no," I shouted, "the storm is getting worse!"

"We need to save him," said GI Michael.

"No, he's way into the current. You're get sucked into it as well!"

"But I can't leave him behind."

"Yes, you can."

GI Michael dove into the water and pulled out Jacob. Both of them rested by the edge of the tub, gasping for breath.

"Thanks, Michael. I owe you one," said GI Jacob.

"Anything for you."

Suddenly, Michael leaned toward Jacob. Jacob didn't move, his plastic body lying motionless on the white fiberglass.

"No!" I shouted, my action figure coming to the rescue. With a huge kick, it knocked Jacob over, back into the tub.

"What are you doing?" shouted Michael.

"Let him drown!"

I watched the plastic figure sink to the bottom of the tub. It rested by the drain, expressionless. Suddenly, I splashed water at Michael—knocking him off the edge of the tub and onto the floor. GI Michael landed safely on the blue carpet, so I continued to splash water on him until the whole carpet was dark blue, with water leaking from beneath. When I stopped, I noticed how the floor had a clear film of water almost a half inch deep. I jumped out of the tub and tried to dry the floor with my towel, but the water soaked the towel in seconds. After coming back to the bathroom with several towels, I was able to dry the floor. Later when I went into the kitchen, I saw there was water on the floor. Above, the ceiling was dripping.

As I was resting on the living room couch—my head feeling as swollen as a balloon—I realized I hadn't taken a bath in years. I mean, I could've taken a bath anytime I wanted to, but I never did again. Truth was, I wanted Jacob to drown that day in the bathtub. I know it was just an action figure. But the guilt of that thought bothered me so much, I never took a bath again.

I could have told Shah and Bella everything and Michael would wipe Jacob off the face of the Earth. But I cared about Michael too much. I didn't want to hurt Michael and knowing the truth would have destroyed him.

Instead I chose lies. I told Shah I didn't know who attacked me. I felt my face. When I touched my cheek, a sharp pain exploded in my head. Suddenly, I felt really tired again and I decided to go back and stare at the kitchen ceiling. Why weren't my parents home? I know they had to go to work, but didn't one of them want to look after me? Maybe it was the story that Bella told, about me being drunk or something. What was it exactly? Oh, I was fooling around with Bella, and we snuck off somewhere in the woods. Bet my Dad was proud of me for that. I smiled to myself—like I'd ever make out with that slut. Moving my cheeks to smile made the pain on my face flare up. I winced. I shouldn't be mad at Bella, I thought. After all, she did cover for me. More lies, lies on top of lies. How many lies could we build before the whole thing would topple over?

My phone buzzed. It was on the coffee table, and I reached out to grab it. My hand couldn't reach from where I was, so I stretched out while still laying down. Just as I was right about to fall off the couch, I grabbed the phone and pulled it toward me. Shah had sent a message:

—I hope you're feeling better.

I replied back:

—I am. My head is a bit sore.

—I'll be over after school to see how you're doing. Bella said it went well...

—Haha, you could say that.

—God, she'll do anything. It's incredible.

—So, how's Michael doing? He never found out, right?

It took a long time for Shah to respond. Finally, my phone buzzed.

—No, Michael's just his normal self.

—Good. Hey, I'm going to sleep for a bit.

—Yeah, rest up. And don't worry about anything.

I let my head sink into the side of the couch. 'No, Michael's just his normal self'? Why did she wait a bit to respond? All the other texts were instant, but that one took the longest to reply. Was she holding something back from me? Quickly, I sat up on the couch. My head pulsed in pain. Something was happening and they left me out of it. I didn't have Bella's number, and there was no way in hell I was calling Jacob. That left Michael. What if he didn't really know about last night? I had to use my words carefully. I texted to him:

—Hey, I'm sorry about last night.

After some time, I sent another text:

—Please talk to me.

Michael finally responded.

—I have to do something.

—Like what?

—I have to hurt the guy who hurt you.

After I tried several additional texts, and no answer, I knew he was ignoring me. I threw it back onto the coffee table. Was Shah a part of this, too? Were they going to hurt Jacob? Should I warn him?

I reached for my phone, but then stopped. I couldn't get myself to contact him. I thought of his fists pounding my face. A part of me still wanted him to drown in that bathtub. Still, I couldn't lay here while another person was going to get hurt. This had to stop. Struggling to stand, I managed to stumble across the living room and into the garage. When I turned on the light, I saw it was empty. All that was there was my old bike, covered with dust and cobwebs.

47
Bella

He wanted me to be a whore. It took me a minute for the concept to sink in. As Michael and I had been walking down the hall, we saw Marshall and the wrestling team pushing and shoving one another against the lockers. Usually, I'd see Jacob and Michael with them—laughing up a storm with the guys. But today, when they saw us, Marshall and the boys stared us down like a wolf pack. We could've walked a thousand different ways to get to our next classes, but Michael wanted to face them head on. I didn't know if this was brave or incredibly stupid.

"I want you to act like you're into him," Michael whispered to me.

"What? Why?"

"Because it's the only way I can get him alone."

"I don't know."

"This is the best way to get back at Lionel—we can't take on the entire team."

Michael wasn't wearing his innocent smile today. He was terrifying to look at. How could a man who was wearing a black dress look more menacing than the entire wrestling team?

"Here he comes," said Michael. "Be fake. You can do this."

Be fake? I suppose I could do that. What was acting "real" at this point anyway?

Marshall sauntered over to us, while the rest of the team encircled us. It was a good, old-fashioned brawling circle. While Michael was a good wrestler, it was hard imagining him holding his own against a bear like Marshall. One punch from Marshall could send Michael flying into the lockers. Still, Michael kept his gaze level and stared down the man who beat up Lionel.

"Hey Michael," sneered Marshall. "Where's your little lover boy?"

"You should know."

"What? Why would I know that?" Marshall said, tilting his head.

"It doesn't matter. Just leave us alone."

"Michael, you got to make this interesting for me. I got to get my laughs in today, and you acting all Wonder Woman always gives me a good chuckle."

I laughed. Marshall looked at me, puzzled. I gave him side-smile and brushed back some of my hair. Out of all the people I've slept with, the things I've tried over the years, this had to be the dirtiest. I truly felt like a *puta* now.

"Damn," said Marshall. "Did your girl just check me out?"

Michael shot a nasty look at me, and I stopped smiling. Even though this was a part of the plan, it felt real. I wanted Michael to really be disgusted with what I did, but he was the mastermind who wanted this.

"We got to get to class. Come on, Bella," he said.

Michael pushed through his former friends and teammates. I stayed within the circle. When he turned around, he looked real broken. Was this also part of the act? I couldn't tell anymore.

"Are you coming?" he asked, his voice hollow.

"I don't know. I'll catch up with you later."

"Yeah," added Marshall, "she'll catch up with you later. She probably has too many dresses as it is."

"Whatever," Michael said, dismissively. He kept walking down the hall, head down, and soon turned a corner. It was so pathetic watching him go. Did I really break his heart? What was real at this point? Marshall put his arm around me.

"I never caught your name. What was it again?"

"Bella," I said coyly. The emptiness was replaced with fake charm.

"Pretty name."

"Thanks."

The other boys kept watching me. They scanned me up and down. I had to put on a show, not just to Marshall, but the rest of his team. I felt like a stripper at this point. This was for Michael, I repeated in my head. This was for Michael.

"I have to know," said Marshall, "Why were you so interested in a guy—I mean girl—like him?"

"I like to mix it up, you know. All the other guys have been boring me. Figured I'd try something different."

"And how did that work for you?"

"Why do you think I'm talking to you?" I gave him some soft doe eyes. Marshall melted right there. At this point, I could have this man punch his own face.

I leaned my lips to his ear. "You free later? During lunch?"

His ears reddened. "Where?"

"The boys' locker room. I'm looking for a bit of a thrill."

Then I pushed away from him and walked down the hall. Deliberately, I swayed my hips—placing my feet in a straight line like I was trying to pass a sobriety test. Even though I couldn't see Marshall and the boys, I felt every eye and could hear every thought. This was disgusting, but I had to be the whore for Michael. That was my role.

48

Michael

I finally figured out how to get what I wanted: It was through power. I couldn't expect people to understand me or have some sort of compassion. Instead, I needed to shove the truth down their throats and let them gag on it. At last, I was in control as I walked down the corridor—my black dress blowing like Death's fabric. I didn't care what they thought of me. As long as they didn't start something, I was fine. Intimidation, it scared them away from their ignorant confidence. I could even scare off my own sister!

When she stopped in the hallway, moments after the ruse with Marshall, I couldn't stop myself from laughing. I told Shah the whole story: "… so he thinks he's going to get lucky in the men's locker room during lunch! Oh man, wait until I show up."

I didn't care about Shah's shocked and disapproving face. We tried her way, we tried Bella's way, now we were trying my way. And from what I saw, my way was working the best.

"Michael," said Shah softly. "You can't do this. If you go after Marshall, then you're no better than him."

"But that's the thing: I'm not better than anyone. I'm tired of hoping the whole world sees who I am, because they won't. I'm a freak in their eyes, and I'll play the fool if they want it. It's my stage, with my rules, and I will not back down."

"Is this really you?" said Shah.

"It is!"

"My own brother has turned into—" She paused.

"Oh? What was that? What were you going to say?"

"Michael—"

"Say it!" I shouted. Those who weren't eyeing me in the hallway before were doing so now.

"You're a monster."

My eyes began to well, but I wasn't going to give her the satisfaction. I put a hand over my eyes and wiped away whatever tears were beginning to form. My phone buzzed. When I looked at the screen, I saw the name 'Lionel' in the center with the text: *Hey, I'm sorry about last night.*

"Oh, so Lionel's helping you out now?"

"What? No. I was just texting him."

"So you admit it!"

"Admit what?"

"That you're trying to guilt-trip me from stopping this."

"He's concerned, but I didn't say..." She pulled out her phone, but before she could show me the text, I grabbed it from her and slammed it on the floor. The phone was shattered.

"Don't talk to me. I'm doing this," I said, pointing a finger at her.

"Michael, please. I'm begging you."

"Too late." The bell rang. Lunch had just started. "Don't even think about talking to anyone else."

"Is that a threat?" said Shah, weaker than she usually sounds.

"Yes." Then I walked away.

It was amazing. Usually Shah was the one barking at me. Instead, I controlled the world. It didn't matter who I hurt, just as long as I got to be me in my Goddamn dresses. I got another buzz from my phone. Lionel:

—Please talk to me.

I finally responded back.

—I have to do something.

—Like what?

—I have to hurt the guy who hurt you.

This was truly me, the monster. It was time to show everyone that.

49
Lionel

My vision was all blurry, and I could barely pedal in a straight line. Plus, the sun was like a flashlight right in my eyes, stabbing its rays into my eyelids. My head rung the entire time I rode my old bike down Melanie Ave. Maybe I should just let Michael kill Jacob? Why not? Eye for an eye, right? But I was worried about Michael. If he was to unleash hell unto Jacob, there was no going back. Forever he would be labeled the freak that went on a violent rampage. Michael was better than that, and I had to stop him. This was my problem, and I was going to fix it. No cops, no principals, just me. I caused this mess, and it was up to me to fix it.

I called Shah at least fifteen times, Michael twenty. It seemed they all had the memo to block my calls. Even my texts didn't go through. I bet Michael ordered them to do it, so little Lionel's sympathy didn't affect them. I had to speak to them directly. That is, if I got there on time. When I reached the end of the street, my head was spinning so much that I had to lie down on the concrete. I threw up on some bushes then desperately tried to climb back on the bike. Every time I lifted my legs, they buckled under me.

A car drove past, and I flagged them down. He slowed to a crawl and noticed the vomit on my shirt.

"Sir," I begged, "I need to get to school."

"I don't think you should be in school today, buddy."

"No, it's important I need to help a—"

Before I could finish, my stomach tightened, and I turned—heaving another wave of bile into a bush. When I tried to finish my sentence, the car had already driven off. There was no one else on the quiet street. I was on my own. I breathed slowly and waited for the sky to quit revolving around my head. I could do this, I told myself, it was just a bike ride. You ride your bike all the time. You rode with Michael and Jacob all afternoon every summer. Then, you stopped because Jacob thought it would be funny to put a stick in the spokes while you were riding down a hill. And you flew in the air and landed on some hard asphalt. Jacob and Michael laughed, and you just laughed with them. Ha, ha, ha. "Little Lionel fell," Jacob had said. The bike had been in the garage since.

God, how long ago was that? Things were so different now—three childhood friends wanted to kill one another. I stomped on my bike and watched it give a small bounce. Damn it Jake, you deserved it! All those years, and nothing changed. Jacob needed to pay, and you could let Michael do all the work! Quit being the coward, and let it happen. No. I'm better than this. If I let my guard dog seek out Jacob, I'm just letting hate take over hate. Get on that damn bike, Lionel. Do it!

I lifted the bike from the ground, cleared away the crusted vomit from my shirt, and slowly pedaled my way to school. Could I make it in time? I didn't have a clue. Still, I had to try.

50
Shah

What could I do at this point? Michael ran off with this holier than thou attitude—and I'm pretty sure he went full on crazy at that particular moment. It's hard to imagine that this was the same guy who I helped shop for bras for only a few weeks ago.

How do you stop a tidal wave? You can't punch a tidal wave, even if you had a big fist. Truth was, I secretly wanted Michael to seek revenge. Deep down I wanted Michael to do it. That night, seeing Lionel bloody and bruised, I couldn't imagine why Marshall stooped so low. Seriously, I just thought he was all talk.

Halfway through thinking about tidal waves, big fists, Michael, and what not, I desperately needed a cigarette. Thankfully, I had a spot outside just for me. It's not my proudest idea, but I prefer to hide behind the dumpsters. That way no one would smell the smoke because they didn't want to go anywhere near the dump. While others opened the cafeteria door to head toward lunch, I slipped to the right and headed toward the exit. I didn't have to worry about any teachers, because they didn't want to bother kids during lunch. Hell, they wanted to be left alone too. Even the noon-aids stayed within the cafeteria, talking to one another. They won't admit they're turning a blind eye during lunch, but it's certainly when the teachers are the most lax. Besides, no one thought perfect little Charlotte would do something stupid like smoke on public grounds.

I walked out the side entrance and hid behind the giant green dumpster. Ugh, the smell. Try to imagine rotten eggs, but with just a hint of puke. It took me a while to figure out the exact concoction, but I'm pretty confident that I could simulate that experience by up-chucking and breaking some shells. Suddenly, I started shivering all over. I wasn't cold, but it was the thought of Michael repeatedly smashing Marshall's head into a locker that chilled me. That's probably how he would do it. First, he'd throw him with some crazy wrestling move. Then—I don't know—punch him in the stomach a few times. The whole thought made me queasy, and it wasn't just the dumpster motivating it. How did this change so fast? We went from being peaceful to full on violent. Does someone really break that fast? I wasn't any better, because I wasn't doing anything to stop him. But Michael literally changed overnight—when Lionel was at the house. Is it that easy to fall? I guess so. All I wanted was for Michael to be happy, not become some bully. He was a monster now, I didn't regret what I said. How much different was he from Marshall—especially after what he'd do to him during lunch. Michael was going to beat up someone who was different than himself. Granted, this was more of revenge, but when would it stop? Nothing good would come with this decision, and I was just waiting. I would just be watching as a tidal wave came crashing down, with no idea how to stop it. Hell, I wasn't even trying. I kicked the dumpster. It let out a long note that lingered in the parking lot.

I could have talked to the assistant principal, and maybe he would hunt Michael down before anything crazy would happen. But I was tired of getting in the way. This was Michael's war, and I was done. When I ashed the cigarette out and threw it in the dumpster, I was right about to head inside. Then, I saw a bike slowly wobbling toward the school. Was the guy drunk? I cupped my hand over my eyes like a visor, and I noticed it was a weak-looking kid with marks all over his face.

"Oh no," I groaned. Why the hell was Lionel here? I walked around to the front of the school entrance—completely ignoring the fact that I'd be spotted—and yelled at Lionel.

"Your stupid ass should be in bed. I don't care how much you like school!" I shouted. Lionel just seemed confused. He looked all over for the sound, but it wasn't hard to spot me in an open parking lot. "Lionel," I called, waving. "Lionel!" Finally, he looked my way and dropped the bike on the ground. He looked like he just survived being a horror flick.

Cuts hardened to red gashes and his face was more swollen than after a bee attack. It was a miracle that he could even walk.

"Please don't let Michael hurt him!" he begged, stumbling towards me.

"Lionel, shhh. I don't want anyone else to know I'm outside."

"Please," he was right next to me. "Not like this."

"Not like what?"

"Tell Michael to stop!"

"I thought you'd be happy. Michael's getting revenge for you."

"Is it worth it?"

I had a hard time answering that, but finally creaked out, "Yeah."

"You'd beat up your best friend?"

"Wait, what?"

"You'd beat up Jacob?"

I felt a shiver run down my spine. What was he talking about?

"Wait," I said quickly. "Did you say Jacob?"

"Didn't you get any of my texts?"

"Michael threw my phone on the ground and broke it.

"Oh no! We have to go find him. It's probably too late."

"Why?"

"Because I don't want him to hurt Jacob, okay?"

"Jacob?"

"Yes, yes, Jacob! I don't know how you figured it out it was him, but please don't hurt him."

"So … it wasn't Marshall?"

"Marshall?"

"Yeah, the guy on the wrestling team."

"Oh God." Lionel's eyes grew wide and he legs buckled. He grabbed for my arm to steady himself. "No. Who said it was him?"

"Oh no, no, no," I said, pacing back and forth.

"What?"

"Was Marshall involved at all?"

"No," he said incredulously. "Jacob—"

Michael's Black Dress

I ran back into the school. I had to stop the tidal wave.

51
Bella

About ten minutes after lunch started, I wandered into the boys' locker room. Thankfully, there wasn't anyone around, so I awkwardly sat on the wooden bench and waited among the red metal lockers. What the hell was I doing? Did I seriously turn into this? I had to wait until some gross ringworm wrestler molested me long enough for Michael to arrive? What if Marshall didn't show up at all? No, he'd come.

A lot of guys told me I have those "eyes." When I have that look in my eyes, guys will walk to the ends of the Earth for me. I can't really will myself to do it, and it's only when I really like someone. I tried my best to think of Michael when I talked to Marshall—hoping that the look would crawl its way over my face. If it did, then Marshall was a sure thing. Then I thought of a completely different problem: what if *Michael* never showed up?

Eerily, I imagined sleeping with Marshall. Nope, I couldn't do it. Here I was trying to justify that I wasn't this out-of-control promiscuous girl when I was secretly luring a boy into the germ-infested locker room. Seriously, would I catch a disease if I stayed here any longer?

I heard giant thuds coming from outside the locker room. He walked like Bigfoot. The door swung open and his smile was almost as wide as his neck muscles.

"So, you showed up."

"Yeah," I said shyly. "Guess I did."

He took a few steps forward. "Alone at last! I have to admit I wasn't expecting a surprise like you today. It's a treat."

A treat? God, he was making me nauseous already.

217

"I suppose you can call me a dessert, if you are into that." He laughed and started undoing his shirt.

"Wait," I said.

"What is it?"

"Just talk to me first." I had to stall.

"Oh, I thought you were…"

"I am … it's just … I need to get warmed up first."

"Well, what do you want me to talk about?" he left his shirt unbuttoned.

"About you, I want to see if you're the man everyone's been talking about."

"So, they've been talking about me?" Marshall sat down next to me. His meaty fingers played with my hair. I shivered uncomfortably but let him continue. "Well, I'm the star player for the wrestling team."

I smirked. "I think everyone knows that."

His fingers moved down my hair and he lightly touched my arm. *Please*, I thought, please show up Michael.

"I'm 55 and 2 this year. Not so bad of a record."

"Uh huh,"

"Threw down a guy with a fireman's carry last week."

"Fascinating," I said dryly. His whole paw was caressing my fingers. I can't do this. Hurry up, Michael! He touched my back then massaged my shoulders. His hands were rough—there was no connection. This felt all wrong. Still, I smiled and let out a slow groan. Marshall was surprised and continued—touching me like someone strokes a cat.

"You like that?"

"Yeah," I said weakly. I was holding back tears. Don't cry, you slut. This is who you are!

"So …" he said softly, "Do you want to?"

"Sure," I tried to say it sexy, but I wasn't into it. Still, it was enough for Marshall to continue. He moved his hands to my waist a put a hand under my shirt. His fingers lifted up the fabric to see my tree—bare of all of its leaves.

"That's so hot." He said, breathing heavily. His eyes were now filled with uncontrollable lust. Marshall kissed me on the neck, rough and impassionate. Michael, I begged to myself, where are you? I'm your good little slut, now do you job. Marshall's hands ventured up, and soon I felt his fingers touch the bottom of my bra. He hesitated for a moment, but since I didn't resist, he continued. Soon, he was reaching for my breasts, and that's when I snapped. No, I am not this.

I slapped his hand from my chest and punched his square on the jaw. Even though I was sitting, I threw my upper body into the swing. Somehow, it knocked Marshall to the ground. He was cradling his jaw—his eyes wide in shock. *Padre* would be proud—if he still had a daughter.

"What the—" said Marshall.

"No, this is wrong. I'm not a slut!"

"But—I didn't—you were."

Finally, the tears came. I let out giant, ugly rivulets and cried into my hands. Why did Michael want this? Is that what I was to him, only an object. That's not how I viewed him! I thought he understood me—but that couldn't be the case. I was only a slut to him. I felt like an idiot.

I continued to cry—forgetting where I was. Then, someone was sitting beside me. My water-filled eyes saw Marshall's giant frame.

"Please don't," I said weakly.

"Shh," said Marshall. "I'm so sorry. I didn't know. I thought that's what you were into."

"Well, it's not!"

"Okay, okay. That's fine. I think I misunderstood I'm really sorry." I brushed away my tears. Marshall had his head down, rejected. There was a giant red mark where I landed my fist. He noticed I was looking at it and grinned. "Good punch."

"Thanks,"

"Can I ask you a question?"

"What?"

"That wasn't you earlier, was it?"

"What do you mean?"

"You aren't into me, are you?"

"No, it was all to—"

"Hey, I get it. You got an image, or something, and you have to hold up to it. Trust me, I get it."

I was about to tell him the truth—I didn't care about Michael's stupid plan. But I wanted to know what the hell he was talking about.

"Get what?"

"I used to be called Broom."

"Huh?"

Marshall looked away. Was he blushing?

"It's a little embarrassing." He took a deep breath than said, "I used to be picked on a lot. I was as skinny as a broomstick. They used to call me Broom, actually. All the kids used to beat me up at my old school. Then, when wrestling came around my freshman year, I really wanted to play, so I stacked up. And now you have this…" He flexed his bicep and with a movie-star smile. I laughed, and then felt a huge pain in my stomach. What was wrong with me? This wasn't good, but I kept listening. "Then I grew up, became the tough one, and switched schools. I knew I had to be on top of the totem pole if I wanted to survive. I have to act like tough so people will like me."

"I switched schools, too," I said abruptly.

"What?"

"I said, I switched school, too."

"Well, now. We got something in common. What did you switch for?"

"I don't want to talk about it," I said.

"That's fine."

Marshall hesitated as to what to say, and then blurted it out:

"Look, please don't tell anyone that I was called Broom."

"Why?"

"It's just that I have appearances to keep up, and if word got out that—"

"It's fine, Marshall."

"Good." We stared at each other for a moment, not sure what to say. "You know, you seem better than this."

"Better than what?"

"Uh … a slut."

"Excuse me?"

"I'm sorry. I'm sorry. I just meant that you seem really sweet, and I don't get why you want to act like this. I wouldn't want to treat you badly."

"Great, *and* you're nice!"

"Uh, thank you?"

"*¡Coño!*" I said suddenly. "If you're such a nice guy, then why do you deliberately pick on Michael?"

"Look, I feel bad about it, all right? Honestly, I couldn't care if he wore a panda costume to school."

I clenched my fists. "Then why did you do it?"

"It's just words. I'd rather be the one calling the names. I know it's not the best person to be, but if I want to stay up here, I need to play the game."

"It was just a game to you?"

"I game I need to win. I will never go back to being the loser. If I have to burn some people, then I don't give a damn. Don't you understand, it's survival of the fittest. You need to be the toughest to survive. It's just words."

"It's just words?" I felt angry rise inside of me. I wanted to punch him again. "Did you see what you did to Lionel, or did words just do that?"

"What?"

"Lionel, you jerk! You beat that poor kid into oblivion."

He slowly tilted his head to the side.

"Lionel? I didn't touch Lionel. Why, what happened to him?"

"You … you beat him up. Right?"

Marshall put his hands up defensively.

"I didn't hurt Lionel. I told you, I only say words."

"But—"

"Wait, I didn't hurt that kid. Is that why you brought me here?"

I looked at the exit. Maybe there was still time. I grabbed him by the arm. "We need to leave, now!"

Suddenly, the door flung open. Outside the light was so bright that I only saw the silhouette of Michael's black dress.

Before Michael charged, he shouted. "It's my turn now!"

52

Michael

I charged at Marshall until I heard the satisfying crunch of lockers being pressed against his back.

"Michael!" Bella yelled, but I ignored her. Even when she grabbed my arm, I pushed her aside until she too crashed against the lockers. I slammed Marshall's head into the metal frames. Each time his skull smashed, I grinned. Suddenly Marshall punched me in the stomach. The wind was knocked out of me, and I crumbled to the ground. With a shove, he pushed me onto my back on the floor.

"Don't you touch me!" he shouted. It was more of a shrill than his typical tough-boy demeanor.

"What's the matter? You hate it when someone does it to you?" I stood up and again charged at his stomach. The force drove him back to the wall of lockers. A short breath of air fell out of his mouth—it was just long enough for me to drop to my knees and lift his hips. It didn't matter if he was heavier. I lifted him up with ease and threw him to the floor.

"Michael," Bella said weakly. I didn't realize she was still on the floor. I straddled Marshall and punched him in the temple. Usually I don't throw punches, but I was fine with destroying the man who destroyed Lionel.

"How do you like this?" I said. I punched him again. Weakly, Marshall lifted his arms, but I batted them away. After a few more punches, Marshall's head stopped moving. That didn't matter. I continued to pummel him against the concrete floor. Once his face looked similar to Lionel's, I stopped—out of breath, heaving like an animal.

The door opened, and I looked at the glowing light. I looked down. Marshall's blood was on my fists, and my dress was torn and ruined. It didn't matter. All I knew was this was going to spread the message. No one would mess with me.

"My name is Michael!" I shouted. "And I wear dresses. You hear me? I am a freak!"

"Jesus Christ," said a voice.

"Oh God," said another one.

I looked down at Marshall. His breath was soft, but he was alive.

"Michael," Shah pushed me off Marshall. I rested against the cool metal of the lockers. It was then I noticed that Lionel was there too. Both were kneeling next to Marshall—checking his pulse and eyes. Suddenly, Bella let out of another groan.

"Check on Bella," I said. I just wanted to relax. I did my job, and I just wanted to bask in the satisfaction. Lionel and Shah didn't seem so pleased. In fact, they looked terribly worried. Didn't they know this was the plan? Wait, how did Lionel get here?

"You idiot!" shouted Shah. She jumped up and charged at me. When she threw the punches at my body and face, I let her do it. I was tired. There was such a wave of relief. It was all over. I had revenged Lionel.

"It was Jacob! Not Marshall."

Instantly, my eyes shot wide open.

"What?"

"You stupid idiot!" Shah continued to yell. "Marshall didn't do anything!"

"Jacob?" I could barely get the word out. My best friend attacked Lionel?

"I'm sorry," said Lionel. "I'm so sorry I didn't tell you. I'm so sorry."

I looked over at Marshall, who was faintly breathing. God, his face was a complete mess. Why did I do this? Shah backed away, disgusted. I couldn't stand her face, it needed to go away.

"Get out!" I shouted. "Everyone get out!"

"Michael," said Shah. "You know we have to get the teachers, right? We can't just leave him here."

"I said get the hell out! Now!"

Shah helped Bella stand up and together all of them left the room. Lionel even closed the door. As Marshall continued to breathe softly, I cried. I didn't cry because of what I did to Marshall. I cried because of what I did to myself. I was a monster. A freak.

53

Jacob

I was an idiot. It didn't really click until I heard the cops were at school. So many people skipped their afternoon classes and stood outside and watched the ambulance pull up to the front entrance. They carried Marshall down the flight of stairs—the students capturing every second on their phones. His eyes were closed, sealed with caked blood. The paramedics tried to cover up the body the best they could, but the massive wave of teens had to see the mess. No one spoke. Everything went beyond words. I didn't really get it, why did Michael beat up Marshall? This wasn't a couple slaps and punches, but a planned attack. What the hell was going on?

The teachers tried to get us to move, but we didn't. The assistant principal tried to cover up the fact that Michael and the others were involved, but word spread pretty quickly. That was when I saw Michael being escorted by two cops down the long stairway from the entrance of the school. Michael's eyes were hollow. His dress was torn. His hands were coated in blood. This was Michael? This was the same guy who gave me wet willies in front of his house? It couldn't be. Ever since he started wearing these dresses, he changed. Maybe I never knew the real Michael, and this new figure was deep inside him all along. It was too much. When he passed by me, I tried calling out, but my lips were dry and and my voice was empty.

Suddenly, a figure turned me around and slapped me. I imagined Shah having soft hands, but it felt like she was wearing lead gloves.

"Don't ever come near us again!" Shah shouted. Bella was holding her back. Still, Shah was screaming at me. "Why didn't you tell me?"

"Tell you what?"

"You know what!"

That was when Lionel joined them in the crowd. His face was worse than I imagined. Did I really cause all that damage? I felt light-headed and tried to sit down, but there were people everywhere. I was now the center of attention. I looked down the stairs and toward the ambulance. They were just about to lift Marshall into the back. Barely conscious, he tossed his head back and forth, as though still caught in a terrible dream. For a moment, I imagined myself on the cot. Oh God. This was Michael's revenge. Marshall was supposed to be me!

I pushed back the people and rushed down the steps. Several cops were standing around and saw me running at them. One of them stood guard like a statue, but I juked around them and toward the cop car holding Michael. By the time I reached him, he was pushed into the back seat. I slammed on the glass, trying to break it with my palms.

"It was me! I'm sorry!" I shouted. A cop grabbed me front behind, but I continued to scream. "It was me!" I was lifted into the air and dragged away from the car. It began to drive away, and, for a moment, I saw Michael's face. He was soulless. Michael, who once had a smile that could warm a crowd, now had a permanent frown. Everything I knew about Michael had drained away. Now, he was a criminal.

Part 4

Epilogue

Speak of me as I am

54

Lionel

I sat on the island, waiting. Around me were the various rejects in the lunchroom. I had no idea what I was waiting for. The loud noises and the florescent lights still hurt my eyes, even a month since the accident. I wouldn't call it an accident, but that's what the lawyers were calling it. My mom and dad wanted to sue Jacob and his mother for all they had—calling it a hate crime. Oh, this was also that moment when I came out to my parents. Thanks again, Jake.

"He beat you senseless," my parents had said. It didn't matter. How could I possibly burden Jacob's mother with more problems? Besides, when I saw Jacob's face in that conference room, with the lawyers going back and forth, he was ghostly. Before my parents stole the show, like they always did, I said, "Let him be. I won't press charges."

"What?" barked my mom.

"I don't want to press charges."

"Son," my father put a hand on my shoulder, "You're still recovering from all of this trauma, you don't truly understand what—"

"Oh, I know what he did." I stared down Jacob, who kept his eyes on the table.

"Lionel," added my mother, "You think that—"

"You don't know anything about me. You didn't believe me when I told you I was gay. You thought that was the concussion talking! So, don't you dare tell me what I think!" The lawyers from both sides looked awkwardly around the room. It was time to end this. "I will not be pressing charges. I egged Jacob to attack me, and I pushed him to the edge. I didn't think he was going to cross over it. Just get him away from me."

And that was the deal. Jacob would transfer to a new school—he wouldn't have to move—and he couldn't be within 100 feet of me. I thought that was more than fair. He would still have to live with the guilt. Even though we lived on the same street, I hadn't seen Jacob since.

As for Marshall, he sat with his group of friends in the cafeteria. His face was worse than mine. There were still bandages on his jaw, which Michael had dislocated that day. Finally, he could eat solid foods that week, but could barely open his mouth. That didn't stop him from laughing and joking with his friends. Both of us were beaten beyond pain, and they treated him like a hero! Everyone felt bad for him, and he quickly became the most popular boy in school.

Meanwhile, I was still on the island with the rejects. I gave up painting during lunch because people now knew who I was. I was the gay kid who fell in love with the freak they once called Michael. No one calls him that anymore. Instead it's Michaella. Michaella was going to be the stuff of urban legend—the cross-dressing freak that attacked anyone who was in his way. Soon, people would forget all about Michael, the young man who just wanted to wear dresses. Instead, they will immortalize the enemy: the boy in the black dress. No one felt remorseful. After all, it was Michael who attacked Marshall, who was completely innocent. Just lay low and hopefully people will forget all about you again, I thought.

"Hey Lionel," one of The Rabbits shouted. I didn't look up. I was used to people calling me out now. Before, no one knew my name, but now I had an identity. I was no longer invisible and had become a target. I concentrated all of my focus on my baloney sandwich, hoping they'd get bored and forget all about me.

"Hey Lionel," said another Rabbit. "Where's your lover boy?" They all started to giggle. I couldn't believe these were once Shah's friends. I continued to stare at my sandwich, like it was a piece of art. I threw away my paints and easel at home too. Everything reminded me of Michael. I was too afraid to call him, and my parents told me not to anyway. I imagined that Michael was completely unstable at the moment, and I didn't want to set him on edge. Now what do I do? He filled my thoughts constantly, but now there was a vacuum where my love used to be. What do I fill my thoughts with now?

"Hey Lionel, sit down with us. We want to hear all about your new boyfriend."

"Stop it," I whispered. No one heard me.

"Lionel!" they kept shouting. When will it end, I just wanted to be left alone! "Lionel, sweetie, come chat with us." They all giggled again.

"Stop it!" I said. The rest of the people on the island turned to look at me. The girls wouldn't stop.

"Oh, don't be mad. We just want to talk."

"He said stop it," called a deep voice.

Marshall stood up and walked over to The Rabbits. Even though his jaw was bandaged, he still had a powerful voice.

"We didn't mean anything, Marshall."

"Yeah you did, and I said to stop it."

"Fine, you don't have to be so rude about it."

Marshall gave them a nasty look and walked over to me. I went back to looking at my mutilated sandwich.

"Hey, Lionel," said Marshall.

"Hey," I said softly.

"If anyone gives you trouble, you let me know, alright?"

"Yeah."

"Seriously."

"I know."

He sighed. "Look, he's gone now. He's not going to bother you anymore. Got that?"

"You think he bothered me?"

"I just think it's time to move on. For both of us."

"All right."

"And get back to painting."

I looked up at him, surprised.

"What?"

"Bella told me you were good at it."

With that, he walked away. He was right. I had to move on. Every canvas I filled was only of Michael, and now I had an empty canvas. I could fill it with whatever I wanted. Tonight, I'd buy some supplies and start fresh. Before I had a chance to thank him, Marshall was sitting back down. He put his arm around Bella and kissed her on the forehead. Bella and I exchanged looks. I couldn't tell if she was happy or not, but she smiled at me. I smiled back. Perhaps I wasn't on an island after all.

55

Bella

I move around my plate of soggy fries. I tried, for the life of me, to figure out why Shah invited me to a rat-hole place like this. I texted her the night before, and she thought it would be better to talk in person. But here? At this place? Half of the seat cushions were damaged—its guts spilling out like massacred teddy bears. We sat in silence. Shah had BBQ sauce all over her face. She stuffed greasy fry after greasy fry into her mouth. I wanted to laugh at her dumb face. She didn't care that blackish-brown globs were dripping down the side of her mouth.

"So," I said slowly. "Are we going to talk or not?"

"Eat your fries first." Shah said without looking.

"I'm watching my weight."

She stopped eating to look at me. I knew that stare too well. It was that don't-play-with-me look. I gently grabbed one fry and ate it.

"No, with the BBQ sauce. It's mesquite."

"I'm good."

Shah dropped half of the fry she was eating and stared up at me. With the back of her wrist, she whipped away the sauce on her face.

"You know, Michael and I used to come her all the time. Whenever there was trouble, we sat here and ate fries. Now, Michael wants to forget everything: you, me, this whole town. It's horrible."

"I'm sorry," I said, but I didn't mean it. Shah picked up on it right away.

"I thought," she looked away, then back at me. "Maybe you decided to hang out with me again—eat disgusting fries together and chat. But, it's not the same. What happened, Bella?"

"I came here to talk."

"But you ain't talking."

"Because…" I wanted to throw that stupid plate at her face. But, I kept my cool. "I thought you would apologize."

Shah cocked her head to the side. "For what?"

"Your brother threw me against a locker. You see this?" I pointed to my forehead. There was still a purple line. I had a splitting headache for days. "It still hasn't gone away."

"What am I supposed to apologize for? It wasn't me!"

"So, you don't think he went a little nuts?"

"Don't call him nuts!" She pointed a brown stain finger at me.

"What? You think this is about the dresses? He treated me like garbage, Shah! It was only after—"

"After you fooled around with Marshall?"

"What is your problem?"

"Bella, I lost Michael and now I lost you. What the hell are you even wearing? Michael used to dig you for your clothes, but you're being pretty basic right now."

"This is coming from the girl whose wearing track pants."

"Yeah, because I don't care, but you do. Well, you used to."

I looked at my clothes. It was wearing a loose, black T-shirt and some khaki pants. It was true, but I wasn't going to get angry. I was different now. The past was dead, and I was starting a new life. That night, after the attack, I came home and apologize to *Padre*. He was still angry at me, but when he saw the scar on my head, his mood suddenly changed.

"Bella, *¿Que pasó?*"

"I'm sorry, *Padre*. I'll do whatever you say."

"What happened to your head?"

"I did something very stupid, and I won't do it again."

"Do you want to—"

"No, I'm going to change, you were right. I was a *puta*."

"Oh, Bella, it's okay. I didn't mean—"

"Please, let me change, let me be your daughter."

We hugged, tears streaming down my faces. Everything rapidly changed after that. I dressed more appropriately, studied hard, and covered up my tattoo. It took a few treatments, but *Padre* and I thought it was best to block out the tree with a black box—just like he did all those years ago. I could have had it laser-removed, but I wanted a reminder: You must cover up your past life, Bella. You will have the urge to see that tree every day. But that life is gone now. It's all black.

Shah snapped a finger at my face, trying to get my attention.

"Hello, Bella?"

"Yeah, sorry."

"Bella," Shah put her hands on mine. "This isn't you. I know we haven't been friends for that long, but this new life you're living … and dating Marshall. It's just—"

"Don't. I like him, okay?"

When Marshall was in the hospital, I stopped by a few times. For a while, he couldn't talk—his mouth was so swollen. However, he listened, and I talked. I told him the whole story: about my past, why I fell for Michael, and why I tried to seduce him to go to the locker room.

"Listen," I said to a bandaged Marshall. "You must think I'm crazy, but do you think you could be interested in me? When you get out of the hospital, maybe we could hang out or something?"

Even though Marshall couldn't speak, he nodded his head. I smiled and immediately went home to tell *Padre* how I met a normal guy and we would do normal things from now on. Marshall was the perfect guy to date. No one called me a slut anymore—Marshall chewed out anyone who spoke badly about me. Life was, I guess, pretty great.

I pulled my hands away from Shah.

"I'm sorry," I said.

"Don't do this," pleaded Shah.

I ate one more fry and reached for my wallet.

"I'm sorry, Shah. But you, your brother, that's a side of me I have to end. Maybe down the line, we can try again, but not right now. More than anything in the world, I just want to be normal. If doing this is the closest thing I can get to being normal, then I'll do it. I lost, Shah. I'm broken. I didn't think it was possible, but it is. Michael lost too, and you don't want to admit that. I thought people would come around, maybe eventually understand. But I realized now that life doesn't work that way. Tell Michael … that I'm sorry."

With that, I put money on the table, and walked away. My covered-up tattoo began to itch, but I refused to scratch it. Never again.

56
Shah

After meeting Bella at the restaurant, I drove the two hours back to our somewhat new apartment. New is subjective, because it's new for Ma, Michael, and I, but this apartment must have been around for a hundred years. It's in a three-family home—each floor for a different tenant. The first-floor tenants just immigrated to the United States and they were happy to have whatever apartment was available. The top floor was lived-in by the landlord—who always gave me the eye every time we crossed paths. It could have been me, acting all pissed-off with our new living situation. I really wished I could've been as grateful as our foreign neighbors below, but this place was a dump.

The wood was worn and cracked—probably because it was older than all of us combined. The floor was even lighter in some places because people have been walking on it for decades. The rooms always smelled like spoiled milk. No matter how much I cleaned the floors, the walls, and even the ceiling, I could not get rid of the stench. It was like the smell was sealed in like a steak on a grill. Ma didn't seem to mind.

When I walked up the wooden stairs to the second floor, I waved to one of the neighbors coming down from the third floor.

"Afternoon," I said and smiled.

He looked straight forward and didn't wave back. When someone blows you off like that, it's hard to tell—for me at least—if being black has to do with it. For the past month, I've said "afternoon" to that guy and he never says anything back. One of these days, I'll get him to respond. It might take another month, or even a year, but I'll keep trying.

When I opened the door to the apartment, the strong smell battled with Ma's cooking.

"Who's that?" Ma yelled.

"It's me."

"Who's Me, I don't know no Me? You one of the people from below?"

"Oh ha-ha, very funny Ma."

"Just in time Charlotte, I made some of my famous meatloaf."

"What if I wanted some normal meatloaf?"

"Then you're going to have to eat somewhere else," Ma snapped, but it was playful. It was nice to see the energy that Ma used to have back. After the accident, Ma decided it was best if we did move out of town to a different neighborhood. Also, she cut back to only one shift. She still worked unusual hours, but somehow managed to get Saturdays and occasionally Sundays free.

I sat down at the kitchen table—which was old and held together by years of glue and luck. My chair made a creaking noise like a tree branch about to snap. Ma placed a plate of steaming hot vegetables and meatloaf on the table in front of me. For a moment, I watched the steam dance and vaporize into the air. It was nice having a home-cooked meal. For years, Michael and I relied on take-out, microwaved meals, or cereal for dinner. With Ma not heading off to work until eight at night, we finally had a chance to have a family meal.

"Is Michael still in his room?" I asked. It was a stupid question, because I knew the answer.

"Yes, but today he came out for a bit to grab some food from the kitchen. So you know that was good."

"Yeah, for a raccoon."

Ma looked back in disgust for a moment, but then cracked a smile.

"You've always had my humor. But it will get you in trouble one day."

"We'll see."

I reached into my pocket and fished around. Then I realized that my smokes were missing. I panicked and patted both pockets to see if I misplaced them. Then I remembered that I decided to quit a while ago. I let out a groan.

"What's wrong?" Ma asked. She sat down next to me with her own plate of food.

"I keep padding my pockets for a smoke."

"Oh, honey."

"Seriously, it's been over a month, and I could still go for a smoke at any moment."

"Then don't. I'm right there with you. Remember, we both decided to quit at the same time, so I'm hurting just as much as you."

"You are?"

"Charlotte, when I was cut off heading home today, I wanted to drive over to the nearest convenience store and buy out every carton."

"Why didn't you?"

"Because I promised you that I would stop. And you promised me that, too."

"I know."

"And I'm really proud of how things are looking."

"I don't feel better. I constantly feel like I'm on edge—like I'm going to snap at any moment. Everything has changed so much."

"That's life. It's always changing."

"Maybe, I'll just cut back. Just have one smoke a day."

"No. You'll get through this. It just has to take time."

"But what if I always feel this way, so hopeless? What if it's always like this forever?"

"You got to try. Don't give up."

"Michael did."

As if on cue, Michael came out of his room. Wearing sweatpants and a T-shirt, he sleepily shuffled into the kitchen, grabbed the plate of food set at his place, and walked back into his room, closing the door abruptly. Tears welled up in my eyes, but I looked down at my plate and focused all my efforts on eating the meatloaf. Ma looked at me and dropped her fork, grabbing my hand across the table and gently holding it in her own.

"Oh baby, it's going to be all right. Michael will get better soon."

"He's been like that the whole time."

"The psychiatrist said that it might take him some time to get back on his feet."

"But I just want him back. I miss him."

"Me too. But only Michael can get himself out of his slump. We just need to be there for him."

Ma squeezed my hand even tighter. My tears were streaming down my cheeks. I quit crying when I heard a knock on the door. I wiped away my tears, unlocked Ma's hold, and stepped to the door. When I looked into the peephole, I wanted to rip open the door and pummel the bastard behind it. It was Jacob.

57
Jacob

"Hey you!" I said, smiling when Shah opened the door to their apartment. She immediately slammed the door in my face. God, this was stupid. Really stupid. Like the stupidest thing out of all the stupid stuff I could do. I drove two hours with a gift, only to have a door slammed on me.

"Hey, Shah. I have this package for Michael, and maybe if you could just take the package—"

"Me?" She opened the door again. "Me? Take the package? I'm going to burn it if you so much as leave it here with me."

"Fair, that's really fair. But, maybe—and just hear me out—since Michael and I are friends—"

"Were, you *were* friends."

"Fair, once again, still fair in the insult department. Can I just talk to Michael?"

"Michael's not here."

"Oh, so where is he?"

"At … the …"

"Oh, come on. You got to get better at lying."

"At the movies."

"Really? That's the best you could come up with? Here, just take this package."

"No."

"Please."

"Who's there?" called Shah's Ma.

"It's no one," Shah called back. Then she slammed the door in my face again. At this point I wanted to cry, but that didn't mean I was going to. Truth was, life hadn't been that great to me since the … accident.

Honestly, I thought I was going to jail. But for some reason Lionel didn't want to press charges. Can you believe that? I deserved any sort of punishment, but instead I had none. Well, I take that back. The only punishment I had was my mom refusing to talk to me. She practically gave me the cold shoulder for weeks. The only thing she said to me was "dinner's ready." It was hard to tell if she was angry at me for screwing up my friendship with Michael or for beating the crap out of Lionel. One day, I asked her. After I lifted her up onto the couch—I was doing all sorts of nice things for her without asking—I said, "Mom, what exactly are you mad at me about?"

"Do I really have to spell it out for you?"

"No. I just need to know if you're mad for one thing or the other."

"I swear, you better thank Jesus that I have two bad legs because I would kick you in the butt so hard right now."

"Alright, alright. And thank you."

"For what?" She was fuming.

"For getting me into that prep school. I honestly thought we were still going to have to move. Because what school would want me? I'm a horrible person."

"Honey," she said softly, touching my cheek. "You did a horrible thing, but that doesn't make you a horrible person."

"It's close."

"Maybe. But now you have to make it right."

"How?"

"Now that both of them have had time to cool off, maybe you can give them an official apology."

"But I can't even be 100 feet near Lionel."

"Then call him on the phone. The lawyers didn't say anything about calling him."

"I thought it was just implied."

"Too bad. You're calling him."

"Like now?"

"Yes now!"

I unlocked my phone, and I was still surprised to see that Lionel's name was still in my contacts. I looked at my mom, who I hoped would decide that this was a stupid idea. She didn't. I called the number and waited for Lionel to scream in my ear. Instead, there was a quiet, "Hello."

"Lionel?"

"Is this Jake?"

"Yes."

"Don't you ever call this number again!"

"Wait, I know. But I just wanted to say I'm sorry."

"You could have said that a while ago."

"Well, I'm saying it now."

"Okay."

We were silent on the phone for a bit.

"So," I asked. "How's the face?"

"Are we done here?"

"No, wait. I can't undo what I did that night, but all I can say is that I'm sorry."

"That's it?"

"I don't know what else to do."

"You can start by hanging up."

The call ended, and when I looked at my mom, tears began to blur my sight.

"Oh honey," she said, and she hugged me.

"It didn't work."

"Of course it worked, Jake. You apologized. Not every apology is going to fix everything, but at least you did the right thing. An apology is not always for the other person, but for yourself. You have to forgive yourself."

"Then how do I apologize to Michael?"

"You need to figure that out."

I thought I did, with my mysterious package, but Shah wouldn't let me give it to Michael. Frustrated, I started pounding on the door.

"Shah! Give this package to Michael. Shah! Please! I'm so sorry about what I did! I can't explain it away, but all I can do is say I'm sorry."

The door opened again. I was so relieved that I wanted to hug Shah right there, but it wasn't Shah. Instead, Michael—looking like death himself—sleepily stood at the doorway.

"Hey," I said.

"Hey," said a ghost back.

"I ... um ... got you something."

"What is it?"

"You have to open it up."

He took the package and slammed the door on me. I smiled. If that was the best I was going to get, it could have been a lot worse.

58

Michael

I took the package, slammed the door, and rushed right back into my room. I knew my Ma and Shah were worried about me, but I didn't care. I needed to be alone. I forgot how many days passed—each waking moment seemed like a reluctant obligation. The state required that I find a new school within the month. A month had passed, and I still hadn't registered for a school, so Ma said I had to just go to the local public school. It didn't matter, because I only had to survive a couple more months, and then I'd be free. Until then, I'd play the game and dress just like every other guy. Then what? How would I be free? Wouldn't college be the exact same thing? Wouldn't the real world be the same as well? When in my life would I be accepted? I never would. I was right back to where I started. That's why I threw out all of my dresses the day we left for our new apartment.

I threw the package across the room. I didn't care what Jacob gave me. I didn't want to ever see or speak to him again. He ruined my life. He turned me into a monster I never dreamed I would become.

"Screw you!" I yelled and threw the package onto the floor.

"What was that?" Shah said from behind the door.

"Nothing, leave me alone."

"What's in the package?"

"I didn't open it."

"Well you better. I want to see what it is."

"No."

Shah walked away and came back with a thunderous knock.

"You better open the door or else."

"Or else what?"

"Or else, I'm breaking the door down."

"Charlotte," Ma said sternly. "Don't break the door down."

"No, Ma. I'm sick of him being locked up in his room."

I opened the door.

"What do you want?"

"Come on, Michael. Let's see what's in the package."

I sat on the bed, and I left enough room for Shah to sit beside me.

"What if it's bad?" I asked.

"You idiot. Do you think Jacob is smart enough to insult you through a gift?"

"I have no idea."

"Look, I feel bad yelling at Jacob back there. Truth is, despite all the dumb things, he did come all this way to drop this off. So, there must be some good behind it."

"Maybe."

"Yes, maybe," she nudged me. At that point, the tears welled up and were right about to burst.

"Thank you," I said, looking right in her eyes.

"For what?"

"For being my sister."

"You're welcome. Now, let's open this package."

I tore open the cardboard box. Inside was a bunch of tissue paper, with a letter on top. Christ, Jacob had the handwriting of a five-year-old. In terrible lettering, he managed to scrawl 'Michael' on the envelope. I smiled, but then quickly hid it before Shah saw. Gingerly, I opened the letter and read what was inside. Again, his writing was almost impossible to read, but I had been around him enough to know how to decipher this mess:

> *Dear Michael,*
>
> *Hey. It's me. Jacob. Obviously. Sorry I haven't tried to talk to you for over a month. I think both of us were confused and didn't know what to say. I still don't know what to say. You? Dresses? I had no idea. I won't lie, it still bothers me a bit. Like, do you always*

want to be in dresses? Or, is it like a full moon thing, where you turn into lady mode once in a while? Whatever, I don't know. Truth is, I'm over it now. I may not get it, but I don't care whether you wear a sleeping bag wherever you go. I just want you to be happy, and if I have a problem with it, then I guess I'm ruining your happiness. Can you believe that I'm about to give you some words of wisdom? That doesn't seem right, but here goes: it's going to take time. Soon, people will come around. Soon, you'll be happy. But it's in the distance. I hate to say that it's far, like Serbia far. Just keep going and soon you'll be there. Does that make sense? Probably not, but if anyone can understand what I'm trying to say, it's you.

Your friend,
Jacob

I tore open the tissue paper, and underneath it all was a dress. It was a black dress similar to the one I wore before. How he managed to find my size was a wonder to me. Maybe Jacob was right. I wasn't going to win over everyone in a day. It may take a year, even decades. But if I wanted to be happy, I needed to be who I was. But it was going to take some time.

"Shah?" I said.

"Yeah?"

"Let me change."

I thought she was going in for a hug, but then wrapped me in a headlock. She was getting better, I had to quit teaching her things. We both laughed, and I pushed her away. When she left, I quickly stripped off my clothes and started to change. When I pulled the dress over my head, I was surprised how easily it fit. I started laughing, and then I looked at myself in the mirror. I thought back to the first time I looked myself in the mirror, wearing Bella's red dress.

"My name is Michael, and I'm wearing a dress."

I said it again.

Michael's Black Dress

"My name is Michael, and I'm wearing a dress."
And I did it one more time.
"My name is Michael, and I'm wearing a dress."
There was a knock on the door.
"Michael," said Shah. "We want to see."
I opened the door.

Acknowledgements

I hope this book creates a dialogue, whether openly or personally, about what gender and dress actually mean. Although I do not cross-dress, my interactions with those who do encouraged me to discuss this topic and learn more, ultimately motivating me to write this novel.

I first want to thank Sartoris Literary Group, as well as James L. Dickerson, for taking a chance on this book. This was a huge departure from my last novel, *Deacon's Folly,* and I was afraid James would turn it down for being too different. He didn't, and I appreciate it immensely.

I want to thank Randy Rosenthal for editing this book, Diane Wells for being my passionate publicist, and Richard DC for designing the back cover art. A special thank you to Katelyn and KJ, who did a phenomenal job advising me on certain aspects of the book. They are both incredibly talented people and are destined to do some great things.

Thank you to all of my friends and family for their support during the writing process. Dad, thank you for always being there for me. Dave, thanks for being a great brother through all of this. Mom, you would have been the first person to buy the book, and I will always love you.

Lastly, Lauren never left my side during this project—always encouraging me to keep going, even when I thought this book would never be published. There is no one else that I want to share my life with, and I love you so much.

Thank you all!

Michael's Black Dress

www.ingramcontent.com/pod-product-compliance
Lightning Source LLC
Chambersburg PA
CBHW071515110726

47908CB00003B/846